I0658379

THE BARON'S
DAUGHTER

A Novel on the Clash between
Christianity and Islam

by

Theodore J. Nottingham

The Baron's Daughter

Dedication

For my daughter Ashley whose spirit is reflected in this work.

Published by

Theosis Books

© 2010 by Theodore J. Nottingham

All rights reserved.

ISBN 0966496086

Back Cover Art by Dale O'Dell

Printed in the United States of America.

The Baron's Daughter

Preface

The desperate man crawled across the hard dirt floor.
He was covered with sores and dust blowing in relentlessly from the surrounding desert through a narrow
slit in the wall. His legs would no longer carry him and
he gasped for the breath that might keep him alive.
It was dark and humid in the cell. The seasons followed one another, and always the same shadows, the
same silence, the same loneliness. For eight years he
had lived in this hellish condition. His noble birth rebelled against such a gruesome, desolate end. But he
ate the food that was slipped into his cell. He ate it because one image stuck in his mind and kept his heart
beating. "Adela..."
The word escaped his parched lips every day. It was
his prayer, his hope. The face of a beautiful ten year
old girl, frozen in time, was the light of his wounded
soul. She would be a woman now, fully blossomed and
trained to care for herself under the loving supervision
he had provided.
He often tried to imagine the stunning human being

she had become without him.

"Adela!"

He called out to her, wanting to believe that somehow his spirit's anguish could reach her across the vast spaces between them. Beneath the matted curls of his graying hair, a tear slid down his cheek and vanished into the forest of beard that grew wild over his once majestic features.

He was forgotten, left to die in a distant, forsaken land. Only one person suffered his torments with him: his beloved daughter, Adela. He dared to believe that she would come for him some day. He had taught her to master the sword, to bring courage out of fear, and to think for herself even if she had to stand against the whole world.

She was his greatest treasure since the death of his wife, and he had nurtured her growth with rare attention and devotion. Now that she had come of age, he needed her as much as she had ever needed him. But she would have to cross oceans and deserts to find him. There would be armies and brigands, heathens and bloodthirsty crusaders to encounter before she could ever reach him. Dared he believe in such a miracle?

"Adela..." he whispered hoarsely. He had to believe it. It was all he had left to hope for. And he knew that his daughter would move heaven and earth for his sake. He knew that his daughter would go where strong men feared to tread and retrieve him from this living death.

The Baron's Daughter

Lord Reynald's castle was little more than the decaying
shell of a Romanesque fortress, the survivor of many fierce
battles. Prior to his joining the latest Crusade, the Baron
had begun construction of a wide moat and of high turrets
in the new Gothic style that was changing the face of Europe. But the call to the reconquest of Jerusalem launched
by Pope Innocent III had halted all labor and left a deep
crevice on one side of the castle that was rapidly turning into a putrid swamp. The thick walls were disfigured by
massive scars from a violent past and crumbling under the
weight of age, but there were not enough healthy men left
in the fiefdom to bring new life to the Baron's home.

For a hundred years, the Crusades had robbed the entire
Realm of its men in a demonic carnage. The kingdom of
Philip Augustus was virtually drained of its men by the demands of the Holy Father. Orphaned children, widows and
grieving old folk constituted the leftovers of a religious

frenzy begun in the name of the Prince of Peace. Threats
of excommunication had forced peaceful nobles like Baron
Reynald of Vendome to impoverish themselves in order to
pay their way to the lands of the Seljuk emirs, the Zengi
sultans, and the caliphs of Baghdad.

Arm in arm, two youths stood before the disintegrating
castle. Bertran was a lad of twenty-two years of age, a son
of peasants powerfully fashioned by fifteen years of relentless toil in the Baron's fields. Lord Reynald's daughter,
Adela, was in the spring of her eighteenth year. Her beauty
was already legendary throughout the provinces of the
Massif Central mountain chain and was surpassed only by
her strong, independent spirit.

She threw back a whisp of her long chestnut hair and
turned piercing brown eyes upon her companion. Her sight
glided over his muscular shoulders, the aquiline nose of his
Roman ancestry, and came to rest on sparkling green eyes
framed in the foliage of curly blond locks sprung from
Saxon blood.

Bertran felt the warmth of her sweet gaze and smiled in
ecstasy. He remembered the day her birth had been joyfully
announced in the hamlets, pastures, and forests of the
Baron's domain. Since that fourth year of his life, Adela
had been his goddess, the only source of beauty in his miserable, rugged existence.

"Oh look!"

She pointed to a bird's nest above them from which came a delightful melody. Bertran understood that she could not bear the intensity of his passionate affection. He looked up at the winged parents patiently feeding their clamoring newborn. They stood near the castle walls in a small clearing bustling with awakening flowers and enormous butterflies discovering the magic of their recent metamorphosis. The fragrance of this life reborn rose like incense into a cloudless, deep-blue sky.

A shadow suddenly darkened Adela's milk-white features as a stinging pain tore through the wonder of the moment. It was the pain of a bleeding wound that had for so many years invaded her most peaceful days, obscuring them with a profound melancholy.

Bertran noticed the familiar sadness rising like dew in her innocent eyes. He knew what agonizing image stood before her mind's eye: the great figure of her father, Reynald the Lion as the King himself had dubbed him, who had disappeared eight long years ago in the mysterious deserts beyond the Mediterranean.

This very day of May had witnessed his departure at the side of the Marquis of Monferrat in a fourth vain attempt to chase the dreaded Saracens from the Holy Sepulcher. It had been another disaster for the noblest knights of France, England, and Germany.

"Dieu le volt!" -God wills it- those were the last words she had heard from her beloved father, the same motto cried out by thousands and thousands of massacred Crusaders. Bertran knew her torment. It burned within him as well. His sovereign lord had often been merciful upon him and his family. He looked away toward the hillside where Baron Reynald's imposing castle was perched. For an instant, he had the odd sensation that his liege lord's spirit stood there, in the shape of the fortress, staring at him with that dreaded imperious gaze. Bertran stepped away from her. Their friendship was rooted in earliest childhood, but, he had always been excruciatingly aware of the great differences between them.

"It is late...Lady Beatrice will be awaiting you..."

Adela looked up toward the sun. Its path was slowly descending from its zenith, flooding the sky with pastel colors.

"Lady Beatrice has my leave to be patient," she said sarcastically. "It is I who am losing patience with her tyrannical ways. I'm no longer a child."

"You must respect your aunt's wishes, Adela."

"Why? If I followed her decrees, I would be sitting before a tapestry from dawn till twilight. I have no desire to rot between those humid walls as she does."

"But she is merely following your father's requests..."

Adela's ethereal features suddenly reddened with rage.

"No one knows what my father desires for me! I will not have anyone guess at how my life ought to be shaped!"

Bertran did not insist. He was well aware that she carried within her the Baron's stormy moods. Many a man, knight and squire alike, had thanked his patron saint for saving him from the wrath of Reynald the Lion. His colossal anger had been fatal to some, though most often the unfortunates who roused him to such heights were forgiven by a charity of equal size.

It sometimes astonished Bertran that Adela could contain such explosive moods. How many hours had they shared admiring the gentler beasts of the forests who did not consider their togetherness a sin as did the prejudices of their feudal society. Adela could let an entire afternoon evaporate while contemplating a single rose. He knew well the deep sensitivity within her and he loved her for it with all his being.

Bertran once heard that, while on a pilgrimage to Rome at her father's side, they traveled into the hills of Assisi where they met a holy man. Adela often spoke of the monk's smile and glowing eyes, a sight she knew would probably never come her way again. From that time onward, she resolved to discover how it was that the holy man communed so vividly with all forms of life. She described to Bertran how he even touched the stones a certain way -

with love.

The memory of that angelic being rose to the forefront of her thoughts each time her temper would take hold of her.

"Forgive me, Bertran...I did not mean to..."

"I understand, Adela."

She smiled a sincere, grateful smile. She knew Bertran understood. He was a true child of Mother Earth, for his acceptance was all-encompassing. That was why she felt so close to him. He seemed to have none of those ugly demons raging within. Certainly he had pride, but it was a pride born from being a part of the wind and the fields and the mountains. Not that small, selfish pride that turned all the men she knew into crippled beings.

Bertran's sad eyes and tolerance reminded Adela of Tristan, her father's favorite hunting dog who mourned his master's disappearance as deeply as anyone.

"Will you come back with me?" she asked with a coquettish twinkle in her eyes.

"To the castle?"

She nodded and revealed the ivory artwork behind her lips.

"I...I cannot...It is forbidden," he stuttered in bewilderment. He wondered what she was up to now.

"It is high time you visited that old dungeon up there on the hill. How many of your generations have been plowing our fields without ever knowing what the Baron's home looks like? Aren't you curious?"

He blamed himself for being caught off guard, not anticipating this sudden shift of moods. He had noticed long ago that the more intensely her anger roared, the more playful she became afterward. That contradiction was all part of her bewitching charm.

"I was in the courtyard once..."

"Ah yes, that memorable day when our dear neighbor thought to divert himself by plundering our lands. That was not the proper manner of exploring your suzerain's abode! I want to show you the banquet hall, the inner court, the dungeon. Have you ever imagined what it must be like to spend years chained to a pillar in a reeking chamber with no light?"

The words caught in her throat as she suddenly realized that the horrid vision could well be her father's fate.

"The Saracens have no dungeons, do they? "

Her voice wavered and she turned away, walking swiftly toward the hill.

"Are you coming?"

Bertran hesitated, but then decided he could hesitate on the way to the castle. He hurried after her.

"Why are you doing this, Adela? Is it to provoke your aunt?"

"And if it is, what does that matter to you, master Bertran? You told me once you wanted to be a man of learning.

Well, I will show you a chapel built in the days of Charlemagne!"

"Truly?"

"My father came upon it while constructing a subterranean
passage beneath the stables."

Bertran's love of ancient lore convinced him to partake in
her mischievous scheme even though he realized that he
was going to learn more about the craftiness of feminine
warfare than about the famed emperor's wisdom.

"The glory of my ancestors has faded somewhat," she
murmured wistfully as they approached the old fortress.
"My grandfather was of royal blood. He could have
claimed the throne if the plague had not interrupted his
ambitions."

In the past several years, Adela had become more and
more cynical toward the gross stupidity of the brutal world
around her. She blamed her mutilated childhood on narrow
minds thirsting for lands they had no right to claim, and in-
satiable appetites hungering for the gore of senseless battle.

"Damn them all!" she whispered to herself. "The Pope, the
King, the priests..."

"Adela!" Bertran cried out. He could not stand for
blasphemy, not even from her.

"They are such hypocrites, Bertran. A troubadour told me
once that he has seen scores of clerics traveling the coun-

tryside trying to excite interest in yet another Crusade!"

"They follow the Holy Father's edict."

She headed for the gates, true to her habit of abruptly ending conversations that did not support her views. Adela was not a woman of her century. Her spirit was forged from a freedom and natural nobility that was the envy of valorous knights.

The guard looked at Bertran in astonishment as they entered the courtyard. A chorus of frantic chickens greeted them, along with the yapping of protective dogs. An immense hound raced down the stairway, wagging his tail in delight at his mistress' return.

Bertran froze as the beast approached him, growling a ferocious warning.

"He's a friend, Tristan." She knelt and caressed him.

"I don't think he likes men, except for my father, of course. He finds them barbaric, as I do."

She kissed the loyal beast tenderly.

"Bertran is one of us, Tristan. I don't want you to bite his leg off. Not today."

She smiled at Bertran who did his best to conceal his fright.

"Come, let's go to the banquet hall."

"What about the chapel?" wondered Bertran, hoping to delay a confrontation with Lady Beatrice.

"All in good time, dear Bertran. We must save the best for

last."

She led him up the stairs and into a dark corridor. Tristan followed behind, sniffing the young man's heels, assuring himself of his honorable intentions.

They had hardly gone a few steps when a young woman appeared from another hallway. She let out a cry of surprise at the sight of the peasant lad.

"Cecilia, greet my old friend Master Bertran, Lord of the northern pastures."

Adela's merry disposition immediately eased the tension. "This is Cecilia, my confidant and lady-in-waiting. She has been at my side for nearly five years now."

They looked at each other awkwardly. Cecilia was a cute, delicate girl whose life had been spent between four walls.

"Mylady..." Bertran said as he bowed.

"I've seen you in the village before," she stated in a haughty tone. She then turned to her mistress, pleading for her to reconsider. "Lady Beatrice is quite perturbed by your absence."

"Is she now? Well, we must set her mind at ease. Hurry along and tell her I haven't been carried away by roving goblins."

Cecilia hesitated. She didn't want to face the sinister woman's fury. She was of a timid nature, a daughter of Venus born to lay by enchanted streams and dream of tranquil romance. But her comeliness was marred by an unremitting fear of everything around her. The very shadows of her chambers terrified her out of her wits when night crept in.

"Go on, do as I say," her mistress ordered in a tone accustomed to command.

Adela smiled as she hurried away in a nervous fit.

"She's my closest companion and tolerates all my whims. I even bring her along on my clandestine hunts."

Bertran looked at her in amazement.

"I'm an expert falconer, I'll have you know," she told him coyly.

Adela was indeed an endless source of wonderment.

Bertran shrugged his shoulders in resignation. He would never comprehend her peculiar nature.

They entered the large banquet hall. It was fashioned in the Germanic style of the ancient Visigoth tribes: low ceilings, wooden beams crisscrossing in a simple but elegant design. Bertran stood in the doorway, absorbing the novel spectacle. His rich imagination populated it with rugged warriors and proud kings. Adela took him by the hand and brought him to the dais.

"It is said that King Clovis once sat in this chair. It's older than the King's Realm."

Bertran touched it with reverence. He had been taught the saga of the Frankish ruler by a learned hermit who sometimes came down from the mountains to share the peasants' meals.

Suddenly he straightened up, sensing the presence of danger. His back ached as though the Evil Eye were burning its malefic glare into his marrow. An icy panic rushed through his veins. He knew that Lady Beatrice stood in the doorway.

"What is the meaning of this?"

He glanced at Adela whose eyes sparkled with anticipation.

"Who is this boy?" thundered a stern and haughty voice.

Bertran turned around. A tall, bony silhouette stood rigidly beneath the arched entrance. He noticed Cecilia peering from around the corner, eyes glazed with terror. Lady Beatrice was a formidable creature. Her bony features, covered with a pock-marked, crusty skin, were those of a man. A viper's glare shimmered in her yellowish eyes. The long nails of her gnarled fingers were veritable claws. She might have been burned as a witch long ago had she not been Lord Reynald's sister-in-law.

Lady Beatrice had never married and lived for nearly twenty years in virtual isolation high in the Jura Mountains. No one had ever seen the warmth of a smile cross her disdainful lips. The Baron knew of her sour disposition, but could find no one else to care for his daughter. The two headstrong women were forced to share the same home, and it had been war from the very first day.

Adela bowed dramatically.

"What is troubling you, Madam?"

A venomous grimace distorted the reclusive woman's face.

"I shall have this peasant whipped for his insolence!"

Bertran's mouth dropped open.

"He is here by my leave. Shall I be whipped as well?"

"I have a mind to do just that! There seems to be no other method to teach you manners, young lady!"

Adela walked to the center of the room and placed her hands on her hips defiantly.

"And whom shall you find to carry out your barbaric desires?"

"Perhaps I ought to discipline you with my own hand, something your father was too weak to do."

Adela clenched her jaws tightly. It took every bit of her mighty will-power to keep her from striking the woman.

Bertran instinctively searched the room for a way out. He had not expected such violent outbursts.

"This is my home, Lady Beatrice! You have intruded on my ancestral rights long enough. As of this day, I declare your powers of regency absolved and claim the honors due me as Baroness Adela of Vendome!"

"How dare you speak to me in such a way!"

The two enemies stared daggers at each other.

"If I desire a guest in my castle, it will be so!"

"It will not! Cecilia, call the guards!"

Already trembling like a leaf, Cecilia nearly fainted at the shrill command.

"If you were a man, I'd face you in mortal combat!" Adela shouted.

Lady Beatrice snickered.

"Your father made a boy of you. You are an aberration. An unnatural creature!"

For a moment, Bertran thought he was going to witness a bloody fight. He felt sick to his stomach.

An old guard hurried down the hallway, a spear over his shoulder and fear etched on his wrinkled features. Lady Beatrice pointed a crooked finger at Bertran.

"Chain him and throw him in the dungeon!"

The guard took a step forward. Adela blocked his way.

"Gerard, you will obey my orders now. I command you to return to your post!"

The elderly man froze in his steps, confused. He turned to Lady Beatrice.

"Do as I say or I'll have you whipped, old man!"

He glanced at Adela. She softened her glare and addressed him in a gentler tone.

"You know my father would not approve of this, Gerard. She has abused her powers. Don't listen to her."

"Arrest him or, by God, I'll send you to the gallows!"

A tremor seized the old man. He was on the verge of tears.

"My ladies," he pleaded, "have mercy on your loyal servant..."

He looked from one to the other, horrified at their fury.

"The Baron placed you under oath! You swore allegiance to me when he left!" screamed Lady Beatrice, losing control of herself.

"She speaks the truth, Mylady," the old man whispered to Adela. "I must obey her."

"Then you will have to take me along as well!"

She held out her arms.

"If that is your wish!" cried Lady Beatrice, a gleam of victory in her eyes.

The old man threw down his spear.

"I cannot do that!" he shouted hoarsely. "This is madness!"

Bertran suddenly grabbed the spear. He raised it, anger boiling through his veins.

"You are right, old man! This is folly. We will leave these ladies to fight their battles in private."

He aimed the spear at Lady Beatrice.

"Out of my way, Lady Beatrice! No one is going to chain me without shedding blood!"

The woman stared at him coldly.

"You will pay dearly for this, peasant, you mark my words!"

She moved away from the doorway, glaring at him with fierce hatred.

"I'm sorry, Mylady. I meant no disrespect." Bertran said sincerely.

"You don't know how sorry you're going to be, boy! I'll have you skinned for this!"

Bertran shook his head in disgust. He looked back at Adela who smiled at him triumphantly. He scowled at her, resenting her thoughtless use of others in weaving her schemes. But her smile did not fade. She knew he would forgive her eventually.

Bertran hurried out into the courtyard, throwing the spear into a pile of manure. Above him, on the ramparts, he noticed a guard watching him suspiciously. He knew that he would soon be pursued and chastised for Adela's childish prank.

He hurried across the bridge and headed toward the forest. It was the beginning. Destiny's first note had been sounded for Adela and Bertran. Their turbulent future awaited them.

2

Bertran hurried across the Baron's fields, cursing himself for having allowed this breach of propriety to take place. He knew that Lady Beatrice would be merciless in her revenge. As he rushed over the muddy furrows, a terrible memory shot through his whole being. He stopped running. His stomach turned to acid as he remembered what Lady Beatrice had done to poor Roland, the village simpleton who shouted obscenities at her as she rode through the town square.

Lady Beatrice locked him in manacles and left him for days in the darkness of the rat-infested dungeon. A servant reported hearing his screams of terror go on for hours at a time. When Roland was finally released, his spirit was utterly crushed and his body shook uncontrollably until a fever stilled it forever.

Anger scorched through Bertran's veins as he recalled the dreadful incident. The sweet, innocent man with the mind of a five year old child was a friend to everyone in the village. Bertran had known him since childhood. The man's unsightly features inspired fear in passersby who often took him for a demon out to put a hex on them. But the children loved him and often made him the center of their play. In his simple, harmless ways, he had shown Bertran pure acts of kindness and friendship, the like of which he had found in no one else. He seemed always happy despite his handicap and loneliness. For Roland had no family to care for him, and though he was always at the front of the festivities, it was to an empty hovel that he returned at the end of the day.

This relationship with Roland had initiated Bertran into his first real test of courage. In his thirteenth year, while returning early from the fields to mend a broken tool, he came upon three ruffians taunting his dimwitted friend. Bertran shouted for them to leave him alone, but the ragged travelers paid no attention. One of the men, drunker than the rest, struck Roland in the back with his walking stick. The poor man let out a terrible cry, all the more painful because he had thought they were playing with him. The men began to imitate his moans and dance around him with great merriment.

It was at that moment that the peasant lad forgot himself and attacked the strangers. He swung his hoe with such fury that the men were on their knees holding their aching limbs before they could return any blows. Bertran stood over them, fearless, with such fire in his eyes that his adversaries chose to run from the thirteen year old boy. From that day forth, Bertran knew that he had the character of a knight of the Realm, not that of a submissive serf. He would never again accept the humiliation of desperate poverty and groveling servitude. His dreams were filled every night thereafter with visions of a noble and glorious future.

Bertran realized that he too might suffer an ignoble treatment similar to the one inflicted upon Roland. At this thought, his valiant spirit rebelled with all its might. He would not be locked away by that witch! He would not be left to rot in the stench of those awful underground chambers.

Bertran also knew that he could not return home. Lady Beatrice had surely dispatched her guards to retrieve him from his family. So the proud peasant dashed off toward the forests, aware that he might never be able to return.

The sun had begun its fall over the mountain peaks when Bertran reached the clearing. Few people ever wandered this far into the woods, especially at dusk. This was the domain of wild animals and lawless brigands. Darkness signaled their appearance from secret lairs. The young man was familiar with this place for it was here that he had first encountered the strange hermit who shared words of wisdom with him.

He knew that the kind old man lived nearby, though he had never seen his dwelling. He could only hope that Fate would grant him a stroke of luck and that he would come upon the solitary figure before nightfall. The pace of the sun's decline was quickening and Bertran well knew that great dangers awaited him if he were caught in the forests at night. He grabbed an oak branch for protection and hurried to the middle of the clearing.

He stood there, waiting. Perhaps the old man would see him from his hidden home and come to him. Or perhaps he would have to spend the longest night of his life listening to every suspect sound and watching every movement. Bertran knew little about religion though everyone around him seemed to live and breathe it. Like his father before him, he was a hard working, practical sort who had to see and touch things in order to believe in them. But now, in this desperate moment, as he sought to fight off the fear that was quickly rising in his soul despite his mighty courage, Bertran felt an irresistible need to call upon a greater Power than himself. Never before had he felt such a feeling. It was alien to his nature and he would have dismissed it immediately were it not for the fact that it caught him in a moment of overwhelming need. His pride attempted to keep the prayer from escaping his lips, but it broke free and gushed out like a long repressed feeling.

"Father in Heaven, have mercy on my miserable soul!"

Bertran had never experienced such an opening in his heart, not even in the presence of Adela. This feeling, this need sprung from unexplored depths of his nature and revealed for a brief instant, the bottomless abyss of his spirit.

"Have mercy on me!"

The prayer came out again, uncontainable. The sky was now a crimson red and already the thick foliage surrounding him was steeped in darkness. The first howls of the night creatures echoed through the forest.

Bertran stood in absolute stillness, mesmerized by the fire in his breast. A great peace flooded his soul, a peace with which he was unfamiliar. Somehow, he knew that the Angel of Death would not come to him this night. For the briefest moment, he envisioned another land where the Grim Reaper would stand before him. The vision was so real and flooded with sunlight that, as he stood in nocturnal shadows, he found himself squinting. He then felt a strange dirt, fine and hot, under his feet and saw in his mind's eye a vast horizon devoid of trees and mountains.

In the blink of an eye, the vision was gone, leaving Bertran disoriented. He shook his head, wondering what sort of dream would appear before him at such a critical moment. The sound of cracking underbrush pulled him out of his reflection. He turned around swiftly, raising his staff.

A tall silhouette at the edge of the clearing slowly moved toward him. Bertran braced himself for combat.

"What troubles you, my son?"

The vigorous young peasant dropped the branch with a sigh. The gentle voice was none other than that of the recluse he had hoped to find. An overwhelming gratitude filled his heart with joy and his eyes with tears. Without understanding how or why, he knew that he had some greater Power to thank for this blessed appearance. Bertran hurried toward the silhouette which had stopped short of entering the clearing.

"Father! You've come!"

He fell to his knees before the old man whose features were hidden by a black hooded cloak. A hand appeared from the heavy, ragged cape and reached out to the young man.

Bertran looked up and took the hermit's wrinkled hand. Its intense heat surprised him. It felt as though the setting sun had risen again in a human limb. But this night was one of wonders, and Bertran no longer questioned every unexpected event that came his way.

"I hoped I would find you," he stated with relief as the powerful old man helped him to his feet.

"No, you did not."

Bertran was taken aback.

"What do you mean, Father?"

In the shadows beneath the hood, he could see the gleam of scintillating eyes. Bertran had never looked into pupils as striking as those of the hermit. Even Lord Reynald, whose courage was equaled only by the legendary Richard the Lion- Hearted, did not match the patriarch's searching gaze. The old man seemed to know the very contents of the soul before him.

"You did not hope for it. You prayed for it. And that is why I am here. I am never away from my home at this hour. I was called upon to meet you here."

In spite of himself, Bertran could not deny the facts that stood before him.

"Someday you will understand these things, my son," the hermit added with a knowing smile. "Let us be content for now with the troubles at hand. What terrible events have brought you to me?"

"Lady Beatrice...."

The recluse raised his hand, unwilling to hear of the Devil's works.

"Say no more, lad. The woman is evil incarnate. If you have become the object of her wrath, then you must leave the fiefdom."

The hermit took Bertran by the arm and led him into the underbrush.

"My soup should be warm by now. Do me the honor of sharing it."

They moved through the blackness of the forest. Bertran could hardly see more than the mud-splattered cloak of his companion and had to protect his face from the branches and thorns that struck him at every step.

Suddenly, a crashing sound was heard nearby. Bertran jumped in terror, recognizing the approach of a wild beast on the attack. The old man swiftly stepped between him and the charging animal. Bertran noticed that the hermit was utterly calm.

A huge wolf rushed toward them, his great fangs gleaming in the moonlight. Bertran frantically looked around for a stick.

"Be still! Do not make a move!" the hermit whispered.

Despite his unbearable instinctive urge to protect himself, Bertran obeyed his mentor. He watched the savage creature dash toward them. Everything within was screaming for him to defend himself and he couldn't understand why he was blindly following the orders of the recluse.

Just as the wolf came into leaping distance, it slowed and stopped several feet away from them. The animal's eyes lost their fierceness as it stared up at the old man. Astonished, Bertran saw the beast respond to the profound peace emanating from his companion. The recluse and the wolf looked at each other and seemed to communicate!

The animal backed away sheepishly, like a dog ashamed of its misbehavior. It looked intensely at the man whose gentle but stern presence so disconcerted it. After a moment, it hurried away and disappeared into the shadows of the night.

The men stood in silence. Bertran was awestruck. The hermit whispered a prayer. In the deep silence of the woods, Bertran felt the first crack in his sense-based experience of reality. Mystery briefly lifted its veil and revealed to the young man that life was not what it had always seemed to him.

"Can you smell the soup?"

The aroma of simmering vegetables brought Bertran back to what he had always thought to be the only real world. The old man headed off toward a structure silhouetted in the pale moonlight. Bertran followed in a daze. This was a night he would never forget. They ate in silence, sitting on the stone floor of the hermit's home. As Bertran's eyes adjusted to the flickering light dancing in the fireplace, he began to notice where he was. Behind the tapestry of moss, weeds and crawling ivy, he could see thick walls of stone. Above him, a low arched ceiling revealed the identity of this ancient dwelling.

"This is a chapel!" Bertran exclaimed.

"What better place to call one's home?" responded the hermit as he sipped his soup in a corner.

"What is it doing out here, at the heart of the forest?"

"It was built in the days of Charlemagne, some four hundred years past."

Bertran knew little of history, but the name of the great emperor was a central figure of the myths told among all families. Looking more carefully, he could distinguish several Roman columns holding up the dome. In the far corner of the chapel, he could make out a heavy table which once served as an altar to worshipping Franks and Goths.

"You alone know of this place?"

"Oh, perhaps a hunter or two have come across it. But the mountain people believe this part of the forest is haunted, so they stay far from it."

"Haunted? Haunted by what?"

"By the spirits of the Khan of the Avars whose horsemen were slaughtered in these woods by the Franks."

"The Avars?" wondered Bertran.

"Nomads from the Asian steppes who fought the Carolingian kingdom for seven years before the Franks destroyed them forever. They were a savage lot, pushing their slaves ahead of them into battle as human shields."

Bertran had met with the recluse only twice before. And each time, he had been taught from the treasury of the learned man. Their first encounter occurred during a blizzard the previous winter. He had gotten lost in the forest while seeking firewood for his family. The season was especially harsh and every inhabitant of the fiefdom was cold and hungry. Without the presence of their liege, Lord Reynald, there were no more festive occasions on which his serfs were let into the courtyard to dance and drink around a giant bonfire, thereby easing the hardships of the season.

The men of the villages were forced to head out into the deep snow in search of game and dry wood. Only those who wandered far from the hamlets could hope to find anything. On this particular occasion, Bertran had forged a path deep into the woods determined to find a hare who might also be looking for sustenance. His little sister was very ill and there wasn't much hope for her without meat to strengthen her body.

The blizzard caught Bertran completely unexpectedly. From out of the grey, motionless skies came a swirling storm which virtually blinded him within moments. The footsteps he had hoped to retrace vanished completely. It was then that he first saw the solemn silhouette of the hermit.

He had heard rumors of the presence of a holy man somewhere in the mountain slopes, but had taken them to be legend like so many other stories told among the peasants. The village priest, a humorless, grim individual by the name of Guilbert, had taken the report seriously enough to warn all his parishioners to stay far from such a man. He had spoken to the monks of nearby monasteries and discovered that none of their order had established a hermitage in the area. The priest therefore suspected that this recluse might be a "hereticus perfectus," an accomplished heretic, a Perfect One from the Cathar sect which flourished further south in the lands of Raymond of Toulouse.

The cleric's fear only inflamed the imagination of his flock and accounts of the hermit grew into the most absurd fantasies. None of the pious villagers had any idea of the beliefs held by the powerful sect which had established a radical spiritual version of Christianity across the continent and aroused the Pope's furor. To the eternal shame of Christendom, Pope Innocent III, in the name of the Prince of Peace, called for a crusade against the Cathars which was tantamount to a war against the people of beautiful Languedoc who had long accepted the sect in their midst. In return for lands and indulgences, the King of France, Philip Augustus and his knights undertook the systematic slaughter of their fellow countrymen for the past three years.

This bloodbath, occurring only two days journey from his hamlet, was one of the reasons why Bertran secretly renounced the authority of the Church. He was told that the papal legate, at the siege of Beziers, when asked by the invaders whether to spare the Catholics of the city, stated; "Kill them all, for God knows His own." Some twenty thousand men, women and children were massacred. Upon hearing Father Guilbert praise the genocide during the mass, Bertran swore never to set foot in another church.

When he encountered the feared recluse during the blizzard, the independent-minded young man was unconcerned over rumors of heresy. Before heading home, Bertran gratefully handed him the meager catch he had hunted down. Then the strange solitaire with the gleaming eyes spoke his first words: "Your sister needs it more..."

Amazed, Bertran begged the seer to let him return the gift of his life with some gesture. So the holy man accepted a loaf of his mother's bread. On the following day, when Bertran returned, there was no one to be found so he left his gift on a tree stump, hoping that his savior would find it before the bears and wolves. Several months later, he encountered the solitary man again. This time, he came across him on the outskirts of the hamlet in the company of a beggar woman carrying a child who was near death. The hermit instructed Bertran to feed and shelter them until the child recovered. He reminded the reluctant young man that the great heroes of the era, King Richard, Godfrey of Bouillon, even Saladin the valorous leader of the Saracens, were men of compassion. The words and example of the recluse made a profound impression on the young man.

Now, in the ancient ruins of the chapel, a guest of this rare man who had once again saved his life, Bertran listened with great intensity to his every word. Illiterate and starving for knowledge, he knew that this man was a fount of true wisdom, the only education of ultimate importance.

He looked over at the kind old man who had befriended him. The old man had removed his hood and for the first time Bertran could distinguish his features. In the shimmering half-light of the fireplace, the hermit's face resembled that of Zeus, the Roman god whose statue Bertran had uncovered while clearing land for the Baron.

His bony features were sharply chiseled and bronzed by exposure to the elements. A long thick beard lengthened his face and increased the emaciated pallor of one who often fasted. The nose was long and aquiline, almost in the shape of an eagle's beak. It was hard to identify the race from which he had sprung; perhaps a blend of Germanic and Mediterranean blood.

The features were more those of fallen royalty whose kingdom had been overthrown than those of a solitary dweller of the wilds. It was the eyes, however, that revealed the true nature of the man. They were unusually large and protruded a bit from their cavernous sockets. The pupils were an arresting sky blue, almost transparent. But the most striking aspect of this face was not physical. Living fire came from those eyes, an intensity of awareness that pierced through everything they looked upon. Yet a great calm also emanated from them, softening their energy with compassion. Bertran could not avoid a feeling of discomfort when they turned toward him for they saw into places within his soul which he had yet to explore.

This man, so learned and yet so humble, so full of strange powers, was the very opposite of Guilbert, the priest of Bertran's village. There was no humility, no compassion whatsoever in the man who led mass each day for the serfs of Lord Reynald. He was rigid and hard, full of judgment and anger. The words he spoke to his flock were weighed down with guilt and condemnation. Bertran was struck by the fact that both men had apparently devoted their lives to the same God. Both professed to be disciples of the Holy man from Nazareth.

Nestled in the safety and profound peace of the ancient chapel, sharing the hermit's simple meal, it was clear to Bertran that if he had to choose whose religion he would consider following, it would not be the one condoned by Rome.

"Are you a Cathar?"

The question came out before Bertran could check himself. He regretted it instantly, knowing this was an infringement on the sovereign privacy of his host.

The hermit looked up from his steaming bowl of soup and focused his gaze upon the young man. He said nothing for a time.

"Forgive my impudence. I...I did not mean to..."

"I am. But we merely call ourselves Christians."

The words echoed across the humid walls. Bertran felt a tightening in his throat. He was sitting with a man whose every belief was foreign to him and who was condemned to the stake by the Pope himself. At this very moment, not two days ride as the birds fly, thousands of people were being bludgeoned for saying what the old man had so calmly and emphatically stated.

"Does that frighten you, my boy?"

"No," Bertran answered unconvincingly.

The hermit put down his bowl, stood and approached the fire. He warmed his hands over the flames. Bertran virtually held his breath.

"I am what the Inquisitor calls a Perfect One. Believers call us "Friends of God." I have vowed to live for God in service to my brothers and sisters. And I am called to renounced the whore of Babylon."

"Who is that?" Bertran wondered, encouraged by his curiosity.

The hermit remained by the fire, looking pensively into the flames. "The Church, my son. The Church of Rome and all her sacraments. The Pope is the Antichrist, a descendant of pagan emperors, not of Saint Peter. He lives in a palace, while the Son of God had no place to lay his head. His bishops live in wealth while the Christ had no lands, no money. His priests are the Pharisees of old, returned to crucify our Lord once again. The Church is a den of thieves, selling indulgences and displaying relics for the ignorant. Worse yet, they preach a false doctrine to the faithful. The Christ did not come to atone for the sins of men and women through a barbaric blood sacrifice to His Father. We do not worship an instrument of torture like the priests require."

The hermit turned a scalding look upon the young man. "If they had hanged your father, would you worship the rope which brought about his death?"

Bertran shook his head in horror.

He turned away again and added with solemnity:

31

"The Christ came to reveal the Truth...the Truth concerning who we are and who we are to become."

He turned toward Bertran, eyes sparkling with tears.

"That is why my brothers and sisters are being massacred relentlessly. That is why they burned one hundred and forty Perfect Ones, men and women of great wisdom and goodness, in the square of Minerve, the twenty-second day of July last. Now the King will have new lands and the Pope will be free of criticism." The hermit moved with deep melancholy into a corner of the chapel. Bertran knew that he was weeping silently.

"Why? Why are they being murdered?"

The old man turned around, his ashen face overshadowed by a strange peace that rose out of the depths of his soul.

"The name Cathar comes from the Greek Katharos which means "pure." We believe that without charity, our life is nothingness. Charity requires an awakening to the divine within us. Not blind allegiance to superstitious clerics. We are therefore a danger to the power of Rome. The Pope has pronounced his anathema against us as well as against the good people of Aquitaine, Toulouse, Provence: "He who dispossesses you will be accounted virtuous, he who strikes you dead will earn a blessing." Our friends will be destroyed along with us."

"How can the Church commit such horrors?"

The old man returned by the fireplace and sat near Bertran.

"The Church is of this world. And Saint John tells us that this world is set entirely in Evil. We seek the Kingdom of the New Earth and the New Heaven from whence our souls emanate just as rays emanate from the sun."

"You believe this world is entirely evil?"

The hermit looked deeply into his eyes.

"A tree is known by its fruits."

"But it is written that the Almighty created this earth."

The hermit gazed into the crackling fire.

"We understand from Holy Scripture that there are two opposing realities in the universe. The spiritual and the material. The transitory reality which we live in is doomed to corruption and destruction. It is in this world that Evil appears. Vice and suffering are part of matter. But that which is unseen is eternal. The Holy One of God said "My kingdom is not of this world.""

"But God created everything..."

"Indeed. Everything being the totality of Creation. But there is another aspect of Creation, its shadow. Consider the first verse of the Gospel of John:"et sine ipso nihil factum est." The clerics translate it as "and without Him was not any thing made." But we understand it as "without Him, nothingness was made." This is what the Scriptures refer to when it is written that "all is vanity." Nothingness is indeed vanity. Surely, they do not refer to the good Creation, the eternal Kingdom where Love and Mercy reign."

Bertran listened breathlessly. He had never heard such ideas before.

"You are saying that there are two creations, one good and one evil?"

"I will ask you a question: how could an infinitely good God create conditions in which Evil could exist?"

"Then who created this world?" Bertran asked, fearful of an answer.

"The shadow of the Uncreated...The Prince of this world. A demonic force which seeks to destroy the Kingdom of Light by creating its opposite - matter and time. It is the darkness fighting the Light. But it is not equal to the Almighty, merely opposed to Him."

They sat in silence for a moment. The fire was fading. The hermit threw in another log.

"We are celestial beings, my son. You are in this tunic of flesh because you have a journey to undertake. A journey which consists in reuniting with the Spirit and freeing yourself from the prison of mortality. This is why the Son of God was sent among us."

"What becomes of those who do not know this?"

"They remain dimly conscious meat who return to oblivion...But only for a time. Our souls return again and again until they are free, for we will all be saved."

"And what of Hell?"

Bertran was surprised at hearing himself ask such a question. Like his father, he had taken pride in caring neither for the questions nor the answers but simply concentrated on the business of surviving.

"We are already in Hell. There is no other."

"How then does the soul free itself?"

The old man put his hand on Bertran's shoulder.

"Gnosis!"

"I don't understand..."

"The baptism of fire in which the Holy Spirit Himself teaches you the knowledge that will initiate you into the awareness of your divine nature."

"Knowledge will save the soul?"

"Knowledge and great effort."

"And how do I come upon such knowledge?"

The hermit's face lit up with a smile beaming with compassion.

"You have come upon it, Bertran of Vendome."

Bertran felt his whole being shiver beneath the power of the man's gaze.

"We call it Consolation. A new understanding of God is given you by the Comforter sent by the Son of God. Through it, the Divine Spirit comes to knock at your door. You need only open it and receive Him. As I have done."

The fire burned bright in the ancient hearth and the longing chant of the night owls echoed in the darkness. The eyes of the Perfect One seemed to sparkle with an unconditional Love emanating from the realm of the Uncreated. The young peasant felt a new power fill his body, mind and soul. The undiscovered country within him was making itself known. All the fears of the day, the threat of flogging and banishment, had vanished.

35

3

High up in the east tower of the Baron's chateau, Adela angrily paced her chambers. The starkness of the cold stone room was relieved by the colorful presence of feathers from exotic animals, Arabian rugs of great beauty, and immense curtains made of cloth brought from distant shores. Lord Reynald had friends among the Venetian merchants who were amassing tremendous wealth in the footsteps of the crusaders. The Holy Land was not only a place of worship, but a center of commerce. And the unrefined landowners of the northern countries were treated to new splendors in their dark and dreary castles while the blood of the devoted seeped into the sands of the Judean desert.

Adela was the sole daughter of one of the richest barons of France. She had made it a habit to eat rare and expensive fruits like oranges and dates brought across the ocean for her pleasure. These exotic treats represented the life she wanted to sink her teeth into: exploration, adventure, wonderment, new discoveries. The Baron saw to it that her education would cause his daughter to hunger for a life lived to the fullest. Quiet, endless days spent in weaving tapestries were not her destiny. She knew the feeling of wind rushing through her hair, and could quote from memory the divine poetry of the ancients that honored such luscious moments.

Full of energy and abundant vitality, Adela loved to fill her days to the brim with experiences for the mind, the heart and the senses. Already well into her marrying years, the fire of sensuality only intensified her natural desire to know life to its very core. She rarely wore the heavy, restrictive garments that were obligatory for every woman born into nobility. Adela hated the dreary servitude reserved for her sex while men travelled the world and breathed in the excitement of being alive.

She even yearned for the thrill of battle. Not that she wanted to hurt anyone, but her father had instilled within her the taste for competition and the skills of the swordsman. Not one of the guards could stand up to her ability with a blade. The Baron's daughter was a fierce adversary as well as a lover of poetry and music.

Troubadours from the south were by far the most important visitors to her domain. As a child, she would sit next to her father, leaning on his broad shoulder, and listen in rapt attention to the melodious tales spun by a wandering minstrel. From them, she learned of romance, of unrequited love and of that selfless affection that mixed with spiritual wisdom as well as with the flesh. Lord Reynald wanted his daughter to know the world she was born into and to master it just as he had. Some accused him of attempting to perversely turn her into a boy, but he knew that he was only feeding her natural capacities.

Adela's independence of spirit made itself clear from her earliest years, when she insisted on her way with a stubbornness that rivaled everyone's inner strength. Even the mighty Baron, finest warrior in the Realm, found himself overwhelmed with his child's willpower. He was often heard to remark that he pitied the man who some day would seek her hand.

Adela was no shrew, for her sense of humor and contagious enthusiasm caused her to beam with a light that attracted others to her. But she knew herself to be a free person, unfettered by the requirements of her time. This was her father's greatest legacy to her and she held to it with unyielding tenacity.

Most women of her age were already mothers several times over. Though she loved the refreshing innocence of children, Adela was in no hurry to bind herself to a life of caretaking when she had yet to live for herself. Her intuition told her that she would see new lands before settling down to nurse her firstborn. But her plans were destroyed by her father's disappearance and she felt herself a caged animal desperate for the freedom of open spaces.

Her sexuality was also becoming harder to contain as time moved on relentlessly. She channeled the heat of her passion into physical activities that only the men undertook. The young baroness was seen chopping wood on some occasions, a vision that was utterly shocking and unacceptable to her aunt and others in prominent positions. Such reckless disregard for the ways of feudal society were dangerous. Just as the Pope crushed heretics mercilessly, so too did the nobility feel threatened by those who lived differently than the laws of the land. Through her independence of mind, Adela of Vendome could single-handedly upset the balance of power among the lords and ladies of Realm. Their way of life was already fragile ever since the peasant revolts of the last decade and the suspicious eyes of a King who was himself insecure. In their castles, these landowners lived reclusive and carefully guarded lives. Warfare among neighbors, seasonal festivities, and troubadours were the only relief from such repression.

Adela would not accept such captivity. She was a part of great Nature and each season found her communing with the beauty and powers that surrounded her domain. The one field of life that remained foreign to her was that of human love. No man had ever courted her, and her lips longed for the sweet pressure of passion. One of her many admirers sent her spoils of the last crusade. On her humid walls hung treasures pillaged from the glorious city of Constantinople, the pride of the Byzantine Empire and the greatest center of culture and art since the glory days of Roman emperors. Few acts of human history would ever be as ignoble as the devastation of that ancient city. Even her father, a sworn enemy of the worshippers of Allah and of all heretics disloyal to the Church, had been sick with disgust upon learning of the vile desecration of the most beautiful cathedral in the world, the Saint Sophia, and the burning of hundreds of rare documents containing the wisdom of earlier civilizations.

Lord Reynald, tutored under the guidance of a Greek-speaking philosopher, felt the full tragedy of the irreplaceable loss of some of the finest works from the golden age of Greece - the writings of Aristophanes, Aeschylus, Sophocles, Euripides. Magnificent statues centuries old were crushed by the barbarous northern knights who destroyed humanity's precious heritage for all time. The raids of the Visigoths and Vandals, even the terror of the East - the feared Mongols - could not have had a more apocalyptic effect on the great city than the soldiers of the Cross.

These primitive men had, in the name of the Holy One of God, committed sacrilegious acts on sacred altars and gambled for hallowed relics in the very places where saints of old, who had known the Apostles themselves, came to offer their prayers and seek the Divine Presence.

Adela stopped pacing and stared at a golden goblet encrusted with rare stones whose names were unknown to her. It had been pulled from the hands of a dying Greek priest, cut down while preparing the Holy Eucharist. When her father looked upon this object of faith and reverence robbed from holy men by knights wearing the cross of the Lord, his rage was such that he decided at that moment to join this fourth crusade and bring purity of purpose and noble action to its leadership. Men of his rank and intelligence had

long given up on the ideal of the Crusades. The authority of the
Pope was coming into question before the sea of blood oozing into
the sands. Since the siege of Jerusalem during the first Crusade
some hundred years before, when "good" Christians slaughtered
over seventy thousand Muslims - among whom were some of the
brightest minds of humanity - it had become more difficult to sell
the nobility on the religious value of the Pope's call to arms.
Stories were brought back from the Holy Lands telling of Saracens
more pious than the Christians. The great Saladin had proved a
worthy opponent to King Richard the Lion- Hearted, both as a
warrior and as a fair and generous spirit. Lord Reynald had often
told his daughter of the worthy elements of Islamic civilization.
The pillage of another culture in the name of the Lamb of God
disgusted him to no end. From the very first attempts to liberate
the Holy Sepulcher, few crusaders had shown themselves to be as
noble-minded as the legendary Godfrey of Bouillon, the rescuer of
Jerusalem. That humble knight had refused the title of "First King
of Jerusalem" and ruled the conquered land with the wisdom of
old Solomon himself.

Most crusaders were now seeking new lands and treasures to claim
for themselves and the desecration of Constantinople, the greatest
city in the known world at that time, was an abomination before
the God whose will they had sworn to follow.

Nevertheless, Baron Reynald of Vendome still lived by the worn
out myths regarding the apostolic authority of the Pope and the

superiority of the Church over all other forms of religion. Though he sometimes questioned the selling of indulgences and the political bargaining tool of penance, he refused to accept the conclusions of other men of power and education. Men like Raymond of Toulouse, Duke of the richest, most refined culture on the continent - the Languedoc region where heresy was rampant and the mockery of the Pope and the Church's rituals an unbridled daily occurrence. Such worldly noblemen quietly rejected the fetishism of a religious empire more powerful than all the kings and emperors of the West. They had gone so far as to reject the most sacred ideas of the faith and embraced new concepts utterly foreign to the centuries-old beliefs of their societies.

It was the fear of chaos resulting from the destruction of order and restraint, upheld by the Church of Rome, that kept independent minds like Reynald as loyal vassals of the Holy Father, regardless of the Pope's very human faults. The Baron was prepared to lose everything in the name of stability and the survival of his society. Adela was a little girl at that time and loved her father with great passion. They were always together. He was her teacher, her companion, her hero. Adela did everything in her power to dissuade him from going to the Holy Land. But no one could change the Baron's mind once it was set on a certain course. He refused to remain at home and grow fat with indolence while the King's knights made a mockery of the sacred call to free the shrines of the Faith. He therefore joined Simon of Montfort and Count Baldwin of Flanders to head the campaign against Egypt in an effort to free Jerusalem once again.

Now Lord Reynald rotted away in a faraway land with little hope of ever returning to the green pastures of his home.

Tears quietly streamed down Adela's cheeks as she thought of her beloved father. It was impossible to imagine that she would never see him again, never hear his laughter, never feel his hearty embrace. She turned toward the narrow window that looked out upon the Baron's lands. Gentle hills rolled on as far as the eye could see, glowing in the golden haze of the sun. A cow bell sounded in the distance carried by a cool northern breeze rising out of the forests. This was a land of peace in a world at war. The Baron's territories were surrounded by the agonizing screams of the wounded and the dying. And beyond the clash of iron came the tentacles of the Black Death which would decimate a third of the continent in its century-long ravaging of humanity.

How she longed to see her father riding off on his favorite horse to inspect his lands, breathing in the sweet aromas of his fields and orchards. She would be riding alongside him, Tristan running at her side. Perhaps they would race across the fields to the first woodlands. She had finally beaten him the last time. It was their final moment together. As his cortege awaited him to journey to the southern seaports, he had trotted over toward his little girl who was weeping uncontrollably. A rainbow appeared through the mist in her eyes when he challenged her to a race as he had so often done since giving her a magnificent Arabian stallion for her eighth birthday. The royal beast was obedient to his young mistress, and had until then never galloped as fast as his great might could take him. But this time, she had thrown all her pain and frustration into the race and the animal responded with thunderous power. Her proud father had cheered her on as she left him behind in the dust.

An unfriendly knock stirred her out of her reveries. Adela quickly dried her tears and called out for the visitor to enter. The door opened slowly and revealed Lady Beatrice and a large silhouette who remained in the shadows.

"I wish a word with you, Adela," said Lady Beatrice in a haughty voice.

"Who is that with you?" the young woman retorted defiantly.

A man stepped out of the shadows. Adela recognized the large frame, the coarse wrinkled skin tough as animal's hide, and the swollen nose crawling with reddish veins as the features of one of the most unpleasant men she had ever known: the priest Guilbert. His thick, curly hair had long turned white and stood out in sharp contrast to the immense black bushes that hung above his narrow little eyes. There was nothing reverent or pious about him. The priest looked more like the town blacksmith than the spiritual leader of the community.

Rumors abounded concerning his predilection for the pleasures of the flesh. If the whispered tales were to be believed, his list of concubines was the largest in the province. Darker stories told of a bastard child born to a poor peasant girl. Its tiny body was found on the riverbank within days of its birth, damned by a father who would have nothing to do it. The peasant girl had hung herself at sunset and the next morning, Father Guilbert was gone, called away on urgent business to Rome.

Such stories had repulsed Adela long before he became adviser to her aunt. The two wretched individuals, mean tempered, lonely and vindictive, had joined in an unholy alliance against all that was good and young and beautiful. They were the only authority throughout Lord Reynald's lands and they terrorized the peasantry and small merchants from the Loire Valley to the rugged hills of the Massif Central.

Now the odious couple stood in Adela's room, violating her last refuge.

"What is he doing here?" Adela asked, throwing a disgusted glance at the gloomy man of the cloth.

"I've requested his presence," responded Lady Beatrice, whose anger was already aflame and ready to leap out at her.

"That man is not to step into my chambers!"

Adela hurried to the door and blocked their way.

"Your insolence knows no boundaries, Adela dear."

Lady Beatrice gave her a venomous smile. She knew her hated niece was digging herself into a deeper hole. His glazed, rodent-like eyes widened in outrage, the priest stepped forward. He stood face to face with the defiant young woman, his ample girth almost touching her.

"How dare you speak to a servant of the Church in such a way!"

Adela let out a mocking laugh.

"You're a servant of avarice and lust, not of the Savior!"

In a burst of uncontrolled rage, Guilbert raised his hand to strike her. But he caught himself and his fist froze in mid-air. Adela stared at him like the true daughter of a noble chevalier.

"There will be pig's blood on the cobblestone if you touch me!"

"Adela!" cried Lady Beatrice. "Is there no end to your insolence? When will you behave like a lady?"

The priest lowered his hand, his features withering into a hideous frown.

"She is a demon, Mylady. The Devil has made her his wench!"

Adela grabbed the door and tried to close it on them.

"Begone!"

Lady Beatrice and the cleric struggled with her, pushing back against the door. Her strength was greater than theirs combined.

"Guards!" the regent cried out.

Adela was about to lock the door when it was thrown open by three soldiers. She fell back into the room.

"How dare you do this to your liege!" she yelled.

"Forgive us, Mylady. But Lady Beatrice is our..."

The embarrassed soldier was interrupted by Lady Beatrice who pointed a sharp-nailed finger at her niece.

"Hear my words, you wretched creature! From this day forth, you are no longer free to roam the lands like a man! You will be confined to your chambers! You will never again set eyes on that peasant boy, and this very evening you will meet your new master!"

Adela turned pale as she leaned against the oak bedpost.

"What do you mean, my master?"

"I have invited the son of the Duke of Tours to honor our dias. We will offer him your hand in return for his family's allegiance and the consolidation of our lands."

A tidal wave of horror crashed upon Adela's soul.

"You cannot do this! My father would have you flogged!"

"Your father is not here," snickered the bitter woman. "He has made me responsible for your upbringing and, by God, you will behave like a woman and learn the ways of Christian living."

Adela began to tremble with fury. For the first time in her life, she feared losing control of herself.

"I will be wedded to no one except the man I choose. I am not a slave nor a chess piece to be bargained away!"

The priest, breathing heavily from the excitement and keeping his distance from the unpredictable young woman, added with solemnity:

"You are a female and you will learn your place according to the laws of Almighty God!"

"Don't speak to me of God, you ignorant blasphemer! You don't even know enough Latin to say the Mass properly! You have no idea what the Christ came to tell us!"

The priest turned to Lady Beatrice, the sadistic shadow of brutish fanaticism darkening his face.

"Is she a heretic as well?"

"Nothing would surprise me, Father," the regent replied, smelling blood.

Guilbert turned back toward Adela, a savage gleam in his eyes.

"I am an acquaintance of the Inquisitor, the Holy Father's newly ordained guardian of the Faith. He is traveling through the territories at this very moment. Perhaps he should have a word with you, child. We would not want you to stray from the right path...Do you know the fate that awaits heretics?"

A chill shook Adela's body. Never in her worst nightmares had she imagined being so threatened and oppressed. She had always taken her freedom for granted. And even though womanhood was synonymous with servanthood in these primitive times, she looked to the great women of her day - Eleanor of Aquitaine and Blanche of Castille - as models of who she could become. But they were the exception among the female population, and though the knights jousted for a lady's scarves, the Church and the law of the land condemned them to low status with absolutely no power and no say in their destinies.

Adela also knew that men of the cloth, though generally reputed to be hypocrites at best, still had the power to torture their enemies ferociously, publicly humiliate them in grotesque fashion, and burn them alive at the stake. Though they professed to follow in the footsteps of the gentle Teacher from Palestine, they showed no sign of his compassion or kinship with the Creator. Pope Innocent's declaration of war on Adela's southern neighbors, who expressed the words of the Christ so clearly through their holy lives, was final proof that religion had gone sour like milk left out in the summer sun.

Lady Beatrice beamed with the joy of victory.

"You will dress in your best gown and have your face made to look its finest for the young Duke of Tours. We do not want to disappoint him."

Adela suddenly stepped forward and slapped her aunt's face. The smack echoed loudly in the chamber, for her hand was hurled on by eight years of mistreatment. Lady Beatrice let out a great moan and fell in a heap on the cobblestone.

"Seize her!" Guilbert cried out, horrified. The guards moved hesitatingly toward the child of the mighty Reynald, but she evaded them. The priest tried to block her way as she rushed toward the door. Fighting for her life, Adela kicked him in the shin with the power of a horse's hind leg. The man's face turned purple and he sunk to his knees.

Adela grabbed a silver broadsword hanging on her wall, a gift to her father from the King of Aragon. She swung around and faced the three soldiers. The men froze before the gleaming, razor-sharp weapon.

"I know how to use this!" she shouted.

One of the guards smiled sadly at her.

"I know, Mylady. I saw your father teach you well."

"Don't force me to strike you!" Adela added, swinging the heavy blade toward them.

The guard who had spoken held his companions back.

"She means what she says. We'll let you go, Lady Adela. But I beg of you, think of what you're doing. Where can you go?" He looked at her with melancholy, remembering the days when the little girl and her beloved father filled the castle with joy. She seemed to read his thoughts and her eyes filled with tears. But the sudden shriek of her evil aunt quickly brought her back to the present.

"Chain her! Chain that beast!"

Adela hurried from the room.

She ran wildly down the spiraling stone stairway.

"Adela! What is wrong?"

Cecilia stood in the hallway, stunned to see her mistress rushing like a frightened deer.

"Cecilia!"

Adela hurried toward her.

"Quick! Have my horse saddled!"

"Where are you going?" her lady-in-waiting asked.

Adela leaned against the wall to catch her breath.

"I don't know...I don't know where to go."

Tears filled her eyes as she realized how powerless she really was.

"Where can I go, Cecilia?"

She began to weep bitterly as the rattling weapons of the soldiers in pursuit echoed into the hallway. The unspeakable agony of nearly a decade of her aunt's oppression came to the surface along with the desperation of a woman's position in this society of feudal lords where wife beating was a law of the land.

Cecilia caressed her dearest friend, hoping to soothe her grief.

"Can I help in any way, Adela?"

The young Baroness made a supreme effort to master her emotions. She knew the guards would be upon her any moment.

A thought came to her and she suddenly grabbed Cecilia with both hands.

"There is, Cecilia, there is! Find Bertran! Go to his mother for she will surely hear from him. Send a message to him that I'm to be sold to the Duke of Tours like a miserable slave of the heathens. Tell him to come for me! Tell him to take me away!"

Cecilia's eyes widened with each word. She had never been asked to participate in such a mad adventure.

"But, Mylady, I...I've never been to the village. It frightens me. The people there are so...wretched."

"Travel with the cook when he goes to market in the morning. Have him show you the way to Bertran's hamlet."

"I cannot, Mylady..."

The hurried footsteps were nearby. Adela stared fire into her frightened lady-in-waiting, trying to penetrate the young girl's soul with her courage.

"You can!"

Suddenly, the soldiers appeared at the end of the hallway. Adela turned to them. They stopped, uncertain as to what she would do. The proud young woman of noble blood stepped forward, sword in hand. She motioned for Cecilia to hurry off and fulfill her mission.

The soldiers studied her with worried expressions. Each one of them would have thrown himself on his own weapon before doing battle with the daughter of their liege lord, despite their orders from Lady Beatrice.

Adela dropped her royal sword.

"I will not shed the blood of my father's soldiers," she said with simple honesty.

"And we would not lay a hand on the daughter of Lord Reynald," one of the soldiers answered.

Lady Beatrice suddenly appeared from the stairway, disheveled and as full of rage as she had ever gotten in a lifetime of anger.

"Will you follow my orders, or will you be imprisoned in your chambers?" she cried out, trembling with outrage.

Adela looked at her calmly, as though resigned to her fate.

"I will obey you, Lady Beatrice."

Her aunt was astonished. For a moment, the shock kept her speechless. Then an evil grin darkened her face.

"Very well, then. We are pleased that you have come to your senses. And I will overlook your attack on my person. Return to your chambers and prepare for our visitors."

Adela could not help but smile sadly at her aunt's immense hypocrisy. After years of mistreating everyone under her control, she was still trying to put on a magnanimous mask that could only fool her. Adela stepped forward, bowed to her victorious regent, and returned to her rooms as the soldiers respectfully moved aside.

In the steep, narrow stairway, Adela encountered Guilbert who was still in pain from her kick. They glared at each other silently as they neared. The stairway was such that one had to stop so that the other could pass by, bodies virtually touching. They stopped and stood in silence, eyeing each other defiantly.

"After you, Mylady."

The priest's voice turned Adela's blood cold. Those common words were filled to the brim with a vicious hatred of womankind in general and of her in particular. He reminded her of a poisonous spider weaving its deadly web.

Adela took a step closer to the large man who smelled permanently of cheap beer. Her whole body tensed as she passed him by. She could feel his wheezing breath on her face and had the queer sensation that he emanated the presence of death.

"Your peasant boy will not live to see this Lord's Day unless he gives himself up to the Baron's guards."

Adela continued on her way, trying hard to keep her attention from the priest.

"I warn you, Mylady. Stay away from the heretics. They will all per-
ish, everyone one of them, as well as all who associate with them."
"I have never even laid eyes on a heretic," Adela stated as she
moved away from him.
"You can never be too certain. They are everywhere, like rats. And
they all started as free thinkers!"
Adela turned back. The priest was eyeing her with the depraved
look of a sadistic interrogator eager to employ his barbaric meth-
ods.
"I am sorry for you, Father Guilbert. You're such an unhappy creature."
With that, she hurried off into the shadows.
Guilbert reacted as though he had been hit with a hammer. Animal
rage shook his entire frame.
"I am very happy these days, Mylady!" he called out coarsely.
"Good Christian knights are carving up heretics from Albi to
Carcassone!"
He let out a frightful burst of laughter and continued his slow
waddle down the stairs. In the humid darkness, eyes gleaming with
satisfaction at the horrific mutilation and murder of men, women
and children who worshipped God in their own way, Father
Guilbert seemed the very incarnation of that which he spoke
against so often - Satan, Lucifer, the Destroyer of Good.
As Adela and Guilbert cursed each other under their breath, they
both sensed that their battle was far from over. And they knew that

it would be a struggle to the death.

4

Excitement filled the gentle spring air as news of the noble
visitor spread through the villages and hamlets of the
Baron's domain. Soon after the first cockcrow, servants
from the castle were in the town square, shopping for the
great banquet in honor of Aimery of Tours, heir to the fer-
tile fields on the southern border of Lord Reynald's
fiefdom.

Such festive occasions were very rare under the rule of Lady Beatrice and the people rejoiced at this event that would
briefly distract their attention from the endless toil and
miserable condition of their lives. While the marketplace
was still being set up, gossipers were guessing at the purpose of the visit. The young Baronness, so admired by the
people for her beauty and friendly manners, was of marrying age and the linkage of the pastures of Vendome and
Tours would create a wealth and power rivaling that of the
King himself.

Cecilia sat silently on the hard bench of the cook's wagon,

trying her best not to tremble. Fear already held her in its clutches and made it difficult for her to breath even though they had only left the confines of the castle a short while ago. She was horrified by the thought of having to travel beyond the town to Bertran's home. The nervous young woman rarely left the courtyards of the Baron's home and had never been to the outlying hamlets. But she had seen the serfs in the fields. Their ragged, unclean clothes and haggard faces made a deep impression on her. This was a level of human misery that she never wanted to come near for fear that it might somehow be catching and cause her to fall into the pit of their desperate poverty.

She found it preferable to spend her days in the dark, safe rooms of the castle, weaving tapestries with the other ladies, rather than breathe the fresh air of the countryside along with the peasants, beggars, and cut-throats who wandered the woodlands. The servants at court had told her blood-curdling tales of this dark world that lay on the other side of the stagnant mote surrounding the castle walls.

Life had always been hard, bitter and short for the vast majority of the people. But the departure of all the mightiest knights of France for the Holy Land removed the only barrier against the barbaric instinct seething beneath the wretched life of feudal society. Death was always present, always overshadowing the few little pleasures of earthly life.

If it wasn't to be the plague, then perhaps it would be a brigand's rusty blade or the horse's hooves of a renegade baron plundering the lands of his neighbor.

Cecilia felt exposed to all these dangers at once as she sat in the open wagon. The town lay ahead of them, perched atop a hill. Beside her, the cook hummed an old ballad. He was a large man, Gasconian by birth, beaming with jovial good nature. His natural warmth was tempered by nearly a decade of feuding with Lady Beatrice who found something to criticize in everything he baked. The grim woman had worn him down and taken that southern joy from his soul.

Worse yet, the daily massacres of his fellow Gasconians, and the destruction of that gentle culture that had arisen as a true child of the Mediterranean climate, was crushing his spirit.

Every few days, a pilgrim, a traveling minstrel, a wandering knight seeking the Baron's famed hospitality, would share another gruesome story about the perverse crusade. Never had the Church declared war so openly against an enemy. Never had the Pope and his clerics revealed the extent of their savage hatred for anyone who dared question their version of religion. Bohemond the cook knew of cousins who had suffered torments at the hands of so called Christians. No Saracen would every commit such acts, not even the fearsome followers of the Old Man of the Mountain who were known the world over for their skills in the black art of murder.

The cook was all the more miserable this day because he was to prepare a feast for the son of a man reputed to have personally taken part in the slaughter of the people of Beziers only two years before. In the bloody streets of that sun-drenched town, the strength of the gentle Cathar believers had been crushed. Though the final massacre at their stronghold of Montsegur was still to come, the ghastly murder of innocent townspeople had broken the back of the finest culture of the age. Men like Bohemond who had left their native land before the butchery began knew that there would never be a time of going home, that all their sweetest memories of childhood, the very way of life that bred them to manhood, had drained away along with the blood of the brightest souls of the century.

The silence between Cecilia and Bohemond spoke more than any words they could have said. He guessed that the young woman was up to something dangerous when she made the unusual request of joining him on his trip to town. Having known her mistress Adela from the day of her birth, he could well imagine the intrigue to which she exposed her friends. Though Bohemond was a bear of a man, he would never consider doing anything to displease Lady Beatrice for he had seen the results too many times these last eight years. One of his assistants was flogged for dropping a plate of her favorite venison just as he was about to serve it to her. The regent was certain he had done in on purpose and she made him pay for all the hateful feelings she sensed from the servants at the castle.

The poor boy never recovered from the lashing because she refused to let his wounds be treated while he lay for hours in the mud of the courtyard as an example to the others. He died in agony a few days later in the arms of his only friend and taskmaster, Bohemond.

The cook's repressed hatred for Lady Beatrice was matched only by his cowardice. The castle's kitchen was a safe place to spend one's life while the world around roared with battle and destruction.

As the wagon approached the crossroads that would lead them up the hill toward town, Bohemond noticed that his passenger's nervousness suddenly increase. Cecilia was glancing toward the other road which led to the tiny hamlet on the banks of the river.

The aging cook caught himself staring at the crossroads as though they were a symbol of his own destiny. He knew that if he took the path leading to town, he would be expressing his obedience to a person he despised like none other. The other road was one of danger and uncertainty. Bohemond's heartbeat increased threefold and sweat appeared on his balding forehead. "What are you doing?" he thought to himself. "No one has asked anything of you. Just go to the market as you always do."

A scarlet shade flushed his round face as shame took hold of him. He realized that Adela had simply assumed his cowardice and not even considered asking for his help. Instead, she was placing her dangerous demands on poor Cecilia, a girl who screamed at the sight of spiders. Surely, some terrible plan was afoot if this scheming was occurring on the very day of the young Duke's visit.

With a sudden jerk of the reins, Bohemond guided the horses onto the road leading down to the river. Cecilia nearly leaped out of her seat and turned to him with terror in her eyes.

"Is this not the direction you want to go in?" he asked solemnly.

Cecilia didn't answer. She looked back at the road that would lead her to Bertran's home.

"How did you intend to get to the hamlet from the marketplace?"

The young woman could barely control her fear. She couldn't tell if he was helping her or would betray her to Lady Beatrice. The cook looked at the frightened girl with great sadness in his eyes.

"Let me help, Cecilia."

"Why?" she asked in a barely audible voice.

Bohemond looked out at the peaceful countryside. Sweet birdsongs sounded through the foliage and the aroma of spring's rebirth filled the air. He tasted a salty tear running down his cheek. The goodness of creation was so evident in everything around them, from the lazy clouds above to the tiniest wisp of grass dancing in the breeze. How then could such evil reign over their lives? How could humanity live in such darkness and cruelty? The beasts of the fields were better off!

He turned to Cecilia and put his large, soft hand on her cheek, soothing her fear.

"I was not born to be a servant of wickedness. It is in the name of our Good Maker that I help you."

Cecilia kissed his hand and smiled. His kindness and courage lifted her fear like a magic spell. The wagon creaked loudly as it descended toward the river below. The horses struggled down the steep mud path, snorting in discontent. Bohemond's soul filled with a strange peace, the kind that could only be reached after a difficult choice. He sensed, however, that his decision would forever alter the course of his life. He had stepped out of the security of the Baron's kitchen and there was no turning back.

Soon the hamlet came into view. A dozen peasant huts squatted by the river. Smoke rose here and there from a busy hearth, reminding Cecilia of fumes from a manure pile. Several dirt-stained children ran about the hovels chasing piglets and chickens. This was a world as removed from the castle courtyard as the encampments of nomadic tribes in the deserts of Palestine.

The wagon approached and the stench of open sewage became more evident. Cecilia involuntarily brought her hand to her nose.

"A sad sight this is," the cook muttered as he observed the half-naked children playing in the filth. "You are witnessing the result of our regent's new taxes on her people. Baron Reynald would never allow such misery in his lands."

The wagon stopped at the edge of the hamlet. Several forlorn elderly serfs sat on crude benches, eyeing them suspiciously. The playing children ran toward them.

"What now?" Bohemond asked his companion impatiently.

"I must find Bertran's home."

The cook looked at her in horror. Everyone at the castle knew that the brash young peasant had called upon himself the merciless wrath of Lady Beatrice. He was as good as dead.

"Are you sure of this?" he whispered, hoping to protect the terrified girl.

"He alone can save Adela."

"No one can save the Baroness from the schemes of her

aunt. Certainly not that unfortunate peasant boy."

A toothless widow approached the wagon, making her way through the excited children.

"What do you want with us?" she asked in an angry voice.

"I must speak with Bertran," Cecilia called out, trying her best to overcome her revulsion and fear.

The old woman's wrinkled face suddenly darkened. Her bony hands tightened around a heavy walking stick.

"Have you come to take him back to the castle?"

"No," replied Cecilia with new hope that they might help her on her mission. "I have a message for him."

"What sort of message?"

"It is for him alone."

The woman came closer. Cecilia instinctively leaned back.

"I am his grandmother. His sister and I are his only family."

"Where is Bertran?" Cecilia asked.

"In a safe place," the old woman retorted defiantly.

"Do you know how to reach him?"

"Maybe..."

Cecilia was losing patience with this game of secrecy. The children were pulling on her sleeves and touching the soft fabric of her clothing which they had never felt before.

"The message is from Adela."

A spark of warmth appeared in the old woman's cavernous eyes.

"Come with me."

Cecilia looked at Bohemond for help. The thought of stepping down from the safety of the wagon and entering into
this putrid world of unspeakable poverty made her skin
crawl.

"You have come this far," the cook whispered to her. "You
must see your mission to its end."

"I can't," the young woman responded in a trembling
voice.

"May I go with her?" Bohemond asked the old woman.
She looked him over suspiciously. His kind nature was impossible to mistake. The widow nodded and turned toward
the huts, expecting them to follow. Bohemond stepped
down from the wagon and assisted Cecilia. She winced as
her dainty leather boots sunk into the oozing mud and
sewage. They walked behind the old woman as she painfully limped through the little maze of dismal homes. The
children skipped alongside them, unable to take their eyes
and hands from the luxurious cloth of Cecilia's skirts.

As they walked by the huts, Cecilia made the mistake of
looking into one of them. In the darkness of the tiny room,
where animals and humans shared a common dwelling, she
saw a mother and her infant sitting near the hearth. The
dim light revealed diseased features and desperation the
like of which Cecilia had never imagined. For the first time

in her life, she felt a searing sense of guilt for not helping in some way. In spite of the superstitions and idolatry of her faith, the words of the prophets and of the carpenter from Nazareth flooded her selfish heart.

Such misery contrasted to her comfort shook her out of her childish self-interest that had never been disrupted before. She noticed that muddying her dress was no longer a concern and she remembered the tenets of the Church which offered indulgences for acts of mercy. How many times in her childhood had she gone to confession and admitted her disinterest in the welfare of others? She had said uncounted numbers of "Hail Marys" and done penance by purchasing candles and praying beyond the normal time limit. But she had never reached out to another human being.

Her mother was a devout believer in the teachings of the priests even though her father and brothers only rendered lip-service to the institution. For decades, perhaps centuries, the Church had been losing the loyalty of its congregations as it amassed wealth and power in opposition to the teachings of the Savior. New relics were always being brought forth as objects of worship and the priests were increasing their control over the people's lives while at the same time falling into worse debaucheries than the laity. Nevertheless, Cecilia remained unquestionably faithful to the religion with which she had grown up. It was the source of her poor mother's only happiness, and the agony of her last illness was alleviated only by the rituals of the clerics whom she trusted as much as the saints to whom she prayed fervently. It was a priest who saved little Cecilia from a brutal lashing by her drunkard father. He had come to visit her dying mother and found the child cowering behind the bushes in their garden. Her father came charging at her, belt in hand. She had refused his perverse advances once too often and, in a drunken rage, he had decided to destroy the life he considered to be his possession. Only the timely arrival of the priest had saved her. She was then put in the care of a nearby convent where her blind loyalty to the Church's dogma increased in zeal.

They came to one of the larger hovels perched over the river. The old woman motioned for them to wait at the entrance as she stepped into the dwelling. Bohemond and Cecilia stood in the mud, surrounded by children and several crippled old folks who eyed them with great curiosity. Though the children's faces were still bright with youthful innocence, most of their features were misshapen by generations of malnutrition and endless toil.

After a moment, the woman re-appeared followed by a hooded silhouette. As they came out into the sunlight, Bohemond suddenly genuflected three times. Cecilia's entire frame shivered with terror at this frantic behavior coming from the usually quiet, slow-moving cook. He remained on his knees in the mud, trembling like an autumn leaf until the hooded figure gently touched his shoulder.

"Rise, my son."

Cecilia looked up and saw the blazing eyes of the hermit. The noble spirit in beggar's clothing helped Bohemond to his feet. Fifteen years had gone by, but Bohemond could never forget the unique impression made upon him by one of the Friends of God who were the teachers of true believers. They all had an aura about them, a humility, a strength of character, and a profound serenity unmatched by any clerics of the Church of Rome. A saint or two might have reached those heights of spiritual awareness, especially the founders of the new lay orders of poverty like Francis and Dominic, but they too lived in sharp contrast to the Pope and his Empire. Their communities would become the Church's way of accommodating the kind of apostolic lifestyle found among the Cathars and so longed for by Christians who could not find it among the priests and the commerce of the cathedrals.

Among the Cathars there were hundreds of ascetics who had vowed their lives to poverty, chastity, and service in the Name of a loving and ever-present God. More than any other Elder, the hermit had struck young Bohemond with the dazzling light in his eyes and the uncontaminated kindness of his gentle spirit. He was the first to help him on his way as a believer in the spiritual journey of the Cathar. It was the hermit who initiated him into the secret transmission of the Prayer that brought the believer into a new stage of intimacy with the Divine Spirit.

The two men looked at each other with an intensity that spoke more eloquently than words. They shared a deep bond that nothing earthly could sever. Bohemond the cook was a Cathar believer who knew the holiness of a Perfect One.

Cecilia saw a metamorphosis take place in the face of her traveling companion. New life seemed to lift the heavy burden in his soul that had lined his features prematurely. She could almost hear his heart pounding with the joy of having met a beloved ghost of his past.

"How came you to this place, Master?" Bohemond asked when the use of his voice returned to him.

"Our friends insisted that one of us must escape the stake for the sake of the teaching. So I find myself in these northern pastures, far from our earthly home."

Bohemond suddenly realized that he was revealing his beloved mentor's identity. He looked at all the witnesses gathered around them. The hermit smiled, reading his thoughts.

"We are safe here. These poor folk have nothing but their loyalty to each other. And you find me here for the sake of one of their own."

"What do you mean?" asked Bohemond, confused.

The gentle old man turned to Cecilia.

"You are here to see young Bertran, are you not?"

Cecilia nodded, dumbfounded. He approached her and put his hand on her shoulder. She felt her fear subside.

"I have come to his home on his behalf. He asked me to comfort his family before his departure."

"Where is he going?"

"Far away...To a place where he might find new life."

"And you have endangered your life for his, Master?" asked Bohemond, astonished.

The old man smiled.

"It is not for us to decide how Providence will make use of our unhappy time on this earth. I merely follow what is given me to do."

"But the Inquisitor is traveling through the Baron's domain at this very moment! You must hide!"

Cecilia suddenly realized that she was standing before a hunted heretic, the enemy of the Lord according to the edicts of the Pope. She had heard too many stories of the heresy that desecrated the altars and crosses in the churches of the Languedoc and in the lands of the Count of

Toulouse. It was said that they rejected all the external expressions of the Faith, all the most sacred rituals including the Eucharist which they mocked as the silliest of superstitions. Such blasphemies were more monstrous than the atrocities of the heathens who at least were not condemning the Holy Roman Church in the name of its Lord!

"You have a message for my unfortunate companion, gentle lady?" the hermit asked.

Cecilia stepped back, afraid that the heretic would contaminate her.

"Fear not, my child, we are not devils despite the lies you've heard. Now tell me what Bertran is to know."

The young woman felt the gaze of the hermit penetrate deeply into her being. For the briefest instant, she saw a glimmer of melancholy flash in those eagle eyes as the seer read something of the future in her soul.

"Mylady Adela is to be given in marriage to the Duke of Tours. She wants Bertran to....take her away."

Cecilia blurted out the words as best she could. Her mind was swimming with terror and confusion. She did not have the constitution to face such unspeakable dangers. Helping a runaway serf was one thing, but consorting with heretics was quite another.

She swiftly turned away and headed for the wagon.

Bohemond watched on, concerned with her reaction.

"Do not fear for my safety, friend," the hermit said softly. I know that death must come to this wretched body. Leave it in the merciful hands of the One who knows only Goodness."

"May I be of service to you in any way, Master?"

Bohemond would have given his life in that instant for this grand Elder of his martyred fellowship.

"Yes, dear friend. Keep the true faith alive by not hating those who revile us and do us harm. Without the charity of our Lord, we live in darkness as they do. Whatever is to occur in these dreadful times, remember to seek the Kingdom above all else."

He took Bohemond's hand in his. The cook could feel a healing energy rush through his arm to his beleaguered spirit.

"Do not fear the agonies of death. They are but the birthing pains of a new, glorious life. Our journey is short here in this vale of tears, and has only one great purpose. Awaken therefore to your true nature and live as a free spirit even now."

Bohemond's heart leaped at these words of spiritual wisdom coming from the fires of a soul united to its eternal spirit. He realized that in this very moment, standing in the mud of desolate poverty and surrounded by the stench of misery, he was receiving the Consolation of the Spirit from one who had awakened to its Presence while still in the flesh and blazed a trail for others to follow.

Unable to control his emotions, Bohemond hugged the kind mystic who had given him the most precious of all gifts, that of discovering his true Self beyond bones and blood and anxiety. The good man held his face in his hands and looked a final time into his eyes.

"Be free, my brother, be free of the oblivion to which so many are headed."

Bohemond walked away, flooded with a new joy. It seemed to him that all the agony of these last eight years was justified and healed in this brief encounter. He would suffer it all again for this moment of enlightenment.

As he climbed into the wagon, he was struck by the expression on Cecilia's face. There was something new on her gentle features, a harshness that he had never seen before. They rode back to the crossroads in grim silence, just as they had earlier that morning. But there was something different between them. Something that felt like the imminent arrival of unutterable tragedy.

5

Golden rays of the late afternoon sun were drawing great shadows across the land. The Baron's turrets shimmered with the fading light like faithful torches. In contrast with the quieting of nature at the end of another day, the castle walls echoed with incredible noise.

The courtyard was packed with the animals and entourage of the Duke of Tours. Servants hurried to and fro making final preparations for the banquet that was to celebrate the arrival of the illustrious guest. The chateau's kitchen was the center of the pandemonium as Bohemond ordered his assistants about, readying the courses of the feast. He had not masterminded such a meal in years. The last visitor of importance was the King's Chancellor sent by Philip Augustus himself in a last attempt to rouse the Baron's loyalty to the cause of the failing Crusade. Though the roast venison was a great success, the Chancellor's mission had come to nothing. It would take the desecration of the greatest city on the continent to convince Lord Reynald of his duty.

Bohemond was usually very calm in these proceedings for he knew every detail of his art. But on this day he was a nervous wreck, sweating profusely as he hurried through the vast kitchen, shouting with rare irritability at his apprentices. The great joy of meeting an Elder of the True Faith was replaced with the sheer panic of learning that there would be an additional place setting at the dais. Arnald Almaric, the Abbot of Citeaux and leader of the Crusaders' armies against the heretics, was heading home from the bloodbaths he had mounted against the entire civilization of the South. By coincidence, he crossed the boundaries of the Baron's domain on this very day. Bohemond did not hear of the arrival until he was beckoned by Lady Beatrice and told of the need to feed another guest and his retinue. The Abbot stood next to her, his harsh, fanatic spirit smoldering in eyes that had witnessed some of the most gruesome scenes in human history. The jovial cook knew of the man's reputation from the very beginning of the blood-letting. It was Arnald Almaric who preached the war against the heretics some seven years before and was heard to say: "May the man who abstains from this Crusade never drink wine again; may he never eat, morning or evening, off a good linen cloth, or dress in fine stuff again to the end of his days; and at his death may he be buried like a dog!" The fierceness of the

Abbot's rhetoric forced the King himself to reluctantly participate in the massacre of his own people.

Bohemond learned of this violent monk long before, when he was Abbot of Grandselve, one of the largest Cistercian monasteries in the cook's native Languedoc. It was there that the man had developed his fierce hatred of the Cathars who were free to live their beliefs under the protection of the southern nobles. Even then, Bohemond wondered how a follower of the holy Bernard of Clairvaux, vowed to the sternest monastic requirements of austerity, obedience and prayer, could exhibit such a warrior-like, hostile spirit. Everyone in the region knew the Abbot to be an unscrupulous, dangerous man. It was only shortly after Bohemond came to work for Lord Reynald that he was shocked by the news that this same cold-hearted fanatic was made Papal legate in charge of wiping out the Christians who had turned away from the decadence of Rome.

Standing now before him, only hours after meeting a notorious leader of the hated sect, the cook saw his life flash before him. The presence of the Angel of Death himself could not have made him more horror-stricken. He found himself imagining that the bloodthirsty monk could smell the presence of a heretic. And when the heinous glare of the Abbot's dark eyes fell upon him and studied him suspiciously, poor Bohemond thought he could already hear the creaking of the rack.

Perhaps the deadly monk recognized the features of a southern-born native. Or perhaps it was the man's visible fear that put him on the alert. As he returned to the kitchen, the cook sensed that he was being watched by some beast of the wilds ready to devour its prey.

As the hour of the banquet approached, the terrified cook desperately tried to devise a strategy that would keep him far from the murderer of his countrymen. There was a long-standing custom in the Baron's domain calling for the chief cook to make an appearance at the end of the feast and receive the applause of the satisfied guests. It had always been a moment of great anticipation for Bohemond because he took great pride in the skills passed on to him from generations of cooks. His family had worked for most of the great nobles across the south and his grandfather had been brought to the court of King Louis VII.

But the thought of facing the Abbot again was too much for him. He began to curse the fool hearty courage that had made him choose the path to the hamlet. Even the encounter with the Perfect One was losing its luster as he found himself trapped like a chased rat in the same walls with the most notorious killer of heretics ever to disgrace the pages of history. Three years had barely elapsed since the hideous slaughter of the citizens of Beziers. Bohemond had not slept for a week after hearing the stories. Twenty thousand people hacked to death! Hundreds more burned alive! And now the man responsible for these gory deeds was hungering for food prepared by his own hands. If there ever was a force of Evil fighting the goodness of the Creator as the Cathar believed, it was making its appearance here in this castle!

In his panic, Bohemond found himself thinking like a man caught in a feverish delirium. Maybe he could poison the monster! But how? Who would be serving the wine at the head of the dais? What would happen if it fell in the wrong hands? How could he avoid standing before the Pope's official cut-throat? Why in God's name had he taken such chances? In God's name indeed...

Bohemond wiped the sweat from his brow which was now running like raindrops down his cheeks. He paused from his supervision of the meal preparations and tried to catch his breath. He felt his heart beat like the attack drum of a Roman warship. He breathed deeply and slowly, remembering the advice of an Elder in his youth. With trembling hands, he poured cold water into a towel and held it against his face. Slowly, he felt a ray of peace return as he whispered a prayer to the God he still believed in even while His faithful children were being decimated.

As his mind tried to wrestle the fear to a standstill, he re-

membered the words from a secret rite of his beloved faith:
"You must understand that Our Father wishes to have pity
on his people and to receive them into His peace and harmony...You must understand that if you wish to receive
this holy prayer you must repent for all your sins and forgive all men..."

Forgive all men! This was where Bohemond knew that he
was far from the purity of heart to which every true Christian aspired. Both his fear and his anger conspired to keep
him from anything but foul hatred for the man who was
systematically destroying all that was beautiful and dear to
him.

Bohemond raised a goblet of wine to his lips and drank
deeply. The hot sensation ran through his chest like a fire
burning through his jungle of fearful emotions. For a moment, he felt better. He was about to turn back to his
duties, when the door opened and a silhouette appeared on
the wall before him.

His brief oasis of calm shattered instantly. Cecilia stood before him. Never before had the presence of the frail young
woman frightened anyone. But there was a look in her eyes,
a look that came from a place never seen before by those
who knew her. In that soft, round face was the shadow of a
familiar expression that so haunted the cook. It resembled
the harsh glare of the evil Abbot himself! The zealot's look

of rage when his sacred idols are being threatened. In those large feminine eyes was the dark light of Le Malin - Satan the Trickster - who made religion his instrument of choice for the perpetration of his most cruel deeds.

"How may I help you, Cecilia?" Bohemond asked as best he could. The sour young woman eyed him silently, then said in an icy voice:

"Lady Beatrice wishes to know if you are ready to begin serving."

The cook swallowed hard and looked back at his busy apprentices.

"We are...Are the guests seated?"

"The minstrel is about to play. After his song, we will be ready for the meal."

"Very good. I shall have Hugh watch for the signal."

He motioned for one of his young assistants to follow Cecilia back to the banquet hall. The lady-in-waiting, who only hours ago was so grateful for his generous help, had become transformed into an ominous creature full of unspoken venom. She swiftly left the kitchen.

Bohemond watched her disappear and involuntarily muttered a prayer out loud.

"What did you say?"

Young Hugh was standing beside him. Bohemond, pale

and trembling once again, motioned angrily for the boy to follow in Cecilia's footsteps.

* * *

Adela remained in her chambers until the last possible moment. The young Duke had been at the castle since mid-day and still she had refused to see him, claiming some disabling illness. As the time of the banquet grew near, Lady Beatrice sent guards to forcibly take her from her room. Adela assured them that she would come peacefully but needed a bit more time to dress.

She sat by her window, looking out at her beloved country. Her conversation with Cecilia kept returning like a nightmare that would not leave her alone. Her lady-in-waiting reported to her that she had indeed delivered the message, but almost immediately she entered upon a frightful condemnation of Bertran.

"He is in the company of heretics!" Cecilia had cried out.

"Bertran? That's not possible! I've never known him to give much attention to anything religious. He worships me and there ends his creed."

"I saw a Perfect One! He tried to touch me! I could tell he had the Evil Eye when he looked at me. And Bohemond is one of them!"

"Our Bohemond? The cook?"

"Yes! He recognized him. I watched him genuflect before the heretic to receive his benediction! Have you ever heard of anything more blasphemous? He kneeled before him in adoration like a worshiper of the Devil!"

Adela had always liked the kind cook who was so skilled in the kitchen and so loyal to her family. He was a special friend to her every since her father had left for the Holy Land. It was he who assisted her when she fell from her horse in the courtyard on a slippery winter's day, and he who snuck food to her chambers on eves when Lady Beatrice forbade her from dining as punishment for some impudent behavior.

Not in her wildest imagination could she have believed that he was a follower of the Cathar and the Albigenese as they were also called in the region. She knew little of their teachings and, until the Pope's anathema was pronounced, thought that this was an accepted form of discipleship as did most of the nobles and nearly all the citizens in the southern lands. It was only the murder of the Papal legate, Pierre of Castelnau, some five years before that had turned the tides of popular acceptance. The Pope's envoy had been inciting Barons to hunt down the heretics, and when the greatest Count in France, Raymond of Toulouse, had refused, the Pope's envoy called for the knights to rebel against their liege lord.

At age eleven, Adela still remembered being aghast at the legate's condemnation declared against the most cultured man she had ever met. For Raymond of Toulouse was an acquaintance of her father's, and he gave her the first falcon she ever wore on her arm. To learn that a priest had proclaimed that "he who strikes you dead will earn a blessing," then excommunicated the Count and put his vast territories under interdict, was inconceivable. With a child's innocent awareness, she knew that Raymond the Sixth, Count of Toulouse, cousin of the King of France and brother-in-law to the Kings of England and Aragon, Duke of Narbonne, Marquis of Provence, feudal sovereign over seven of the richest counties in the known world, was a good, virtuous man of high birth and spirit.

This great prince of Christendom was forced into a humiliating submission before the Pope's representative. It was one of the Count's officers who cut down Pierre of Castelnau, Legate to the Apostolic See of Languedoc, to save the honor of his lord. From that day forth, the fury of the Holy Father raged across that peaceful world where alone among the Frankish lands there flourished culture, art, and high civilization. While the northern epics praised bravery and the joy of battle, the gentle troubadours of Albi and Carcassone sang of the purest love.

Adela always associated the lofty spirituality of the Cathars with the sophistication of those regions. In her youthful fantasy, she imagined that only noble men and women took part in the mysterious initiations led by the Perfect Ones. It never occurred to her that simple folk like Bohemond would be attracted to the radical discipline and profound understandings of this way of living. Yet upon hearing this revelation from Cecilia, she recognized that all his many small kindnesses were not merely the luck of natural character, but the efforts of a soul on the way to conformity with its Divine origin. The cook's unselfishness was above all an offering of himself in the name of the Unconditional Love of the Creator.

"Why would Bertran be among heretics?" Adela wondered.

"I have often felt a darkness about him, Mylady," Cecilia admitted.

Adela was stunned. She would not have suspected sweet Cecilia to hold such feelings.

"My Bertran? He's as good as the earth and trustworthy as the mountains!"

"I don't know, Mylady."

Adela studied Cecilia's eyes. They had a look that disturbed her - a look of dementia - the very look she had seen on the priest's face that awful day she watched him come from the dungeons where a confession had been torn out of some poor wretch.

"What has come over you, Cecilia?"

The girl looked away from her.

"Speak!" Adela called out with booming authority. She
could not stand the insolence of disobedient servants.

"Serfs are thieves and cutthroats!" she cried out with
haughty contempt. Adela's face turned scarlet.

"You arrogant sot! Do you think because you were bred in
a disease infested town instead of the open fields that you
are better than the noblest friend I have ever had! Begone
with your brutish ignorance!"

Cecilia looked up at her sheepishly. Adela grabbed a belt
draped over a chair nearby and raised it with intent to use
it.

"Out!"

The girl ran as fast as she could. The belt whistled in the air
and caught the edge of her ear. Cecilia cried out in pain as
she slammed the door behind her. Raging like a mad bull,
Adela whipped the door again and again, mentally tearing
the flesh from her domestic's back.

She suddenly stopped, arm poised in midair for another
blow. The strong-tempered Baroness felt ashamed, as
though she were standing outside of herself observing her
primitive, uncontrolled behavior. She sighed deeply and
threw the belt in a corner. This was the first time she had

ever wanted to beat Cecilia, though not the first time she had raised her hand on a servant. Aggression was in her blood and, though born a woman, combat was second nature. Her inherited anger had multiplied fourfold since the loss of her father and her aunt's repression had destroyed the joy of her privileged childhood.

Adela dropped into the great oak chair. It wasn't merely the impertinence of insulting her friend that had so incensed her. She wanted to whip all the dull-minded, vulgar sentiments of her fellow humans which caused such misery to their brothers and sisters. The gross stupidity of the Crusades which had drenched with blood the sacred ground where the Anointed One of God once walked, the desperate poverty of the serfs who were plundered by knights, brigands, and priests alike, the loathing of women and their vicious enslavement: all this she saw in Cecilia's intolerant grimace. Somehow, she understood that this was the cause of evil in the world, the demonic side of humanity which would lay asunder peace and harmony to the end of time. Looking out her window, Adela now felt the invasion of dark despair. There was no sign of Bertran and the hour was upon her to enter into the snares of her hated aunt. And besides, what could he possibly do? How could he even make his way into the castle? The two guests had brought with them dozens of men at arms who filled the courtyard with the eerie sound of clanging metal.

A harsh knock at the door reminded her that the guards were in the hallway, still waiting for her. She looked across the horizon painted by the early colors of sunset. This was a view she had known since infancy. It was like a mother's face, radiant with security, steadfastness and unconditional love. Adela was seized by the terrible sensation that this might be the last time that she would look upon this cherished sight. Stepping away from the window, she hurried to her mirror.

She quickly straightened her hair and adjusted the folds of her blood-red tunic embroidered with gold. She needed the assurance of looking her best before facing the ordeal ahead.

The banquet hall was packed with gruff visitors. The castle dogs growled as they roamed through the corridors, suspicious of the intruders. Every servant was anxious, having rarely dealt with such a show of luxury. The Duke of Tours had brought a multitude of entertainers and domestics to impress the Baron's family, for the young noble knew that the sister of the mighty Reynald would respond only to wealth.

Aimery of Tours was a strapping lad of twenty, full of a knight's vigor and a noble's haughtiness. He was ruggedly handsome, his face framed in perfectly square jaws. Straight black hair fell upon broad shoulders, and his princely features revealed a powerful Norseman heritage. He had established a firm reputation as one of the finest jousters in France, having never lost to any man. His uncle, the powerful Duke of Burgundy, had brought to his court the best swordsmen of Aragon who trained the boy for glory. It was known that he had the makings of legendary prowess and his entire youth was spent in intense training for the noblest chivalry.

Aimery stood in the Baron's courtyard and smiled to himself.

The castle, though unkempt, reflected the worldly ways of its absent master. Influences from Provence and the lands of Islam had softened the harsh, imposing presence of the chateau fort. This was more than the lair of a warlord, built for protection against the assault of enemies. This was the home of a man of knowledge who was familiar with the best his times had to offer. Moreover, the proud knight knew that a young woman of mythic reputation lived within these walls. He had never seen her himself, but the presence of such beauty and character was a subject of conversation from the shores of Normandy to the banks of the Rhine. In this era of sickness and death, of famine and plunder, a woman so harmoniously formed in body and spirit was as rare as the most precious stone of the East.

This very evening, Aimery would be meeting her and winning over her heart. He had no doubts concerning his own attractiveness for he too was a prize possession in an age where high-born knights were being slaughtered by the hundreds under the hot sun of the Egyptian and Syrian deserts. He had been too young for the last Crusade and had yet to be convinced that there was glory in butchering his southern neighbors.

Aimery headed for the stairs where his host awaited him. Lady Beatrice watched him swagger through the courtyard like a young lion sure of his power. He was dressed in black and gold, his body armor of interlaced silver rings gleaming in the setting sun. The young man was first and foremost a warrior and always in combat dress. His immense sword never left his side for it was an extension of himself and without it he felt only half a man.

The regent wrung her hands in delight as she prepared to greet her noble guest. This was her greatest scheme yet in a lifetime of scheming. She would become fabulously wealthy in the merger of these mighty families and would be rid of her niece once and for all. This evening would bring perverse happiness to her hardened heart for the first time since the days of youth.

"Welcome to our humble home, Sir Aimery," she called out as he came up the stairway. "I pray your journey was a good one."

"The lands of Lord Reynald are magnificent territories to travel through, Mylady."

"It is a great honor to have you grace our castle, Sire."

Lady Beatrice escorted him into the main corridor. Within moments, the sounds of scurrying servants, clanging goblets, lutes and song rose toward the vaulted ceilings and echoed across the ancient stones.

The great platters of venison and wild boar had already been served when Adela made her appearance. Silence fell over the banquet hall as she stepped forward and approached the dais. The Duke's soldiers gasped at the sight of the young noblewoman. These rugged men of war had never seen such high-born beauty before. But it was her look of defiance as much as her soft features which made such an impression. Dressed in flaming red, Adela was the very incarnation of a queen's demeanor in the grand tradition of Eleanor of Aquitaine.

As for Aimery, he nearly choked on his wine upon catching his first glimpse of her. Here was the vision of his dreams, the reason why men seek glory and set out for war. Yet at the same time he felt a cold wind rush through his soul as she came nearer. In the very intoxication of her sight, there came a premonition of calamity. The thrill of passion was matched with a strange fleeting dread of mortality.

The mysterious feelings left him almost immediately as she sat next to her aunt several chairs away. Lady Beatrice pointed to Aimery and she turned to him. Her coldness suddenly melted as her eyes met his. He was indeed the fairest lad in the land and his noble bearing was unmatched by his peers. Adela turned away quickly, frightened by her unexpected reaction to the man who was to take her captive. Somehow, her aunt's plan didn't seem so awful after all.

She looked at the other faces surrounding her. Lady Beatrice, at her side, watched her closely, seeking to read her mind. Guilbert the priest sat next to her, a brutish grin on his ugly features. Then Adela's gaze fell upon the man seated beside the cleric. She felt her breath cut off as though invisible hands had grasped her throat. The Abbot of Citeaux glared at her like a buzzard about to tear the eyes out of its victim. He had the face of a wild bulldog, reminiscent of Viking pirates of old. But it was the glaze of his eyes which took her breath away. It seemed to her that a dead soul was peering at her from its catacombs. Long forgotten tales from her childhood of the living dead flooded her mind. Horror stories of bloodthirsty ogres, wizards and vampires flashed before her as though they had all come to life in the features of Arnauld-Almeric, the butcher of Beziers and Carcassone.

"We are honored to have another guest with us," Lady Beatrice whispered to Adela, embarrassed by the expression frozen on her face. "The Papal legate himself, Abbot of Citeaux and defender of the Faith against the heretics." The Abbot forced himself to offer Adela the slightest nod of the head. He was clearly another one of those monks who hated womankind and blamed the Fall upon Eve and her sisters. Adela represented all that made his blood boil, right down to the very color of her tunic. Her fiery gaze was perhaps her worst offense and the more he looked at her with disdain, the more she glared back defiantly.

Lady Beatrice clapped her hands for the meal to begin and to interrupt the awkward situation. Everyone turned to their plates and goblets, except for the priest whose ears were red-hot with outrage at the insolence of the young woman. He turned to the Abbot and shook his head. The warrior-monk took up his knife and sliced into the meat as though he were assaulting Adela and destroying her unacceptable beauty and pride of character.

Aimery sipped his wine, watching Adela closely. He hadn't missed an instant of the interchange and found pleasure in her courage and disgust with the mass murderer. Like most educated nobles, he had no patience with the clergy which was either soiled with wealth or perverse behavior. Adela had already won his heart.

"What news have you for us, Sire?" the priest asked the man he admired more than any other in the land.

"I can tell you that our Crusade against the heretics will be a glorious success. It has not been easy to gather large armies for the task, but the soldiers of the Lord are now under the able leadership of Simon of Montfort. He will lead us to victory against Montsegur, the heretics' last stronghold."

"What of a new Crusade to the Holy Land?" Aimery asked, revealing his impatience to be done with killing other Christians and the Frankish instinct for war against the Saracens.

The Abbot snickered as he chewed on a large morsel of meat.

"There is another Crusade being preached this very day, young sir. But I doubt if your lordship would care to join it."

Aimery's anger flared at the thought that he was being insulted by the piggish cleric.

"What do you mean?" he called out, his hand automatically moving toward his trusted blade.

"There is a shepherd boy in Saint Denis calling for a Crusade of children."

"Children?" Adela cried out. She couldn't believe her ears.

"He claims that our Lord Himself charged him with this

mission and he says that where glorious knights have failed, children bearing only peace and faith will conquer."

"What a lovely thought," added the priest sarcastically.

"Do they truly mean to walk to Palestine?" Adela asked.

"They have already begun, Mylady. They are on their way from Paris and every other region in the Realm. I am surprised you had not heard. They are planning to gather at Vendome."

The Abbot wiped his greasy, stubby fingers on his cloak. "Though it makes for a fine legend, I must say that the sword will always be more efficient than the faith of children in dealing with the heathens."

"They are gathering at Vendome? On the boundaries of our territories?"

Lady Beatrice was stupefied.

"We have few visitors these days, Sire, and know little of the events in the King's realm."

She turned to the servants who were bringing more courses.

"Have such rumors reached you?"

They shook their heads nervously, not wanting to reveal how much they kept from the hated woman. Lady Beatrice spotted Bohemond as he gave orders to his assistants by the stairway leading to the kitchen.

"Bohemond! Come here!" she called out.

The cook looked up and did his best to control his sudden terror.

"Did you hear me? Come here!" she cried out angrily.

The cook anxiously wiped his hands on his apron and hurried to her, trying to stay out of the Inquisitor's view.

"Is the food not to your liking, Mylady?" he whispered.

"The meal is fine. I want to know if you've heard of this Crusade of children we have just learned of. The good Abbot tells us they are traveling through our lands."

The Abbot turned his vicious glare toward the cook, stuffing his face with venison. Bohemond looked away from him, fearing some kind of recognition.

"I have only heard tell of young Stephen of Cloyes and his visitation. The townspeople speak of a Crusade of children from Cologne which has ended in the death of thousands."

"You mean to say children tried to cross the mountain passes of the Alps by themselves?"

"Yes, Mylady. And their failure has only increased the excitement for a second effort among our children."

"Where are you from, cook?"

The Abbot's voice rang out like a death knell.

The cook felt his whole body shiver.

"The region of Albi, Sire."

"I thought I recognized the accent. You were born among heretics then."

"That is why I left, good sir. My family has always been loyal to Rome."

He crossed himself awkwardly, hoping he had followed the right ritual.

"It is not Rome, but the Lord that we must be loyal to. The Holy Father is merely the servant of the Son of God."

"That is what I meant to say," Bohemond stated as his stomach churned painfully.

"It is a good thing you left your country then, cook. It is a field of corpses these days. The heretics have damned all the good citizens of Occitan."

"Forgive me, but I must return to the kitchen Lady Beatrice."

With that, Bohemond hurried away, wishing he had never had to looked upon the odious face of evil incarnate.

Lady Beatrice called for a troubadour to entertain them as they ate. A young man appeared with his lute and stood in the center of the room. He began to sing a soft, melancholic tune made famous in the courts of Toulouse and Montpellier. The sweet melody rose above the clanging sounds of the diners and filled the shadowy room with enchantment.

"Far more it pleaseth me to die

Than easy mean delight to feel.

For what will meanly satisfy

Nor can nor ought to fire my zeal."

While few turned their attention from Bohemond's deli-
cious artwork, Adela lost her appetite instantly upon hear-
hearing the heart-wrenching lyrics. The gentle man's voice
was as soft as his blond curls and as sad as his sky-blue
eyes. He sang to himself more than to his audience, reminding her of an exotic bird

held captive in its cage and forced to please its jailors.
Aimery, filled with the energy of springtime, found his attraction for Adela increase with every pluck of the lute
strings. In his egotistic world where he alone was king, he
assumed the words were meant for him.

The troubadour sang louder as he played a chorus full of
deep emotion.

"O high and glorious King, O Light and Brightness true!

O God of Power, Lord, suppose it pleases you,

Make my comrade welcome, and grant him all your aid.

For him I have not seen since fell the night's dark shade,

And soon will come the dawn."

The sorrow-laden minstrel had hardly finished his last note,
when a loud crash broke the spell of the mesmerizing melody. All eyes turned toward the Abbot of Citeaux who had
risen from his seat, eyes bulging with wild rage. The monk
had smashed his goblet on the cobblestone. Everyone
stopped eating. The minstrel plucked a final note and

looked at the wine spread across the floor like the blood of a dying man.

"He sings of heresy!" the Abbot cried out.

"What do you mean, good sir?" Lady Beatrice asked, bewildered.

"Did you not hear what he said? Praying to the "Light"! Seeking to be united with his comrade! Is that not the soul you sing of, minstrel? The "comrade of the body" longing for a return to its Spirit?"

The troubadour looked at him without fear and said nothing.

"It's not love between a man and a woman which he sings of. It's love with the Uncreated Light, a mystic love given, they say, by the Power of the Holy Spirit."

Guilbert was shocked.

"They sing of the Lord in Heaven as they would of a fair-haired maiden?" he asked with repugnance.

"Indeed!" Arnaud-Almeric cried out, the deadly poison of his hatred surfacing from the darkness within. "They worship the Holy Goodness. They make of our Father a feminine deity!"

"What blasphemy!" the priest retorted.

"You mock us all, heretic! You Mediterraneans think we Northerners are too barbaric to see through your tricks! But you are wrong!"

He approached the singer and slapped him harshly across the face. The young man did not blink.

"Do you know who I am?"

"The Devil," the minstrel answered calmly.

The Abbot's face was now deep red and blotted with rage.

"Worse than that! I am the angel of your apocalypse! The herald of the Judgment Day! Your perversions of the letter of Scripture are ending in the fires of purification!"

He turned to the audience which was transfixed by the eruption of his brutal energy.

"They have tampered with the Word of Holy Scripture for too long! Turning straightforward commandments into symbolism full of spiritual meanings! As if the Lord would speak in secret messages meant for the "enlightened ones"! They are the devil's disciples, sowing discord and doubt among the faithful!"

"Antichrist!" yelled the priest.

Every man around the banquet table jumped to his feet.

"Destroy him!" the Abbot barked at his soldiers.

"Silence, monk!" shouted Aimery, springing from his seat. "This troubadour is in my company and has done nothing to deserve your insults!"

"Mylord!" Lady Beatrice whispered nervously. "Please remember that you are addressing the Pope's envoy."

Guilbert stood in turn and pointed to the minstrel.

"The good Abbot is an expert in the realm of heresies, young sir. He knows all their ways and their blasphemous beliefs. Consider his song of death as preferable to earthly rewards. The boy is preaching a sermon to us from the Cathars' doctrines!"

Aimery looked at the young man who remained unmoved at the commotion he had caused.

"Is this true, Godfrey?"

The minstrel answered only with a melancholic, peaceful look of friendship.

"Don't bother with questions," the Abbot said. "These heretics are sworn to secrecy upon initiation. I have tried many times, I assure you. But perhaps this one will be different on the rack. Guards! Seize him!"

"Stop!"

Adela slammed her fist on the table.

"You are in my home under my lordship! This boy is in my protection and no one will lay a hand on him!"

"Adela!" cried Lady Beatrice, " you are not to contradict his Holiness the Abbot!"

Adela turned to Aimery, suddenly inspired.

"Sire, I call upon you to come to my aid. You have the means to uphold the authority which is rightly mine under the laws of the fiefdom."

That was all Aimery needed to hear. The young knight leaped over the table and shouted for his men to draw their swords.

"We are at your command, Mylady."

The priest gasped with horror as the Abbot turned a terrible scowl upon Lady Beatrice.

"In God's name, do not do this, Sir Aimery," she said in a trembling voice. "I know my niece is a lovely maiden worthy of your chivalrous protection. But she is misguided. If this minstrel is indeed a heretic, he must arrested."

"There are no heretics in these regions!" Adela insisted.

"This is not the province of Toulouse!"

"Yes, there are!"

All heads turned toward the far end of the banquet table where stood Cecilia. She stepped forward as Adela's blood ran cold.

"No, Cecilia!"

"You are eating the food of a heretic!"

Shockwaves ran through the crowd. Lady Beatrice was speechless with horror at this turn of events. Cecilia rushed to the front of the dais and bowed to the Abbot.

"Sire, I have seen Bohemond the cook ask a benediction from a stranger who is hiding in the woodlands."

Arnauld-Almeric's eyes flashed with victory. A grisly smile twisted his face into a freakish grimace. He motioned for his men to hurry to the kitchen.

"This cannot be!" cried Lady Beatrice, beside herself.

"Bohemond has been in my service for ten years!"

Guilbert put his arm around her to support her as she faltered.

"Heretics are as sly as demons. Have I not told you often not to trust anyone?"

Adela covered her face with her hands, unable to control her emotions. Aimery rushed to her side.

"Tell me your wish and I will stop all this madness!"

Adela looked at him through her tears. For the first time in her life she couldn't think.

The Abbot's guards hurried into the kitchen. Bohemond had heard the commotion and escaped into the courtyard. His terrified assistants pointed the guards in his direction. The heavy-set man stumbled down the outer stairway, panic-stricken. Two of the Abbot's soldiers appeared in the doorway.

"We've got you now, heretic!"

They ran down the stairs as the poor cook sprawled into the mud. Suddenly a loud thud echoed across the courtyard. The first guard crashed onto the cobblestone, unconscious. Bohemond turned around in time to see the second guard receive a savage blow to the head from a heavy staff. As he fell over, his assailant stepped out of the shadows. It was Bertran.

"Save me, Bertran!" Bohemond cried out with new hope.

The powerful young peasant swiftly removed one of the guards' belt and sword and strapped it around his waist.

"Do you know how to saddle a horse, man?"

"I do! My father was squire to the Viscount of Foix!"

"Then hurry to the stables and ready Tancred for me!"

"Tancred? Adela's stallion?"

"No other horse can carry the three of us."

Bohemond was thunderstruck.

"You're...You're not going after Adela, are you? There are a dozen men at arms in there!"

"Stop your babbling and get to the stables!"

Bohemond ran off as fast as his fat legs could take him. An arrow suddenly whistled through the courtyard and struck the cook in the back. Bohemond fell on his face with a scream. Bertran looked up in time to see the soldier placing another arrow in his crossbow. The young man leaped up the steps letting out a wild yell. With all his might, he threw his staff like a javelin and hit the man in the forehead. The soldier fell over backwards, falling into the courtyard. Without a second thought, Bertran dashed into the castle, running toward his fate. The old castle guard appeared in the corridor. Seeing the crazed look in the young man's face, he jumped out of his way, throwing his spear to the floor. Three of the Abbot's men came out of the banquet hall, sword in hand. Bertran's weapon hissed out of its scabbard as he threw himself on them. The clash of iron knocked the first guard's sword out of his hand. He shouted for mercy as Bertran swung his weapon in the air. The banquet hall doors opened widely, revealing the scene to everyone in the room.

"Bertran!" Adela shouted.

"Stand back all of you or by God I'll strike this man dead!" the young peasant cried out. He held his sword over the man's head, ready to drop it with all his force.

"Kill him then!" the priest called back. "Soldiers! Run this ruffian through!"

"No!" Aimery shouted. The knight stepped forward toward the doors.

"That man is my squire. Let him go, peasant."

Bertran and Aimery stared at each other, unflinching. Time seemed to stand still for an instant as both sensed that each had met his nemesis.

"Adela! Come to me!" Bertran suddenly shouted.

A roar went through the crowd. Lady Beatrice grabbled Adela's arm. The young woman tore it from her hands.

"Adela, if you go to this serf, you will disgrace yourself and your family forever!"

Adela smiled sadly at her.

"You have already done that for me, dear aunt. I will have nothing more to do with your evil ways!"

She hurried to Bertran. As she passed by Aimery, he called out to her.

"Mylady! I will die before I see your honor soiled!"

He drew his great sword with lighting speed.

Adela held up her hand and he froze under her commanding glare.

"You will do no such thing, Mylord. This good man is here at my beckoning. He is saving me from the vile schemes of my aunt. You and I are merely pawns in her perverted games."

"I am no one's pawn, Mylady! I am here because I chose to come and see the most beautiful noblewoman in the land!"

"Stop her, Sir Aimery! Stop her before she escapes!" Lady Beatrice cried out.

The young knight was confused. Such a queer situation had never been presented to him in his training. He felt terrible humiliation at his helplessness even though he held the mighty sword which had never failed him. But those feelings were quickly replaced with unbounded hatred for the miserable serf who was now his rival.

"What would you have me do, Mylady?" he asked almost sheepishly.

"Let me leave freely, Sire. There is nothing more precious

to me than my freedom."

"You pay a heavy price for it, Adela of Vendome!" Guilbert called out. "If you leave with that wretch, you will forfeit your dominions!"

"They have already been stolen from me, priest! I will return some day and take back what is rightfully mine!"

She hurried to Bertran's side. Cecilia suddenly rushed toward the Abbot.

"Your holiness! Bertran knows the whereabouts of a Perfect One!"

"What's this?" the fanatic monk roared. "Take him, guards!"

Adela turned to Aimery with pleading eyes, asking him silently to let them go. The young knight cringed. It was the one favor he did not want to do for her. His sword whistled through the air and paused before the oncoming guards.

"I will come for you, Adela! Wherever you may be, I will come for you!" he shouted as the men backed away from him.

She sadly shook her head.

"You are too noble to go where my destiny is taking me."

Adela stepped into the corridor. Bertran grabbed the captive squire by his long hair and dragged him along as he backed away slowly.

"Peasant boy!" Aimery shouted. "I swear on all that is holy that my sword will find your heart! You will die for this outrage!"

In the flash of an instant, all the horrors and injustices Bertran had witnessed and been subject to at the hands of feudal lords crashed upon the shores of his mind. Warring knights plundering their fields, priests filling them with superstitious terrors, taxes reducing them to a life of beasts, and above all, the obscene scorn which the wealthy held toward the poor, made Bertran's long repressed anger overflow and flood his tormented heart.

"A curse on all of you! Damn your souls to hell!"

Holding his sword ready, he ran toward the door. For the first time in her life, Adela was uncertain of her actions, but she followed him as though pushed on by the force of Destiny.

"What sort of peasants to you breed here?" the Abbot asked, disgusted. "That insolent boy needs to be crushed! After him!"

Aimery lowered his sword and led the guards into the corridor, eager for Bertran's blood. Adela's request had been forgotten beneath the unthinkable disgrace of being cursed by a peasant. They came to the door in time to see Bertran lift the wounded cook onto the back of the Arabian stallion. He leaped on and wrapped his arms around Adela's waist as she kicked her mount into a gallop. Aimery jumped from the stairway as the mighty animal thundered across the bridge.

"Get your horses, men!" Aimery roared.

His soldiers dashed for the stables. The young knight walked up to the moat and watched the white stallion disappear in a cloud of dust. He wrapped his strong right hand around the golden hilt of his weapon and slowly raised the heavy blade toward his vanishing enemy.

"You will be mine, Adela. Mine alone!"

6

The white stallion galloped furiously across the vale and tore into the woodland. The fugitives were temporarily safe. Under the cover of the heavy foliage, their pursuers would have great difficulty in tracking them.

"Where to now?" Adela asked as she guided her mount through the underbrush.

"Head for the waterfalls!" Bertran replied in a breathless voice as he strained every muscle to hold onto to Bohemond's limp body and Adela's waist. In the heat of the escape, he had not even noticed that he was holding her more intimately than ever before.

The great beast trotted up the rocky paths leading to the heart of the forest. Its whole body glistened with sweat from the extra weight on its back. Branches whipped their faces and arms as they raced through the woods. Adela pressed her stallion onward, escaping from herself as well from her pursuers. She didn't want to have to think about what she was doing. Her doubts would be too painful.

Soon, they came upon the ruins of the ancient chapel buried in the dense foliage. The tall, gaunt silhouette of the hermit stood in the arched doorway, awaiting them. As Adela violently reined Tancred to a halt, he hurried toward them and assisted Bertran in dismounting with Bohemond's body. The hermit paid no attention to the young woman who eyed him suspiciously as though he were a dangerous brigand.

They swiftly carried Bohemond into the chapel.

"Tie Tancred to the oak tree behind the chapel," Bertran called out as he disappeared within the moss-covered walls.

They laid Bohemond on his stomach next to the hearth and the hermit immediately examined the wound.

"Is he alive?" Bertran asked, horrified at the sight of the arrow deeply imbedded in the man's back.

Bohemond let out a painful sigh and began to shake.

"He will not be with us much longer," the hermit whispered. "There is no reason to cause him more pain by removing the arrow."

They turned him on his side and propped his head up with animal

furs. Bohemond grimaced in agony. But when he caught sight of
the hermit, the muscles of his face relaxed as though the pain had
magically vanished. A strange light came into his bulging eyes.

"Bless me with the Consolation, Good Christian," he muttered
hoarsely.

Adela entered the room and hurried to Bohemond's side.

"Don't die, Bohemond! Stay with us!" she whispered tearfully.

The cook's body shook again as he tried to hold the Angel of
Death away. The hermit gently motioned for Adela to hold her old
friend's head.

"But we must give him medicines!" she said in protest.

Bertran shook his head and motioned for her to be silent. Perhaps
for the first time in her life since the disappearance of her father,
Adela obeyed an order. In the presence of a dying man, within
reach of a hunted heretic who looked like a brother to the man
from Assisi, and with her life in shambles, the young baroness tasted the bittersweet feeling of humility in her proud soul.

The hermit held out a large, tattered Bible for Bohemond to touch.
In a voice vibrant with solemnity and deep affection, the hermit
spoke to the dying man.

"Bohemond of Albi, you wish to receive the spiritual baptism
through which the Holy Spirit is given in the Church of God with
the holy prayer and the laying on of hands by those who received
the consolation before you. Holy Scripture tells us that John indeed
baptized with water, but you shall be baptized with the Holy Spir-

it."

In the flickering half-light of the fireplace, Bertran and Adela, each holding the shivering body of their dying friend, found themselves lifted into an otherworldly sphere. The sounds of the forest seemed to silence themselves in reverence toward the grave words of the saintly man as he addressed the soul about to enter Eternity. The hermit touched Bohemond's forehead and seemed to ease his pain.

"The Church of God has preserved this holy baptism by which the Holy Spirit is given from the time of the apostles until this day, and it has passed from Good Men to Good Men until now, and the true Church will continue to confer it until the end of the world. And you should understand that the Church has the power to bind and to loose, to forgive sins and to fix them on men, as Christ said in the Gospel of Saint John: "As the Father sent me forth, I also send you.""

Tears fell from Bohemond's eyes. But they were tears of joy, not of sorrow. The hermit leaned forward to be sure the dying man could hear him.

"If you wish to receive this power and this might, you must keep all the commandments of Christ and of the New Testament to the utmost of your ability. Know that He forbade men to commit adultery, to kill, or to lie, to swear oaths or to steal, to do unto others what they would not have done to themselves. He commanded them to forgive those who do evil to them, to love their enemies, to pray for and bless those who denounce and accuse them, to turn the other cheek to those who smite them, to give up one's cloak to him who takes away the coat. He forbade them to judge and to condemn."

Adela looked up at Bertran. In this unique atmosphere where life and death were meeting on the fringes of time, she saw him not as the kind serf who always obeyed her wishes, but as an equal created in the image of the Almighty. The young peasant turned his gaze upon her. The slow, powerful voice of the hermit seemed to be blessing both the dying man and their love, the departure of one existence and the arrival of new life.

"You must hate this world and its works and all things which are of this world. For Saint John says in his Epistle: "My little children, love not the world, neither the things that are in the world. If any man love the world, the love of the Father is not in him. For all that is in the world, the lust of the flesh, and the lust of the eyes, and the pride of life, is not of the Father, but of this world. All the world passeth away, and the lust thereof: but he that doeth the will of God abideth for ever."

A strange new feeling began to spread through Adela's soul. Though the words of the hermit condemned life in the flesh, her heart heard them praise true love, pure love, the goodness of the human heart. And those qualities she saw reflected in the eyes of her brave Bertran who had risked everything for her sake. She felt in her breast the birth pangs of that self-transcendent love and she looked away to shield the transmutation taking place in her soul. She saw Bohemond's face suddenly radiate with an unearthly vitality, as though his soul had surfaced from within. The man was in ecstasy while still in the throes of mortal agony. The hermit continued the sacred ritual.

"These texts and many others show that you must keep the commandments of God and hate this world. And if you do these things well until the end of your days, we have hope that your soul will attain everlasting life."

In a last burst of life, Bohemond whispered with great conviction.

"Have mercy on me. For every sin I have committed by word or deed, I ask pardon of God, and the Church, and all here present."

The recluse touched his cheek with deepest tenderness.

"May they be forgiven you by God and by us and by the Church, and we pray God to forgive you."

The old man placed his right hand on Bohemond's head and blessed him.

"Our Father, receive thy servant in thy justice and send thy grace and thy Holy Spirit upon him."

The hermit kissed the Holy Bible, then gave the kiss of peace to Bohemond.

"May the Father, Son, and Holy Ghost forgive us all our sins."

As the hermit spoke the rite of Pardon, Bohemond's eyes filled with a profound, unconquerable peace. He looked up at Adela and gave her a beatific smile that revealed all the good will he had held toward her these many years. He then grasped Bertran's hand and pressed it with warm affection. Turning again to the hermit, he kissed his hand with one last effort.

Bohemond let out a deep breath and fell limp. His soul was released. To her surprise, Adela did not weep. She was certain that he was somehow alive in a spiritual realm, knowing a joy which he had never found in this life. As she thought upon these wondrous things, the hermit stepped away into the shadows and bowed in prayer. Bertran dared not move least he should wake from this prodigious moment which had brought him into the vicinity of unspeakable mystery.

"You must leave now."

The hermit's voice brought them back into the harsh realities of existence in the earthly realm. Bertran jumped up, realizing that, in his wonderment during the Consolation, he had completely forgotten that men with drawn swords were furiously whipping their horses to catch up with him. Adela turned to him, suddenly jarred by the insanity of what she had done.

"Where can we go?" she asked, revealing a vulnerability Bertran had never seen before.

The hermit noticed her barely restrained panic and understood that her nerves might shatter at any moment, for she had stepped out of her cocoon of wealth and security for the first time in her life.

"You know what you must do, Baronness."

Adela looked up at the kind features of the Perfect One. She was no longer afraid of the fact that he was a hunted heretic who re-jected all the trappings of the Church of Rome. She had seen him bring the joy of Paradise to her dying friend and felt the depths of reality open onto infinity in a way she had never experienced in the cathedrals.

"I do?" she asked with a quivering voice.

The hermit approached her and held out his hands like a prophet of old about to speak the revelation of the Almighty.

"Adela and Bertran, you must go to the Holy Land, to Terra Sanc-ta, and bring back the man who will restore peace and order to this troubled Realm."

"The Holy land?" Bertran cried out, both frightened and thrilled at the same time.

"How could we undertake such a journey? How would we know where to look for my father?" Adela asked, unprepared to consider such a dangerous adventure.

"You will have to trust, my child. You have no other choice. That is how it must be."

Bertran hurried over to Adela and excitedly placed his great hands on her shoulders.

"He's right, Adela. This is the only way you'll find freedom!"

"But...what if my father is..."

"Hush, now!" Bertran said gently. "In all these years, I've never heard you say such a thing. You've always told me that you were certain that Lord Reynald would return some day."

"I never thought we would be the ones to bring him home!"

"Who else is there? Who else cares for his fate? And what else can we do? We are fugitives now!"

Adela turned away to hide the tears welling up in her eyes. The sands of Palestine were a harrowing world for one bred in the sweet climate of central France. Uncounted thousands of pilgrims had met grisly deaths on their journey through heathen-occupied territories. The bravest knights of five kingdoms had perished far from their homelands. How could two youths do any better?

"You will not be alone, child," the hermit whispered in a soothing voice. "There is a sea of children coming together at this very moment to journey with you."

Adela peered into the hermit's eyes. They radiated a contagious peace.

"Are you telling us to join the children's crusade? That is madness in the making!"

"All the more reason for persons of good faith to go with them. They will need your help."

"But there will be so much suffering!"

Adela shivered with a premonition of the horrors of such a journey.

"We must all learn to make of our lives a living sacrifice. Give yourself to this venture in the name of the Good Creator."

Adela backed away. "I do not have the strength!"

The hermit smiled and looked at the two young people standing over the precipice of new possibilities.

"Perhaps not. But together you will find all the strength you need."

No longer restrained by the social mores that had kept them apart in spite of their affection for each other, Bertran put his arm around the love of his life.

"I'll protect you, Adela. We will make it!"

Adela searched the knowing look of the holy man.

"Will we make it?" she asked.

The hermit smiled sadly.

"It is not for me to tell you. You must discover your future for yourself."

The peacefulness of the forest was suddenly torn asunder by Tancred's frantic neighing.

"Tancred senses our pursuers!" Bertran said in a jittery voice. "We must be on our way!"

"Go, my children. Find your father."

Adela and Bertran hurried to the entrance. They turned back to thank him, but he raised his hand and interrupted them.

"May the grace of our Lord be with you."

Intuitively, they bowed and received the holy man's blessing. Renewed strength and hope filled their hearts as they mounted Tancred and galloped off toward the town of Vendome.

The old man watched them disappear. A shadow of melancholy tinged his radiant eyes. But a profound serenity returned as quickly as it had left, and the hermit looked down at the Bible he still held in his hands.

"My time has come," he whispered to himself. "I will be with you soon, dear brothers and sisters."

Resolutely, he walked away from the chapel toward the fields from which could already be heard the sound of galloping horses.

With every step, a great peace seemed to expand through his spirit. It was as though his soul was separating from his body and watching it from afar. He had never known such freedom before.

The hermit came out of the forest and headed through the meadow. He heard the song of birds, crickets and bees and his heart rejoiced at all that was good in Creation. Then he saw the demonic side of matter rushing toward him.

A dozen soldiers raced through the meadow in his direction, their swords and spears gleaming like laughing furies. The young Duke of Tours led the pack of angry men, his black tunic flapping in the wind. The Perfect One stopped and watched them approach.

Within moments, he was surrounded by snorting horses and shouting men of war.

"Have you seen a white horse?" Aimery tried to ask him, but he was interrupted by one of the Inquisitor's men.

"Who are you, old man?"

The hermit studied the soft clouds floating by in the sky.

"You know who I am."

"Do I now?" the soldier snickered. "Let me guess. A black cloak, a pale face from too much fasting, and the Holy Scriptures. Would

you be a Perfect One, an Elder of the Cathar heresy perchance?"
The hermit turned a solemn gaze upon the soldier.

"And you, with your weapons and stained armor, would you be
one of Simon of Montfort's killers, damning your soul with the
blood of the innocent?"

The soldier was taken aback and for the briefest instant felt the
anguish of guilt slice through his darkened conscience. But his vicious nature took charge again and he yanked the reins of his
horse, trotting up to the old man. He kicked him in the face with
his heavy boot. The hermit fell to the ground.

"What are you doing, man?" Aimery cried out, aghast at the ignoble act.

"This is a leader of heretics, Mylord. He is good only for the
stake."

The soldier jumped off his horse and approached the hermit who
was rising to his feet, letting the blood flow freely from his mouth.

"I've roasted many a Cathar, old man. But today I'll chop one to
pieces!"

He raised his sword. The hermit stared fearlessly at his assailant. As
the blade whistled toward him, a great clash of steel resounded
through the meadow. The soldier looked up in time to see Aimery
block the blow with his glittering sword. The young Duke's stallion
rammed the soldier with its chest and he fell to his knees. Aimery
whirled his steed around and faced the other soldiers.

"There will be no killing in this field unless it is by my sword! We are not barbarians here! And we still punish soldiers who strike defenseless old men!"

Shame colored the faces of the guards and they backed their horses away from the outraged knight. The fallen soldier rose to his feet and picked up his sword.

"You're a fool, young Sir. Protecting heretics is a mortal sin!"

Aimery dismounted swiftly and hurried to the man.

"Calling Aimery of Tours a fool is a mortal sin!"

The two broadswords met in mid-air, sending sparks among the flowers and swaying grass.

"Stop in the name of God!"

The hermit stepped between them and miraculously avoided being hit by the swinging blades.

"Do not shed blood on my account, kind sir. If you wish to be chivalrous toward an old man, return your sword to its scabbard."

Aimery was struck by the man's penetrating gaze. It disturbed some mysterious place in his soul and he found himself lowering his weapon. His adversary did the same, grateful at this opportunity to escape certain death. He had felt Aimery's power in that first clash and sensed that the fight would not have lasted long.

The hermit approached the young Duke.

"Nobility will never be gained at the tip of a sword, my son."

The words resonated in the abyss of Aimery's heart. He felt a tidal wave of sadness flood his being. For he knew that he was doomed to follow a warrior's path all the days of his life. And he knew that, somehow, the hermit's words were linked to the fate of his greatest desire - gaining the hand of Adela.

"Do you know where she is, old man?" he asked on impulse.

The soldier grabbed the hermit and roughly tied his hands behind his back.

"Don't bother, Mylord. These Perfect Ones don't reveal anything. We've tried to loosen their tongues many a time."

Aimery walked up to the good man and confronted him again.

"Do you know where my Adela has gone to?"

The hermit could read the lovesick heart that already haunted the young man.

"As with all worthy things in this life, young sir, seek and you shall find. But seek with a pure heart."

The old man knew that Aimery of Tours would play a vital role in the future of the two lovers whom he had solemnly blessed.

7

The city of Vendome was in an uproar. From its outer walls to the far edge of the horizon, it was besieged by a swarming ocean of children. Never in the long history of the region had such a bizarre and disturbing sight been witnessed. Sons of the noblest families in the Realm walked alongside the poorest serfs. Boys and girls, none older than twelve years of age, wore the tattered cloak of the pilgrim with a red cross sown on the right side of their breast. Fifteen thousand came from Paris. Another fifteen thousand came from the shores of Normandy, the Vosges mountains, the sun-baked lands of Provence. Every dialect of the country was heard among them, yet they were all unified around a common goal: to liberate the Holy Sepulcher from heathen hands with the weapons of love and faith. Their leader, Stephen of Cloyes, only twelve years of age himself, had told the crowds at Saint Denis: "For the last time have we heard of defeat! Hereafter shall children show brave warriors and proud barons how invincible are youths when God leads them!"

In less than a year's time, the young shepherd had gone from the solitude of his watch on the hillsides of Cloyes to great fame throughout the continent. He was said to have been charged with this incredible mission by a divine visitation by a pilgrim returning from Palestine who came upon him and shared his meager bread. Stephen had recently traveled to nearby Chartres where he witnessed a procession of the Black Crosses. The sorrowful litanies, the black-draped crosses and grim-faced priests dated from the days of the plague and were now performed to remind the people of sufferings Crusaders enslaved in the Holy Land. Everyone knew of the dismal failure of the Fourth Crusade and the atrocities endured by devout pilgrims. The shepherd of Cloyes was still in the tempest of such emotions when the wandering stranger told him of the wonders and tragedies he had seen on his journey. Then the man told him that he was the Lord Jesus Christ himself and commissioned him to preach a new Crusade to the children, assuring him that victory would be theirs. He gave Stephen a letter and instructed him to deliver to it the King of France, ordering the monarch to help them in this sacred effort.

The shepherd boy traveled to Saint Denis, the great cathedral on the outskirts of Paris where kings were buried since the age of Dagobert and where the Oriflamme, the holy standard of the Realm, was kept. He declared his visitation to the throngs of pilgrims. From there, his story spread across the land and thrilled the hearts and minds of children everywhere. He showed his letter to the King as proof of his mission and the people believed him.

As homes emptied from the Pyrenees to the Rhone river, an edict was issued by Philip-Augustus telling the children to go home. But nothing could stop this growing tidal wave. The more thoughtful clergy also tried to interfere, but were accused of heresy by other priests who saw this upheaval as a way of exciting the parents to a new Crusade. Mothers and fathers in great distress, unable to hold back their impassioned children, saw this as a trick of Satan. Others suggested that it was the work of the Old Man of the Mountain, the all-powerful ruler of a Syrian sect known as the Assassins whose bloody deeds were more terrifying to the world than the threat of Mongol invasion. His followers were trained from infancy in the skills of murder and it was said that he had freed two French children and sent them back to their country to bring him an army of youths for his dark purposes.

No horror tale could stop the children in their race to join the swarm of singing pilgrims waving banners and crosses as they traveled to Vendome, the place of departure for their holy cause. Eight year old boys and girls, wearing the broad rimmed hat of pilgrims and carrying the palmer's staff, filled every road in France and shouted with confidence of baptizing the Muslim infidels. Their prophet, Stephen of Cloyes, promised them that the great Mediterranean would open up before them just as the Red Sea had done for Moses and the children of Israel. Most of the little pilgrims had no idea how far away lay the deserts of the Bedouin tribes and marched toward their fate with tragic innocence.

It was among the hopeless wailing of parents and the final blessing of the Church that Adela and Bertran entered the teaming city. They waded high above the mass of tiny bodies on the back of the white stallion and stared in awe at this sight that no one could ever have imagined. The multitudes of soft, naive faces beaming with ecstasy resembled a poet's description of some lost Paradise. Fresh young souls made equal by a sacred ideal that they only could have the foolishness to believe in, and transcending the barriers of a harsh feudal society, seemed proof enough that some new world was possible after all. The Crusade freed them from the unalterable course of class and family heritage. There was a feeling rising above the sea of youths that they had been blessed with the power to make all things new.

"This is insanity," Bertran whispered in Adela's ear as they slowly made their way through the teeming throngs. "These children should still be clinging to their mothers' skirts."

"There is something very touching in all this," Adela responded. "Perhaps there is a divine force urging them on."

"Not a bearded lad among them," Bertran muttered. "How will they survive the hardships of the journey? Who will guide them to the seaports?"

Adela pointed to a chariot at the gates of the city where the crowd was especially dense. As they approached, a great clamor rose about them. Thousands of little voices were calling out to the chariot and raising their hands in a frenzy of idolatrous worship. As the pandemonium became more distinct, they could make out the words being shouted: "Stephen! Stephen!"

"That must be him in the chariot," Bertran yelled in Adela's ear to make himself heard. "It seems that he will ride in comfort while his followers tear their feet to pieces along the way."

As they came closer they could see that the enclosed wagon was a splendid one, with magnificent carpets and a canopy made of colorful draperies. A number of priests stood nearby, ready to advise and accompany the child prophet on this extraordinary journey. Young nobles on horseback, dressed in their finest and flashing swords and spears, guarded the chariot with great zeal. Stephen the shepherd boy had come a long way in a few short months.

One of the youthful soldiers turned his mount toward the oncoming white stallion.

"Stop where you are! What is it you want?"

"You are addressing Baronness Adela of Vendome whose domain you have entered!" Bertran called out with pride. "She wishes to speak with your leader."

"No one approaches the prophet without his approval." Adela loosened the reins and let Tancred continue his approach. The boy's arrogance was enough to cause her to disregard his orders.

"Halt, I say!"

The young noble lowered his spear, aiming the sharp point directly at Adela's head. Outraged, Bertran drew his sword. His arm swung in a circular motion with great force and the lance flew out of the boy's hand. The sound of clashing iron caught everyone's attention. In an instant, the prophet's guards surrounded them.

"Who are you?" asked a soft, almost effeminate voice. Stephen looked out of his sumptuous carriage. He was a blond haired child with wide green eyes. There was something wild in their gaze, like a lamb lost among wolves. But that was tempered by an intensity beyond his years rising out of a sense of purpose that gave him an unusual radiance. His features were those of a gullible, uneducated boy and his hands bore witness to a life of dull, hard labor.

"I am the daughter of Lord Reynald, Baron of Vendome and suzerain of these territories," Adela announced defiantly.

"Come closer," Stephen stated calmly.

The spears raised and Tancred trotted past the guards and priests who clustered around them. Bertran felt disgust as he eyed the boy who was clearly one of his own people and so out of place in this princely chariot. He knew that if his noble guards had encountered him six months before, they would have despised him and treated him like a servant. But now that he was famous and praised by many, they were his loyal escort, each hoping to win his favor.

"Have you come to bid us farewell?" Stephen asked.

"We have come to join you on your Crusade," Adela heard herself say, still unconvinced that this was happening.

The shepherd boy's eyes brightened and a warm smile revealed the rotting teeth of those bred on poor nutrition.

"The Lord be praised! You are welcome! Ride near my chariot where the children can see you. You and your fine horse will give them confidence."

"Aren't they already certain that they want to undertake this journey?" Bertran wondered, looking over the sea of excited children.

"Who is this?" Stephen asked suspiciously.

"He is my friend and companion. I owe him my life."

Adela turned to Bertran and gave him a grateful smile. It was the kind of smile men died for.

Stephen took an instant dislike for Bertran, perhaps because he sensed that the proud peasant could see right through him.

"Where is your retinue?" Stephen wondered.

"This is all we have," Adela answered. "We come as simple pilgrims."

Bertran winced at the exaggeration. Honesty was the cardinal virtue for him. The shepherd boy turned prophet was surprised and could hardly hide his disappointment. Riches and food were going to be sorely needed on the journey. He waved them away and the guards respectfully guided them from the chariot.

"That's no prophet," Bertran whispered in Adela's ear.

"How do you know? Have you ever seen one?"

"No, but I've seen shepherd boys before. And that's just what he is. Except that he has fooled a lot of sheep."

"Enough of that, Bertran!" Adela ordered. "If this boy leads us to my father, I will be the first to kiss his feet."

Adela led Tancred to a little mound near the walls away from the crush of the great crowds. From there they could see the waves of children, some in pilgrim's garb, some in rags, some in fine linen. Wailing parents could be seen eve-rywhere trying to keep their sons and daughters from leaving. Priests were blessing motley groups preparing to take their first step toward Jerusalem. In his chariot, Ste-phen was eating a bowl of grapes, waiting for departure. Adela suddenly pointed toward the great city gates. A cloud of dust was approaching them. Two riders were hurrying through the multitudes.

"That's Cecilia!" Bertran exclaimed.

Before Adela could respond, Cecilia and the old castle guard rode up to them.

"Mylady!" Cecilia cried out, virtually in hysterics. "I never thought I'd find you!"

The young woman was splashed with dirt. Her hair was a tangled mess and her cheeks were lined with tears.

"How in God's name did you find us?" Adela asked, feeling terrible anger rise in her breast as she remembered what her lady-in-waiting had done at the banquet.

"The heretic told me where you could be found."

Bertran felt a pang in his heart.

"How did you come to speak with him?" he asked in a worried voice.

"The Duke's soldiers arrested him and brought him to the castle. I went to see him in the dungeon."

"Why would you do such a thing?" Adela shouted, suspicious of Cecilia's purposes.

The young woman began to weep. Her whole body shook with sobs as she tried to speak.

"I beg your forgiveness, Mylady...I...I never wanted Bohemond's death! He was so good to me...I feel dirty...evil! And the Pope's envoy, he is not a true Christian. He spoke of torturing and burning the heretic! I'm so sorry..."

Adela and Bertran looked at each other, horrified to hear of the fate awaiting the holy man.

"How could they have caught him?" Adela asked.

"Don't you understand, Adela? He gave himself up to keep them from catching us!" Bertran exclaimed.

The strong peasant youth choked back the tears but found them leaking out nevertheless. He swiftly wiped them away with an angry swat of the hand.

"So why have you come?" Adela asked her former confidante.

"Look what I have brought you with William's help."

The old guard smiled a toothless grin as he pointed to several large saddlebags laid out on their mounts.

""They're filled with clothes for the journey, Mylady," Cecilia said, hoping to see forgiveness in her mistress's stern gaze.

"I will not need all of that!" Adela stated indignantly.

"These are my bags," Cecilia replied. "I'm going with you."

"What?" Adela cried out. "Never! Begone from my sight at once!"

Cecilia cringed under the Baroness's wrath. She raised her hands in prayer.

"I beg of you, Mylady! Let me do penance for my sins! I will care for you on the way to Palestine!"

"I don't need your care anymore!"

"But the servants at the castle...They will butcher me in the night after what has happened!"

"Good!" Adela cried out.

Cecilia began to weep again, uncontrollably. Bertran leaned toward Adela's ear.

"Let her join us. She may be useful."

Adela glared at him.

"I will not have anything to do with her!"

"But she has nowhere to turn now. We're going to need every bit of help."

Adela thought for a moment. She looked out at the masses of children and felt a shiver go through her. This was insanity! There were untold dangers ahead. Many would surely die before reaching the seaports. Even at a glance, she could see that there were wolves in sheep's clothing among the young pilgrims plotting everything from robbery to unspeakable deeds. Adela turned back to Cecilia.

Perhaps she could use her after all since the poor girl was foolish enough to want to join them.

"Stop your crying! I will let you come along."

"Oh, thank you, Mylady, thank you!" Cecilia shouted through her tears.

"Please control yourself, Cecilia. You're drawing attention to us!"

Adela saw several armed men galloping toward them. Behind them she thought she noticed a familiar silhouette. But the bright sun and the clouds of dust made it difficult to see.

"Are you certain that you weren't followed from the castle?" she asked.

"Not at all. Who would follow me?"

As she was still blurting out her question, the soldiers surrounded them. The silhouette by the city gates trotted toward them. It was Lady Beatrice, followed by her constant shadow, Guilbert the priest.

Bertran reached for his sword, but an icy blade appeared inches from his throat.

"You are to come with us, Lady Adela," a guard stated solemnly.

"I will not!" she answered without fear.

"Chain them!"

Lady Beatrice's shrill voice rang along the ancient city walls.

She pulled up beside them, her eyes gleaming with hatred. "This is the last one of your insults I'll be subject to, Adela!" she yelled, barely able to control her seething anger. "You will pay dearly for what you have done! From this day forth you are stripped of all your rights and I am taking full charge of Reynald's fiefdom!"

She trotted up to Bertran who sat motionless surrounded by swords.

"And you, you insolent peasant, will suffer the consequences of your vile behavior! You will pray that life had never been given to you! Take them away!"

The soldiers pulled out heavy chains and began wrapping Bertran's wrists. Adela slapped the first guard who approached her.

"How dare you! My father is your liege lord! He would have you flogged to the bone for this!"

"I'm sorry, Mylady. But I will be flogged if I don't obey these orders," the soldier stated sadly.

Tears filled her eyes as she helplessly watched the man place manacles on her delicate wrists. She began shaking her head, unable to accept this indignity. Suddenly, she kicked the sides of her powerful horse as hard as she could. The great animal bolted forward, knocking the guard from his horse. Several other horses reared and kicked as the white stallion smacked his chest into them.

Just as Tancred cleared the way to gallop off, one of the soldiers pulled Bertran off the horse's back. He fell to the ground and two guards instantly jumped on him.

"Kill him! Kill him!" Lady Beatrice shrieked, losing all control over her mask of nobility.

Bertran threw the men off of him with great force and turned to run but found himself closed in by the horses.

"Run, Adela!" he cried out desperately.

Three other guards fell on him and held him down. Guilbert grabbed Adela's reins as she spurred Tancred on. They struggled fiercely. In a frenzy, Adela clawed at his face like a tiger. The man yelled in agony and pulled back, red gashes across his cheek. In a wild fury, Lady Beatrice seized one of the soldier's spears and aimed it at Tancred's head.

"No!" Adela shouted. "Don't hurt him!"

But her enemy charged forward, thirsting for blood. Adela jumped off her mount and slapped him away. She turned to face the oncoming spear. A muffled cry came from Bertran as he witnessed the scene. Lady Beatrice, a mad grimace on her face, raised the spear over Adela's body. Suddenly, she was pulled off her horse. She jumped up in a fury and shrieked for the guards to kill the assailant. But as she turned around, she found herself faced with hundreds of children's faces. Waves of other children quickly surrounded the guards.

"Get these ruffians away from me!" Lady Beatrice shouted. But the guards were not prepared to raise their weapons on children, especially when there were enough of them to trample their bodies into the dirt.

Like a cornered beast, Lady Beatrice slowly backed away as the children moved forward. Their crusade against evil had begun before ever taking a step toward the Holy Land. An indominable quality lit their eyes, as though each little soul had decided in that moment never to fear demonic power again.

Lady Beatrice began to drool in terror as they neared, hundreds upon hundreds of them at arms' length. She was the symbol of an oppression that had stolen childhood's joy from their young lives. In the spirit of their mission to the Holy Sepulcher, they were no longer willing to accept such evil.

The ranks of children suddenly parted and the young guards came forward on their steeds.

"The prophet says that you are to depart from his sight this moment or he will not answer for your safety."

Guilbert helped Lady Beatrice to her horse. Fear shook her body so violently that she was unable to speak. The priest leaned toward her, holding his wounded cheek.

"Let them go, Mylady. There is little chance that they will

come back alive. The Saracens will take care of them."
He took hold of her reins and turned away. The guards followed closely behind. The sour group made its way through throngs of children who watched on with condemning eyes. A jeer was heard, then another and another until a roar of anger and mockery escorted them to the city gates. The group cowered closely together, terrified of the innocents who had witnessed their dark intentions. As they disappeared behind the city walls, the priest looked back one last time at Adela. She could make out an evil grin on his face.

8

As the days turned to weeks, and children's feet blistered along the roads from the Loire Valley toward the ancient seaport of Marseilles, the initial enthusiasm began to fade. The hymns and victory songs that had echoed across the French countryside, beckoning yet more youths to join their chorus, soon lost all joy and vigor.

Most of the children had no notion of the distance they would have to undertake. This was a great fantasy in a day when harsh labor, wretched surroundings, and hopeless entrapment in a merciless feudal system, made such an adventure seem like a heaven-sent opportunity. But forbidding reality soon set in as food became scarce and hunger and fatigue began to leave little corpses by riverbanks, pastures, and meadows.

Stephen proved to be a crafty prophet. Every day, he would address his devout followers and bring new hope into their exhausted limbs. The children flocked to hear him and drank in his words like cool mountain water. In their tragic naiveté, they believed that simply touching his cloak or even the wheel of his chariot was life-giving, and anyone who tore a piece of fabric from the luxurious drapery cherished it as a precious relic.

Adela and Bertran were faring better than most of the children, taking turns riding on the Arabian stallion. In the be-beginning of the journey, they had kept to themselves and tried to avoid contact with the little pilgrims. But soon the anguish they were witnessing forced them to lend a hand. Each new dawn, Bertran was thrilled to awaken and find the love of his life laying at his side. This colossal disruption of the way things had always been gave him new hope that one day she would love him as he loved her. They lived now as brother and sister, too busy to linger arm in arm and too tired to think of romance under the stars.

The young Baronness had long since abandoned her noble composure and the clothing suited to that behavior. Her garments were a loose-fitting blend of materials fit for rigorous traveling. She had gone without a bath longer than she wished to remember and her hair was in knotted disarray. But her spirit was stronger than ever and it seemed that the open air and the desperate need all around was increasing her strength of character day by day.

She was one of the oldest women in the group and quickly became a mother to the children, wiping away tears and healing sore feet. She would trot Tancred back and forth alongside the motley ranks, looking for those on the verge of collapse. This whirlwind that had lifted her out of her leisurely existence at the castle called forth new depths of compassion within her which she had not encountered before.

Confronted by countless little faces beaming with naive hope and growing fear, Adela felt a new sense of responsibility for the fragile life around her. In the second week of their relentless journey, she had cradled in her arms one of the first victims of the crusade. A little girl not eight years old, dressed in boy's clothing to hide her identity, shivered against her chest with a deadly fever the whole night through. Adela gently caressed her soft hair which still carried traces of infant down. The child managed a brief smile as she looked up into the eyes of her caretaker. This was as close to Jerusalem as she would get. In Adela's eyes, she saw a vision of the Love which had been incarnated in Bethlehem. Adela witnessed the reflection of that same Love in the peace which filled the girl's large brown eyes. The memory of the ritual which the good hermit had performed at Bohemond's side appeared to her mind's eye with all the vividness of that precious moment. It was the same peace that had filled his soul as it wavered on the verge of departure - that holy peace which passes all understanding.

The child died with a glow of serenity on her face. Adela held her for a long time afterward, weeping as she kissed and caressed the tiny limp body. Only Bertran's strong, gentle hands puller her away. Soon afterward, the sun disappeared behind the horizon, as though mourning for the lost child. The procession halted for the night and Bertran called upon a priest with kindly eyes to take care of Adela while he buried the little girl.

As he dug the small grave in the twilight, a great anger thundered in his heart. He knew that this was only the first of many graves to be dug, and the time would soon come when there would be too many bodies to bury. From the day of their departure, he felt that this absurd crusade was riddled with deception. He had no patience for the idolizing of the eloquent shepherd boy. And he seethed at the way his guards enforced the "prophet's" rules with a zeal that forgot the religious reasons for the undertaking. Stephen was worshipped by everyone, including the priests. Bertran noticed that many of them encouraged this blasphemy. They had their own purposes which came to light in every town and village through which they traveled. The singing children and the waving banners were the best possible way to rouse the adults to sacrifice themselves and their goods to yet another assault on the Muslim-held shrines of Palestine. Pope Innocent III had given his blessing to the children because he foresaw that they would generate an emotional upheaval that few of his priests could hope to achieve through their itinerant preaching. The dismal failure and disgrace of the last attempt to liberate the lands where once the Christ had walked broke the spell that held popular imagination captive. It didn't matter how many indulgences were offered, or that lands conquered from the caliphs and emirs would become the wealth of the Crusaders. The military skills of Egypt's great sultan, Saladin, had crushed the spirit of the Crusades and his virtuous character, contrasted with the pillaging of the Christian soldiers, had planted seeds of doubt among the pilgrims over the righteousness of their cause.

Hills and valleys now crawled with little lambs heading for slaughter to satisfy a Pope lusting for the expansion of his Holy Roman Empire. Bertran could feel in the pit of his stomach that this insanity was not for the glory of God nor even to satisfy His Will. He knew deep down in his soul that the "Abba" of Jesus of Nazareth was not a bloodthirsty pagan deity. He had come to wonder whether the beliefs of the Cathars might not be true after all; whether in fact the Church was worshiping a fiendish demiurge full of vengeful judgment. Was this the Maker of matter, the ever-destructive principle striking at the irradiance of the Good?

Bertran's cynicism was growing each day since his escape from the castle. The world he knew was clearly in the service of Evil. His people lived in misery while the sword and the spear were the true lords of earth. Only rarely had he seen kindness in the midst of the works of darkness.

His disgust with the world only intensified upon witnessing Cecilia's rapid deterioration which revealed an even greater sin at the heart of this crusade of gullible children.

She had been morose for days. Then she went from remorse for her actions to moral dissolution. Her face hardened and her clothing lost its discreet quality. It seemed as though some wild demon was taking possession of her and burying the real Cecilia within her own body. A demon by the name of Guilt.

That very evening, the multitudes stopped once again for a night's rest, and the campfires pierced the darkness like teardrops from the stars. Shimmering with other, more graceful worlds, the vast sky gave solace to the wearied travelers. Songs rang across the valleys, carrying the high-pitched delicate sound of children's hopes and dreams. Bertrand stepped away from the large fire he had built with the help of a dozen boys. He sat down for the first time since sunrise and felt his sore muscles relax in sweet repose when, out of the corner of his eye, he noticed Cecilia moving off quickly into the shadows with two of Stephen's guards. Their furtive glances clearly revealed depraved purposes.

Bertran sprang to his feet and hurried after them. The guards walked at a fast pace. Cecilia accompanied them willingly, though a tragic look darkened her features - the look of a lost soul. They wandered through a labyrinth of youths crowded together in small groups. Bertran followed swiftly, making sure he remained undetected.

The guards finally approached a campfire along the riverbank, away from the makeshift city of children. It was a large fire and Bertran soon made out the contours of Stephen's chariot. He knelt in the tall grass as Cecilia and her companions stepped into the circle of light emanating from the fire. He could hear words being exchanged and bursts of laughter echoing in the shadows. But the relentless ritual of summer crickets made it difficult for him to decipher what was going on.

He slithered through the grass with a snake's gracefulness, inching his way toward a great tree rising at the edge of the fire's flickering light. He could see better from that position. And what he saw struck him like a battering ram.

He had never heard of Roman orgies and the worshippers of Eros. Such behavior was foreign to him, alien and repulsive to his spirit. Poor Cecilia! Though he hated her for what she had done to his friends, he couldn't help remembering the sweet, timid young girl who followed her mistress everywhere like a loyal pup. With great indignation, he watched on as she was flung from arm to arm, receiving indiscreet kisses from bestial strangers, releasing a laughter as painful as the cut of a broadsword.

Bertran was not a creature of violence, but his impulse to fight against wrong was as natural to him as chopping wood for the hearth. His Nordic blood still carried the distant echo of battle cries from Viking ancestors. When the winds of anger blew, he was a terrifying adversary, not because he thirsted for blood, but because he never backed away. Not until he set aright that which caused him such righteous indignation.

His father had shown him the meaning of bravery when Bertran was twelve years old. A errant knight was tearing through the hamlet, destroying everything in his path. Bertran's father confronted the armored warrior as he dismounted and attempted to take a young woman in his arms.

He fought with an oak staff against the knight's huge broadsword. Three times he struck the ignoble man with powerful blows. But the iron finally found its target. Yet the boy saw that his father never once backed away. He had often told his son: "Never let them crush your spirit, son! They may kill the body, but not the soul!"

147

When the guards began to tear at her clothing, Bertran jumped up from behind the tree. Just then, Stephen appeared from his chariot, dressed in a silk cape, wearing only a loin cloth beneath. He was drunk with wine and dizzy with debauchery. Bertran felt the sting of outrage rush through his whole being. This boy who commanded the attention of western Christendom, claiming a visitation from the Christ Himself, was using his newfound power to wallow in the abuse of those who admired him.

Stephen eyed Cecilia with uncontrolled lust.

"Bring her to me!" he cried out.

That was all Bertran could take. He dashed from behind the tree and ran toward the guards who surrounded Cecilia. He grabbed the first one by his belt and collar, flinging him some ten feet away. Before the second guard could react, the angry peasant smashed his great fist against his temple, knocking him senseless to the ground. The third guard went for his sword but was stopped by a large foot crashing into his coat of mail. The boy fell back against the chariot.

Bertran grabbed Cecilia by the arm.

"What do you think you're doing, Bertran?" she shouted, tears of humiliation bursting from her eyes.

"I'm taking you away from this pit of sin!"

"She is my guest here, boy! Leave her be!" Stephen cried

out, red with rage at the intrusion.

Bertran tore his sword from its scabbard with a roar. He rushed toward the perverse shepherd boy, and swung his arm back to let loose a fatal blow.

"No, Bertran, don't kill him! They'll tear you to pieces!"

Bertran caught himself. He was struck by her concern for his welfare. He looked back at her. Behind her tears was a pleading expression such as he had never seen.

"Don't throw yourself away for me...I gave myself to him."

Bertran turned to Stephen.

"You're swindling the innocent for your evil desires, shepherd boy! Your life is doomed!"

By this time, the guards were back on their feet and others had appeared from the shadows. Five bloodthirsty young men formed a circle around the intruder.

"You cannot speak to the prophet of the Lord in that way! I've been given a divine mission to save the glorious..." Stephen shouted without conviction.

"Save your lies for the crowds!" Bertran yelled out, interrupting his pathetic self-aggrandizement. "You're a hypocrite and you're leading these poor children to their destruction! I should run you through!"

The guards rushed at him, swords raised. Bertran watched them approach, fearless. They were all half his size and, though well into their training for knighthood, much too

frail to face a son of the earth who had built his muscular
frame from a life of heavy toil.

They slowed their assault, seeing the self-confidence in his
eyes. Behind the fearless calm, Bertran had enough repressed anger in him to explode in a roaring blaze and cut
them all to pieces. He charged the closest guards and
backed them away with mighty swings of his sword. He
turned and faced his other adversaries. Iron clashed, sending sparks into the night air.

Bertran was not skilled in the art of weaponry. But the
mountain people had taught him to use the staff as an ef-
fective instrument of defense. His raw strength and brutal
rage terrified the guards. They all quickly realized who was
going to be hurt. Stephen saw this as well and called out for
them to back away.

"You're a true warrior," Stephen stated nervously, finding
new interest in the courageous peasant. "Our crusade needs
you. I have no desire to see you killed. You are free to
leave."

"I'm taking Cecilia with me!" Bertran cried out defiantly,
his face covered with the sweat of his boiling anger.

"Take her! She's yours."

Stephen had a crafty mind and was already planning how
he could maintain his power with such a one at his side.
Bertran eyed the guards suspiciously as he backed away,

pulling Cecilia by the arm. The boys of noble birth lowered their swords, thankful that they did not have to feel the damage of the peasant's blows on their limbs. But they seethed with resentment for this humiliation. Their parents had taught them to despise the common people, and they had never seen serfs excel over them. From that moment on, the young viscounts, barons, and dukes had a common enemy.

Bertran and Cecilia walked in silence passed the crackling fire camps. She rearranged her clothing, distressed by Bertran's intrusion.

"You had no right to do that, Bertran."

"You're Adela's friend. I did it for her."

"She's not my mother!"

"Someone needs to be! What's come over you?"

Cecilia abruptly grabbed his arm and looked into his eyes.

"What concern is it of yours, Bertran? Aren't you happy to see me punished?"

"No. If you want to do penance, help the children."

"You hate me, don't you?"

Bertran lowered his head and quickened his pace.

"No, I don't hate you, Cecilia. I'm sorry for you. I'm sorry for all of us."

They came upon the small campfire where Adela waited with Tancred. Bertran pushed Cecilia toward her mistress and hurried off into the darkness.

"I have nothing to say to you, Adela!" Cecilia cried out. These last few days, she had taken on the habit of calling her mistress by her name. At first, it seemed to be part of the astonishing equality which characterized the crowds of children. There were no nobles here, no serfs and no princes. All were equal on this insane pilgrimage despite the ways of the world and the laws of the land. Adela accepted this change as she had accepted so much that was new and shocking to her formerly well-protected existence. But the insolence in Cecilia's tone of voice sent fire through her veins.

"Something has happened to you, Cecilia. I'm concerned for your welfare."

Cecilia laughed a coarse and painful laugh.

"Haven't you enough people to care for? There are sick children all around you!"

Adela took her hand in an expression of sympathy that she had not shown for a long time. Cecilia was momentarily taken aback.

"It's too late, Adela," she whispered with great melancholy. "You cannot help me."

"It's not too late! We're just beginning. The Holy land awaits us. And so does my father. When we find him, everything will be set right."

Cecilia shook her head at her mistress' optimism.

"Do you still believe in the success of this crusade?"

"Why, certainly! There are many obstacles to overcome but we are well underway."

Silent tears fell from Cecilia's eyes.

"It says in the Holy Scriptures that you will know them by their fruits...Well, this fruit is rotten to the core."

Adela was stunned. She had never heard her lady-in-waiting speak in such solemn tones before.

"What do you mean, Cecilia?"

"The prophet is unclean."

Her face turned scarlet as she felt Adela's reaction.

"How do you know this?"

Adela felt compelled to ask the question, though she already knew the answer and had guessed it days before.

"He has made me his concubine...And there are others."

"How is this possible?" Adela cried out. "He appears before us every day with new revelations from the Lord!"

"I have seen him with...other boys."

"No!"

Adela could hear no more. She could not accept that the shepherd of Cloyes was a deceiver and a lustful wretch. A terrible intuition came over her, foretelling a gloomy future ahead. If the crusade was poisoned from the start, it had no hope of succeeding. And her own desperate attempt to find

her father might come to nothing, leaving her utterly destitute. Such a thought was to horrific to contemplate and she
forced herself to focus on the matter at hand.

"You must stay away from him if he is as depraved as you
say."

Cecilia smiled sadly.

"I never wanted this from the beginning. I have no choice.
They have all the power. Maybe this is the punishment I
must endure for what I did to sweet Bohemond."

"It cannot be, Cecilia! Our God does not require
such...sacrifice."

Cecilia turned away.

"I must go. They are waiting for me."

She moved into the shadows but then suddenly hurried
back to her old friend.

"If it is not the will of the Lord, then what is it, Adela?
Have I fallen into the claws of Satan?"

Adela gently caressed the girl's cheek.

"No, Cecilia. You've been deceived by liars and hypocrites.
Let us help you get away from them."

"Not even you have the power to do that, Adela. Stephen
is Lord here and there is no law but his. We are his victims."

Adela pressed her against her chest.

"My poor girl."

"Don't give me your pity! Keep it for yourself. You'll need it!" Cecilia cried out, pulling away.

She hurried off, regretting that she had said so much.

A shiver shot through Adela's body as she realized the implications of Cecilia's revelations. The lives of thousands upon thousands of children were in the hands of a depraved boy who had deceived everyone including himself.

* * *

Bertran wandered through the sprawling encampment. The fires were beginning to die out and most of the mounds of bodies were fast asleep. Surrounded by the soft snores of the innocent, he felt his anger flare up again. How could this be? How could so many children be destined to certain annihilation? What malefic force was behind such an atrocity? Surely, this massive exodus of boys and girls from the hearths of France could not possibly be the result of a vain shepherd boy's schemes. There was something utterly demonic about this undertaking.

He suddenly found himself on the other end of the camps were smaller groups had gathered, seeking isolation from the hordes. Bertran recognized some of the faces in the flickering light. They were the priests who had joined the children for the journey. One of them was the kindly man whom Bertran had called upon to help Adela on the day he had buried the first victim.

The priest looked up, sensing that he was being watched.

Upon seeing Bertran, he stood and approached him quickly.

"Good evening, Bertran. What brings you to our fires?"

The young man stammered awkwardly, himself confused as to why he had come to this place.

"It's that "prophet"," he blurted out.

"Stephen?"

The priest took him by the arm and moved him away from the camp.

"What has happened?" he whispered with concern.

"He's an imposter, that's what's happened!"

The priest was silent for a moment. A dark expression overshadowed his kind features and Bertran was suddenly struck with the thought that the man was already aware of the situation.

"You knew this!" he shouted in outrage.

"No, not in the beginning," the priest responded sadly.

"But we knew that his story was false."

Bertran's eyes opened wide.

"How did you know?"

"Well, we believe that the stranger who called Stephen to this mission and gave him a letter was...a priest in disguise."

"What are you saying, father?" Bertran cried out.

The good man put his hand to his lips, and looked back at the campfire.

"You must understand that the Holy Father has been attempting to raise a new crusade for many years. He has many legates who travel the land, seeking every possible way to please his will."

Bertran shook his head in disbelief.

"Why did you not try to stop this madness?"

"Me? I am but a pawn of the Church. I have no power but to give of myself. And that is why I am here."

They walked in grim silence through the dark shadows.

"This is a doomed venture," the priest whispered. "Didn't you know it from the start? This is the blood sacrifice for a new orgy of war that will be waged in the name of the Prince of Peace."

Bertran was struck by the man's honesty. He had finally found someone who was not merely a blind follower of orders from on high.

"Who then is responsible for this disaster?" Bertran asked.

"The spirit of the age, Bertran. We have believed for too long that relics and consecrated places are more sacred than human life. We have made our religion a weapon against every other religion. Christendom has become just like Islam, waging holy wars to expand its power and wealth. We have mistaken Jerusalem the desert town for Jerusalem the heavenly city. The faithful have not understood that the holy city which John of Patmos speaks of in Revelation is an inner state of being, not a place with streets and walls!"

"Why haven't you preached this to the children?"

"It is too late. They would stone me. So I've come to die at their side."

"How can you still claim allegiance to a Pope who..."

"I am vowed to a life of obedience, Bertran. Besides, there are some who believe that the Church is not responsible for this crusade."

"Who then?"

"Have you ever heard of the Old Man of the Mountain?"

"Never."

"He is the most feared man in the world! He lives in a fortress called the Eagle's Nest high in the desert mountains. His followers worship their god through the ritual murder of those who are enemies of their beliefs. They are called the Assassins."

Bertran was fascinated.

"Tell me more."

"It is said that his disciples are trained from infancy to become fearless and skilled in the art of killing. I have heard a tale that he released two of his captives to bring together a new flock for his evil purposes."

"How could such evil exist in a man?"

"Remember that we know only what his enemies have reported of him. But it does not matter if this story is true or
not. We are doomed regardless of who our butcher will be.
If we're not swallowed up by the sea, we will surely be massacred by the Bedouins or the Atabeg warriors."

"Have you been to the Holy Land before, father?"

"I have seen it three times, my son."

Bertran grabbed him by the shoulders.

"Tell me, can a prisoner of the Saracens ever be found and
freed?"

"If that is your intent, my young friend, then I pray that
you will be granted a swift passage from this life to the
next. The peoples of those desert lands are fierce, without
fear, and often merciless."

"I've heard that Saladin was a good ruler."

"He was indeed very devout, but he also had prisoners
killed one at a time before his very eyes. It is not that they
are worse savages then we are. They have been subject to
such butchery from the Crusaders that their cruelty is
vengeance for abominations. Did you know that the great
Godfrey of Bouillon, the first Christian King of the Holy
City, entered Jerusalem riding over the blood of seventy
thousand victims of his siege?"

Bertran had not heard such things before. He had always assumed that the Christians were in the right and that the Muslims were followers of evil.

"I was there in Constantinople when the knights destroyed it as no city has ever been ravaged," the priest continued.

"Did you follow the Crusaders to Acre and Sidon?"

"I did. Why I survived is a mystery I have yet to understand."

"Did you know Lord Reynald of Vendome?" Bertran asked breathlessly.

"Yes, I did. Is he the man you are looking for?"

"I'm here with his daughter. Her lawful inheritance has been taken away from her. Our only hope is to find Lord Reynald and bring him home."

"He was the noblest of our leaders in that army of thieves and murderers. I was deeply saddened when I learned of his capture. The Crusade might have been a success if he had remained at its helm."

"Do you know who captured him and where they may be found?" asked, virtually intoxicated with excitement.

"I do. But Bertran, this is not good news."

"Of course it is, father, of course it is! I thought that we were on a hopeless mission, but now all might be made right!"

"Bertran," the priest said solemnly as he pressed his hands

against the youth, "the men who took your friend's father were members of the Assassins sect! Lord Reynald must be a prisoner of the Old Man of the Mountain!"

An owl suddenly released a deep moan as it fled from a nearby tree. The night creature had given voice to the dread that flooded Bertran's soul.

9

The children soon began to lose all hope of success in their naive mission. Only Stephen could raise their spirits and he did so with surprising skill as he continually improved his impersonation of a divine messenger. Every time his chariot appeared among the young pilgrims, a massive stampede took place.

The frenzied youths rushed to touch the chariot and listen their own little god. To touch the boy prophet was to be assured good luck in the Holy Land. Stephen found it all very gratifying for a time. But, as the ecstatic crowds became more desperate to reach him, he started to fear them and ordered his guards to surround the chariot and beat back his eager admirers. The children of nobility who had the

privilege of carrying out his orders discovered new thrills in wielding such power. They didn't merely hold the young idolaters back, they enjoyed beating them with whips and staffs.

From that day on, a new atmosphere settled over the crusade. Rules were established and enforced with fervor. The guards would trot their horses through the ranks of children, looking for those who disobeyed or were making trouble. Fear now blended with the worship of the prophet, making the children all the more passive to his orders. None dared to question his authority. None reflected on the fact that he was pampered while they suffered; that he lived in debauchery while claiming to be blessed with the visitation of the Son of God.

Under the influence of such absolute power, Stephen's self-indulgence grew worse with every passing day. If he saw a pretty girl in the crowd, he would make sure that by nightfall she was in his chariot. The young nobles thought nothing of carrying out his lascivious commands. Some of them followed his example and turned the pilgrimage into an orgy of rape and brutality.

Adela had caught Stephen's eye from the beginning.

On her Arabian stallion, with her mane of wild locks and her intense expression, Adela was a nearly mythic vision to these destitute souls. But her peasant friend was never far away and watched her like an eagle. Stephen wanted Bertran dead. But he dared not ask for murder from his loyal followers. Not yet.

The boy prophet took his frustrations out on poor Cecilia. When he found out that she was Adela's lady-in-waiting, he humiliated her constantly before his little court. It was as close as he could come to controlling the most extraordinary woman he had ever seen. Everyone was aware of her presence and sensed her strength of character and unrelenting concern for the more helpless among them. The shepherd boy fantasized more about the Baron's daughter than about heavenly visions of a new Jerusalem.

All this was kept out of sight from the mass of children who held fast with innocent faith to the belief that their leader was sent from a higher world.

Only once did one of Stephen's guards attempt to draw Adela into the chariot. The pilgrims had stopped outside the gates of a southern town and were resting during the noonday heat. The brazen young noble approached Adela and showed her a purse full of gold coins. He assured her that there was more for the friends of the prophet.

"Why are you not buying food for the children with that money?" she asked, infuriated.

"Each must look after himself, that is the rule for all who join this pilgrimage. These are rewards for those who please the prophet."

The boy's suggestive gleam stung Adela's pride like the burn of a whip. She slapped his face with great force. Furious, the young warrior grabbed her by the hair, shouting obscenities. He raised his fist and tried to strike her. The first blow missed as she slipped out of his grasp.

A little girl watching on hurried to Bertran who was busy filling his water supply at the river's edge. He raced up the hill to the encampment and found the guard holding his nose as it oozed with blood. Adela stood a few feet from him with a rock in hand. She had evidently hit him with it and was ready to use it again. Bertran laughed and sent the boy on his way with a swift kick in the rump. He was proud of his Adela, though he wished she might need him more. But she was firmly rooted in her own self-reliance and refused to let herself be vulnerable.

The days turned into harrowing trials and the nights into desperate efforts to forget the agonies of this endless journey. Dozens of little bodies marked the paths they had taken through the hills and woodlands of the southern provinces. The summer's heat sizzled like never before in the memories of the old folk. Despite Stephen's daily speeches, the crusade was crumbling into chaos.

The multitudes splintered into groups that survived as best they could, invading villages and towns along the way. The little pilgrims were no longer welcomed by the populace. They were seen as no more than uncontrollable ruffians whose numbers were a fearsome sight.

Bertran and Adela pressed on, growing closer each day as they struggled together against adversities. It had taken weeks for them to come to grips with all that had happened. Suddenly, they were no longer the people they once were. Adela began to see in Bertran a protector rather than a peasant, a man rather than a boy. Yet they were never intimate together though they slept alongside each other. Every night, in the dying light of the campfire, one would watch the other fall asleep, grateful to be side by side. There was a new bond between them, born out of that extraordinary moment in the ruins of the chapel, as though the Consolation received by dying Bohemond had also exposed their souls to a common fount of love that now fed their relationship.

Adela was discovering depths of feelings she had never known before. The dirty-faced children who looked to her as mother had unlocked her nurturing instincts. Under the broiling sun, surrounded by pain and need, the scales of selfishness were melting from her heart. This unforeseen twist of fate had pulled her from her tower of privilege and flung her into the midst of humanity.

Bertran hardly noticed the physical traumas of the journey. His love for the indomitable young woman grew with every new dawn. He witnessed with deep joy the little acts which revealed her rapid blossoming: wiping away tears, sharing a morsel of her meal, encouraging those who were giving up. Since childhood he knew that such a soul burned bright in that strong-willed personality. To see her flower into the full beauty of kindness and compassion made everything else unimportant. At the same time, he also realized that this unexpected adventure might save him from the deadly burden of a serf's life and lead him to the fulfillment of dreams that he had always carried secretly within his heart.

Bertran felt a new fire rush through his veins, an anticipation of great things to come. So many extraordinary opportunities were heading his way, not the least of which were the new ideas instilled in his mind by the hermit. Years of rooting up trees and plowing the Baron's fields had overshadowed the vaster part of his nature.

He now found himself captivated by an exhilarating attraction to the mysteries of life. Behind every tree, mountain and river there was a new sense of immensity, as though the invisible presence of the Great Unknown was making itself known. All the images of his childhood that had once fed his soul now rushed forward from his memory. A painting of the star of Bethlehem in a corner of the cathedral had first sparked his awe of the universe and his place in it. The statue of the Mother of God had spoken to the little boy of divine gentleness and care. Even the candles appeared to him as souls in prayer.

These hallowed moments had been dormant beneath the sweat and hard labor of daily survival.

He spent hours alongside Adela, thinking about Good and Evil. Did the heretics have the Truth in their possession? Clearly, the Church which could be seen was as maggot-infested as the cadaver of a person long dead. The one good priest Bertran met on the journey only made more evident the perversion of so many other men of the cloth. Adela alone brought his thoughts back to the relentlessness of the pilgrimage. A new quality was also permeating their relationship. Though he was still a servant of sorts to the young baroness, he was also becoming a companion.

Bertran wore with pride the sword he had taken from one of the Abbot's men at the castle. Every dawn, before the huge caravan moved forward, he would practice swinging it as he had seen done by knights of the Realm. Adela offered her knowledge of sword-

play, sometimes showing him a move taught to her by Lord
Reynald. It was a relief from boredom, a chance for them to be
close without embarrassment. But behind these small joys was the
ominous sense that they were marching directly into the jaws of
death. Bertran was not merely learning the use of his sword in order to feel more like a man of noble birth. An intuition deep within
urged him to prepare for confrontation with the mighty warriors of
the East.

Lord Reynald had trained his daughter well. Adela shared with
Bertran secrets of parrying and coordination of foot-work. He often walked alongside Tancred, swinging the weapon every which
way as his teacher enjoyed his awkward efforts. At times, when the
pilgrims stopped to rest, Adela would stand behind him and hold
his arms, showing him the warrior's moves which would someday
save his life. He relished those moments when they stood so close.
The heat of their bodies intermingled and stirred within him mysterious waves of ecstasy.

It was on the eve of reaching the city of Marseilles that Bertran
revealed to Adela the information he had gathered from the priest.
He thought the news would devastate her. But the stubborn young
woman was hardly even interested. Wherever her father was kept,
they would find him and bring him back. It was that simple. Adela
had heard of other Christians winning the hearts of a caliph or a
sultan. It was Lord Reynald himself who had taught her to respect
those different than her and to discover what might be learned

from them. She had heard that many a follower of Islam was devout and virtuous. Surely, she would be able to convince such a person to release a true knight.

Besides, there was something not unfamiliar with the idea of being in the Holy Land. From the day her father had left, she felt that she too would travel through the hot sands of the Sinai.

Adela had often imagined, especially when galloping through the meadows on her Arabian stallion, what it might be like to wear the silks and sandals of a Persian princess. An old friend of her father's had visited them years before and told her wondrous tales of those exotic cultures. He was a Knight Templar, a warrior-monk from the Order of the Temple of Solomon, vowed to defend the pilgrims and Crusaders throughout the Holy Land.

Adela had been struck by the man's unusual look. She had never seen a knight in such simple armor, sprouting a great unkempt beard, and smelling like a barnyard animal. His rugged face, bronzed by exposure to the sun and sandstorms of the deserts, bore witness to the knight's incomparable bravery. The Templars always led the charges against the enemy, always fought where combat was the most fierce, and were never spared as prisoners since they refused to be ransomed or relinquish their faith as their captors required.

The young Baronness was fascinated by the paradox of the warrior-monk. They were pledged to poverty and obedience and followed a Rule of Life penned by the great saint Bernard of

Clairvaux. But their self-sacrifice and worship of the Almighty was done with swords and spears, not with rosaries and fasting. At the same time, they respected the Saracens and learned much from them. For years, they had lived in peace alongside them after the First Crusade. No other northerner knew the cultures of the East better than they did. It was even rumored that some of their rituals and beliefs had been infected by the teachings of Muhammad. The Templars were a hybrid creation born from the encounter of these two alien worlds.

New hope ran through the motley ranks of exhausted children as they set camp for their last evening under the stars before reaching the seaport. Jerusalem couldn't be far now. Most of the little pilgrims had never even seen an ocean before and had no idea of the dangers of sea voyage. But their prophet told them that the waters would part before them just as it had for Moses and his people, and in their innocence they believed him.

Bertran watched on cynically as Stephen finished his last speech of the journey, assuring all within earshot that victory was theirs and the Holy Sepulcher would be freed. He reminded the children that Paradise awaited their friends who had died along the way as it awaited them at the end of their days. Bertran shook his head in disgust. Religion always seemed to come down to "what's in it for me?" The Pope gave out indulgences, the priest handed out absolutions, and Stephen of Cloyes promised miracles. It was a commerce, just like the tanner's business in the village who sold his wares in the marketplace with the bargaining skills of a greedy Venetian merchant.

Bertran wondered whether it would always be so. Could the Church do anything more than entice its followers with a vision of things to come while it amassed immense wealth, primarily from its duped flock? Was this world nothing but treachery and lies? Was it only the evil of brute force that gained power here below? He certainly knew that his big arms and his even bigger sword had kept him safe from Stephen's guards. But it also meant that he was always on the alert, always suspicious of shadows around him. This was not the life he wanted. He missed the freedom that was his when he walked in solitude through the hills and woodlands of his home.

Stephen finished his speech by asking that everyone come forth with valuable goods and place them before the chariot. Money would be needed before entering the ancient city. Unlike the towns through which they had marched, Marseilles would not permit such a desperate crowd within its gates unless the pilgrims could pay for their needs. This vast city first built by the Romans was run by merchants who understood life in terms of the jingle of coins. The city's tranquility was bought in gold, for it behooved the wealthy citizens of all the surrounding provinces to keep the seaport active in trade. There was no tolerance for beggars and vagabonds here. The last inflow of pilgrims into the city had been the magnificent cortege of Richard the Lion-Hearted. Their great ships, glorious banners, and silk-laden knights were welcomed with open arms. But an army of ragged children was another matter. Bertran suspected that there was another motive for Stephen's request. The degenerate prophet feared mutiny and wanted to control the packs of children by stripping them of their last relics of independence.

"You there!" Stephen called out to Adela. "Give an example to the others and bring us your white horse."

Adela looked over at Bertran, stunned.

"As you can see, my chariot needs another mount, a strong one. Yours would be perfect."

"But what would I ride then?" Adela asked.

"We are within a day's walk of Marseilles. Surely you can manage to use your feet. There are little children who have been walking all the way from Paris."

"I haven't seen you walk!" Bertran cried out defiantly.

Stephen's pallid face turned red. He peered into the darkening shadows to see who had spoken so insolently to him. One of his guards rode up beside the chariot.

"It's that big peasant, Sire. The one who attacked you once before."

"Come forward!" Stephen shouted to Bertran.

Adela grabbed his arm.

"Don't move, Bertran! I'm scared!"

Bertran looked into her eyes. He had never before heard her

admit of any weakness. His heart leaped as he recognized that her fear was for his welfare. A smile warmed his features and he patted her hand.

"They can't hurt me."

He stepped toward the chariot, his right hand falling to the pummel of his sword.

"Do you see this man?" Stephen cried out as he pointed dramatically to Bertran. "He has tried to interfere with my divine mission! He even

drew his sword on my person! But, as a good disciple of our Lord, I let him go free. Now, he stands again in my way even as we feel the salty breeze of the ocean which will take us to the Holy Land. What would you have me do?"

"Kill him! Tear him to pieces!" a hundred voices cried out.

Adela barely withheld a scream of terror.

Bertran jumped up on a tree trunk and raised his hands to address the multitudes.

"Many of you have come to know me on this painful journey. I carried some of you in my arms until you could walk again. Mark, you remember when I buried your brother for you and gave you my dinner."

A young boy in the crowd nodded as tears came to his eyes.

"I have not harmed anyone. But Stephen, your prophet, would have us give up our last possessions to fill his coffers."

"It's for the good of the Crusade!" a youthful voice

shouted out.

"It's for the good of the shepherd of Cloyes!" Bertran shouted back. "You've all seen how easy this journey has been for him! He lays in his royal chariot and eats grapes while we hunger and thirst!"

"But he is a messenger from God!" another voice yelled out. "He will lead us in glory to the land where Jesus walked!"

"Is this glory?" Bertran responded. "Look around you! Our ranks have broken up and thinned out. No one sings anymore. There are thieves among us! Many of our girls have been violated!"

"Blasphemer!" several voices cried out. "Kill the traitor!"

A number of Stephen's guards spurred their horses toward Bertran. With a great shout, Adela kicked her mount who jolted forward and blocked their way. Bertran ran toward the chariot which was his only escape route and leaped into it. He pulled his sword and stuck the blade against Stephen's throat. A terrible gasp came from the crowds.

"Tell your guards to back away or you'll never speak again!" Utterly terrified, Stephen motioned for his young knights to stand back.

"You'll let us end this journey in peace, without taking our horse!"

Stephen stood motionless, more pained by the humiliation than by the sharp iron against his flesh. Bertran pushed the sword forward, cutting a small line of blood across his neck.

"I will! I will!" the terrified boy shouted.

"You heard your prophet!" Bertran roared at the children.
"He will leave us alone and not demand our horse. This is his word!"

The crowds shouted angrily at Bertran. He turned to find a way to escape the wrath of the deluded children. As his gaze passed by the draped portion of the chariot, he saw a form lying motionless on the silk cushions. It was the body of a woman stiffened with the rigidity of death.

Bertran turned to Stephen, eyes flaming with outrage.

The boy cowered and began to whimper.

"I tried to stop her..."

Bertran flung open the curtains. Before him lay Cecilia. Her scantily-clad corpse was covered with scratches and bruises from head to foot. A deep gash across her wrist revealed the cause of death. There was blood everywhere.

"When did this happen?" Bertran cried out.

"At midday. I couldn't stop her or she would have killed me too."

"And you've sat in this blood since then?"

"I didn't want to scare the children," Stephen moaned in anguish.

"We'll bury her this evening."

The shouting children had surrounded the chariot by then, calling for Bertran's death. Adela rode her horse between them and her friend.

Bertran grit his teeth to restrain his anger.

"Listen to me, shepherd boy! I'll hold up the body of this poor girl for all to see and show them that you're a trickster if you don't give us protection!"

Stephen was no longer the assured prophet idolized by the gullible masses. He was a frightened, simple shepherd boy who had been thrown into a fantasy of self-indulgence with the Pope's own seal of approval. Before the grotesque corpse of the young woman he had abused so bestially, his mask dissolved and he found himself confronted with the monster he had become.

"Stop your whimpering and tell them to leave us alone!"

Bertran had already leaned forward to grab Cecilia's blood-stained leg.

"No! Please don't do that! They would rip me apart!"

"Then talk to them now!"

Stephen stepped to the edge of the chariot, trying to compose himself and play his role.

"I command you to stop!"

The waves of menacing children halted instantly.

The shepherd boy disappeared again behind the face of the inspired prophet.

"This man is under my protection! I will forgive his insolence and I forbid you to harm him!"

Stephen's guards cursed as they put away their swords.

"You will keep your word, Stephen?" Bertran asked suspiciously.

The boy nodded, still terrified by Bertran's physical strength and the fact that he had seen him for what he really was. "One more thing, then. Let me bury her. I don't want her thrown into a pit like the carcass of some animal. I'll return for her when the children are sleeping."

Stephen nodded his approval, relieved that he had not been unveiled before his adoring throngs. But he knew that his feeling of power would never be the same. The foundations of his pedestal were cracked because of the peasant with the big sword. After nearly a year of adulation since his first exhortation on the steps of the cathedral of Saint Denis, he became completely enthralled by the reactions of the multitudes. He lost track of the quiet, religious boy he had once been and given in to the intoxication of human praise. When clothes, money and followers were thrust upon him, he fell helplessly into the abyss of vainglory and lust.

Stephen entered his little chamber in the chariot and began to tear the blood-stained curtains from the walls, flinging them over Cecilia's body. He could not bear to look at her anymore. For most of the afternoon, he had sat next to her and stared at her open, vacant eyes. Now that he no longer lusted for her flesh, he began to notice her gentle, slightly plump features. They reminded him of a girl from his village, a peasant's daughter who had often watched for him on his return from the pastures.

Stephen realized to his great disgust that he had destroyed a lovely human being in order to satisfy his lecherous hunger. He longed for his lost innocence and the simple life he had left behind. And he felt the weight of this young woman's death hanging over him like an executioner's hatchet. All the details of that terrible moment flooded his mind as he sat there and studied the dead body. It had been another night of orgiastic madness involving some of his guards and other girls lured away from the campfires. Cecilia had romped with abandon, throwing herself into the depravity like a criminal rejoicing at the penance of the whip.

By morning, she crawled off into a corner, soiled and wretched, coming face to face with her misery. Stephen could not stop her weeping and finally threw her out of the chariot. She had vanished for a time, and Stephen felt relieved for he knew deep within that her despoilment reflected his own.

Then, just as he laid back on his cushions for an after meal nap, she re-appeared in his cabin. The guards had let her through be-cause she was a regular visitor to the chariot as well as to their own tents. But it was no longer the same woman who stood before him. Her crazed expression, like that of a cornered animal confronting death with desperate determination, frightened him immediately. He sat up and looked her over. Her clothes were torn to shreds, as though she had run through a woodland dense with thorns. Her hair rose wildly over her head like the mane of a charging lion. She seemed demon-possessed.

"What do you want?" Stephen heard himself say.

Without a word she suddenly drew a dagger from her belt.

"No!" Stephen yelled as he jumped to the back of the cabin and cowered among the thick drapes.

Cecilia approached menacingly. Stephen's whole body shook. For an instant, he was deeply sorry for all his heinous sins. The lost young woman laughed at his pathetic cowardice.

"You fool! I didn't come to kill you!"

Stephen let out a great sigh of relief.

Cecilia stepped closer.

"I came to kill myself!"

With that she raised her right arm and swung the sharp knife across her wrist. A jet of blood sprayed across the entire cabin. Stephen shrieked with horror. Cecilia stood there staring at him, holding her arm in the air completely unconcerned with the terrible wound.

"Let this be a warning to you, Stephen! There is divine judgment and it has come for me! I bleed for the death of dear Bohemond and the arrest of that old hermit."

She came closer to the hysterical boy and stood over him, letting the blood gush all around him.

"Hear the words of the dead! There is a Hell, but it's nothing like the lakes of fire they tell us about. It's worse! Hell is the madness in your heart and in your mind when you have abandoned God. The stake would have been easier than the agony I have suffered for my sins."

The blood-stained girl burned with the fury of a doomed soul seeing her errors too late. A mighty seer of ancient Israel would not have instilled more terror and remorse.

"Hear me, Stephen! My fate awaits you! You will pay for every one of your lies and treacheries! Death will be sweet compared to the punishment that is prepared for you!"

She suddenly fell in a heap on the floor. Stephen watched her fade away only a few feet from where he crouched.

"Forgive me," she whispered hoarsely to an invisible Presence, "forgive me..."

Stephen wept uncontrollably for hours. Several of the young barons found him and called for the priests. After a time, Stephen the blessed prophet who was to accomplish what no king or knight, pope or saint, had ever done and fulfill the dark dream of the Crusades, emerged from his chariot healed from his unbearable feelings. The representatives of the Holy Roman Church had forgiven and absolved him of all his sins.

10

The children limped into the great seaport of Marseilles, many weeping with joy thinking that they had seen the end of their troubles. They arrived in absolute chaos, coming into the city in clusters, terrifying the citizens with their mud-splattered rags and emaciated faces.

Stephen sent out his soldiers in an effort to organize their entrance and to insure that they would all come to the same place. But even his authority was overshadowed by the exhaustion and desperation of the children. Fresh and rested, dressed in fine clothing, he led the way like a conquering centurion on a victory parade. Only a distant haze in his eyes revealed that the depths of his being were in great torment. Bertran and Adela rode alongside the children, doing what they could to help those who were collapsing from fatigue.

Tanned by the sun, her hair made wild by the wind, Adela's resolve to find her father was greater than ever. The journey had initiated her into a new strength of character and

181

trimmed the last baby-fat of self-absorption from her nature. She was no longer the spoiled baroness in adolescent
rebellion against everything around her. The human misery
she had encountered face to face had aged her beyond her
years. Cecilia's burial had also been an internment of her
own youth.

The previous night, Bertran and Adela stood side by side
looking down into the grave he had dug for their poor
friend. Adela wept silently and Bertran reflected on the
darkness that had kidnapped Cecilia and dragged her into
this untimely death. He put his arm around the woman he
would love forever and gently filled her with his own
strength.

Her pain left quickly as she felt the support and presence
of the man who was as dependable as the seasons. In the
midst of her sadness for the tragedy of her childhood
friend and confidante, she was surprised to feel a deep
sense of well-being as the strong arm wrapped itself around
her shoulders. Her first impulse was to move away and repress the vulnerability which had frightened her ever since
her father had left for the East. But she remained at
Bertran's side and found herself being healed by his love.
Standing over the grave, there was no escaping the fact that
they were equal in the sight of God. His peasant heritage
and her high birth, a cousin to royal blood, meant nothing

as they peered into the dark pit at the body whose tormented soul had departed for the home they all shared in common.

Adela had always imagined a mighty prince as her companion, one dressed in the finest furs and silks with a gold and silver sword at his side. But on this cold and lonely night, the warm presence of her most loyal friend was a blessing from Heaven. She felt a wave of peace and gratitude rise in her heart and melt away the pain. Though they were fugitives and penniless, with a dangerous future ahead, they were together and that was all that mattered.

As they rode into Marseilles, Adela felt a new certainty that she would find her father and return to claim her rightful heritage. On that day, she would shower Bertran with gifts and perhaps make him an overseer of her lands.

She felt Bertran's arms tighten around her waist as they trotted toward the colossal city gates of Marseilles. She knew that his love for her was constantly increasing. Their proximity through this ordeal had dissolved his timidity and his need to be closer to her was becoming more evident every day. Adela realized that he would never be satisfied with becoming a better paid servant at her castle. She knew that he wanted her and nothing else. That thought frightened her greatly. She was not yet willing to consider the possibility of giving her hand to a serf. Her vanity still held her in its grip.

Adela banished the thought from her mind as was her habit when things became too difficult to deal with. It disappeared in her inner no-man's land of forgetfulness along with those awful thoughts of death under the sabers of the dreaded Saracens. She was still young enough to be an optimist even while walking into the jaws of annihilation.

A great shout of joy rose from the little pilgrims. It was the first time in weeks that exuberance had been heard among them.

"Look! The sea!"

Bertran peered into the distance and saw what looked like a giant rug of sparkling stones surrounding the edge of the city. Some of the children began to run toward the wondrous sight with renewed fervor. Adela felt her heart pound quicker as she scanned the flat horizon which would lead them closer to her beloved father.

The shimmering waters were eerily calm under the blazing sun, awaiting the youths with the semblance of peace. Bertran, however, knew that the sea was a dangerous adversary and would not be bridled for the sake of the innocent.

The city fathers were on hand to greet the famous boy prophet. They stood in the great square overlooking the ocean and awaited impatiently as the cloud of dust in the distance announced the arrival of their odd guests. These men had seen their ancient city return to its former glory through the prosperity generated by the Crusades. The commerce of warfare filled the coffers of the leading merchants of the seaport. It was therefore difficult for them to turn their backs on the tiny pilgrims who were perhaps the precursors of a new era of voyages to the bloody sands of Palestine.

Stephen and his entourage arrived at the head of the twenty thousand strong army of peaceful pilgrims. He was greeted like a visiting dignitary, with all the honors and pomp due to a messenger of the Almighty sanctioned by the Pope himself. The city fathers could not entirely conceal the worry on their faces as they watched the great square quickly fill beyond its capacity. Stephen announced that they were only in their city for a night because he had been promised by God that the sea would open up before them. They would be needing no money, no ships, no extended hospitality.

The welcoming committee looked at each other and tried not to smile. Though they were as religious and superstitious as any good Christian, they had lived by the sea too long to believe in such a miracle. Bertran, sitting atop Tancred with Adela, did not attempt to hide his mockery. He was certain that the time had come when Stephen would be revealed for what he was - a corrupt, ambitious boy with a mighty imagination. At tomorrow's dawn, when the tide came in as it always had and always would, Bertran hoped that Cecilia would have her revenge through the complete humiliation of the false prophet.

The city made room for the young travelers. Stephen and his guards of noble birth slept in sumptuous quarters while others found rooms in convents and monasteries. The majority slept on the Roman cobblestones.

Adela and Bertran took a room at an inn, paying with some of the jewelry that Cecilia had tossed in the saddlebags the day of their departure. They took Tancred to the stables behind the inn and let him feast on fresh hay which he so deserved. The animal had lost much weight and continually foamed at the mouth. The journey had exhausted even his powerful body.

Adela caressed his silky white main as he ate.

"My loyal Tancred...You've been so courageous."

Bertran patted the horse's strong neck.

"He doesn't look the same. I don't know much about horses, but he seems very ill to me."

"Nonsense!" Adela responded. She would not allow any more bad thoughts to overshadow her spirits. "He'll be just fine.

Won't you, my beauty?"

The horse lifted his head and dropped his ears back. His eyes gleamed with a melancholic look.

"I tell you, Adela, this animal is not well at all. See how he perspires. You know he hasn't eaten well for many days."

"This stallion comes from the best stock in Persia. With a good rest and plenty of food and water, he'll be his old self again soon."

"I don't think so..."

Adela turned angrily on Bertran.

"If you're just going to prophecy doom for us, why don't you go away!"

Bertran was stunned by her careless words. He felt he deserved better from her after all he had done.

"Don't talk to me that way, Adela! I'm trying to help."

The young woman's face turned red as her eyes widened.

"How dare you speak in that manner! Do you think that because Fate has forced us on this journey together, you can do away with the respect due to me?"

Now it was Bertran's turn to get angry.

"You aren't due anything, least of all from me! Do you realize that at this moment you've been stripped of all your possessions? You're a fugitive from your regent and are no more important than a common vagabond!"

He instantly regretted his words. But it was too late. Adela's eyes grew cold and sent a shiver up his spine. He felt her suddenly slip away from him.

"I'm sorry, Adela. I simply meant to say..."

"I don't want to hear anymore! Begone!"

With that, she turned her back on him.

Bertran was crushed. All his wild hopes suddenly vanished like a passing dream. He felt his body weaken as though he were sinking into the ground. But after all they had gone through, he couldn't believe that this altercation would damage the only thing he lived for. He placed his hand on her shoulder. Adela pushed it off with unexpected violence.

"Get away from me, peasant!"

Bertran's eyes filled with tears as he watched the seething hatred in her features destroy their delicate relationship.

"Adela..." he whispered desperately.

She backed away from him, head lowered as though aiming horns at his chest.

"I may be in rags and unclean, but I still have my pride! I am still Adela of Vendome, daughter of Lord Reynald! And I will regain my properties and my dignity!"

"I know you will, Adela. That is why I've accepted to endure all this with you."

"I want you out of my sight now!"

"We've been through a terrible ordeal. I understand your anger. But please don't..."

Adela suddenly started screaming for help. Bertran was

horrified.

"What are you doing? It's me, Bertran!"

The sound of boots and the clanging of weapons echoed in the alleyway. Bertran thought for a moment that he would lose his mind. Adela screamed again and again, losing all control. He wanted to take her in his arms and hug her as he had the night before. He wanted to find again that blissful love which he dared to believe they had begun to share. A sergeant of arms appeared at the other end of the stables, followed by several soldiers. They were one of many patrols in the streets, for the city could not sleep soundly with their undisciplined, motley guests roaming about.

"Grab him!" he shouted. Bertran looked one last time at Adela. She was no longer the woman he knew. All the anger and pain of this last month, perhaps even of the last eight years since she had lost her father, was erupting from hidden wounds. With a terrible roar of outrage at this twist of events, Bertran dashed off into the night, chased by the soldiers.

* * *

He wandered until dawn on the shoreline at the edge of the city. The morose cry of lonely seagulls and the soft rhythm of splashing waves coming to die upon the beach expressed the desolation of his heart. He walked barefoot in the cold, wet sand, looking out at the infinite expanse of ocean. For a time, the grandiose wonders of nature soothed his grief. But the distant, hateful look in Adela's eyes always came back, like the waves, to shatter the tranquility of his soul. For hours, under the sparkling stars, he tried to convince himself that all would be better in the morning. Surely, she would forgive him and they would be dear friends once again. Surely, she would recognize that her outburst was exaggerated, that he was not the enemy, but in fact her comforter, her protector. Then an icy fear would set in as he remembered the many times in their childhood when she exhibited an astonishing lack of logical behavior. She was ruled by pride and emotion, not by intellect and logic. Bertran looked up at the vast sky overhead and cried out involuntarily, as he had done once before.

"Blessed Creator, have mercy on me!"

He felt too much agony to weep. A broadsword's blade buried in his chest would not have hurt as much. He wanted to rip his heart out, toss it into the sea and be done with this business of love. Nothing and no one could hurt him as Adela did. She was his joy and his misery. And having come so close to sharing that true love which was rightfully theirs, even though it was spurned by the ways of men, he could not bear to watch it disappear over a trivial argument.

"Damn you, Adela!" he shouted to the stars and the waves.

"Damn you for possessing my heart and soul!"

He increased his pace along the beach, instinctively attempting to release his rage through physical strain. He suddenly realized that he had gone from praying for mercy to curses of damnation. He stopped walking. Something was happening in his soul.

Just as the first red glows of the sun began to break through the mantle of darkness, he felt a new force being born within. His rage and his pain evaporated like morning dewdrops in the heat of the rising sun. As the horizon filled with magnificent colors, he felt his whole being flood with peace.

Even his senses seemed to change. He could hear and see and smell more clearly. The aroma of the sea breeze eased his tension; the rhythm of the tide caressed his heart; and the great expanse of water spoke of the glory of his Maker. Bertran looked up at the golden orb peeking at him from the far end of the ocean. He was struck by the awesome sensation that this splendid birth of day was for him alone, that without his presence on these shores, it could not exist. He was its sole witness.

The solitary figure stood on the beach staring out in silence at the cosmic occurrence, lost in the immensity of the sky and sea. He was standing before the unveiling of the Holy and his soul was humbled like never before. He fell to his

knees, sinking into the wet sand. The first colored ray of
sun shot across the ocean waves and headed directly for
him. He felt its warmth on his face and closed his eyes as a
great tremor shook his being. It seemed as though the hand
of God was blessing His beloved child.

The goodness and sacredness of life made itself known to
him. Alone in the vastness of silent nature, he was filled
with a greater Silence, the dwelling place of the Divine
Presence. Bertran spread out his arms, receiving the gift of
the sun into himself. A gentle breeze cooled his cheeks and
the soft sands cushioned his knees. He knew in that timeless moment that the Creator was Goodness Itself and
cared for him as for an only son, raising him from insignifi-
cance to kinship with the Eternal Spirit. The gentle colors
of dawn had faded beneath the brilliance of the sun when
Bertran stood up. His mind and heart resonated with an extraordinary tranquility, as vast and calm as the boundless
waters before him. His whole body was numb with ecstatic
emotion. He touched his face and found that it was
streaked with tears.

But they were tears of joy for he had been given the gift of
acceptance and unconditional love. More than that, he had
experienced his true home. It was a place within, yet above
all the torments of daily life. It was a sanctuary more sacred
than the greatest cathedral, where he could return at any

moment if ever he remembered who he was and to whom

he belonged.

Bertran headed back toward the walls of the city. Each step brought him a rapture he had not known since early child-hood. Each breath of sea air filled his heart with the thrill of being alive. He had no idea what awaited him in the city of humanity. But that was not important. He knew that Bertran the serf was also Bertran the child of the Universe.

* * *

Adela stepped out of the inn into the southern sunshine. She felt wonderfully refreshed, having slept in a bed for the first time in weeks and lingered in a bathtub of soapy wa-ter. Her clothes were of fine, clean linen, the one garment left in the saddlebags which had not been soiled by the voyage. She was ready to embrace the new day with regen-erated strength and hope.

Only the slightest discomfort remained from her fight with Bertran the night before. Anger still simmered within, like coals from a great bonfire. Her fierce pride and independ-ence had been threatened and had nearly toppled her into a void of vulnerability which she could not live with. She had to stand on her own without anyone's help, just as she had done ever since the tragic day of her father's departure. She repressed any twinge of remorse over her unfair treat-ment of Bertran. Besides, she assumed that he would always come back, like a loyal pet who can always be counted upon. Stepping lightly into the street, she took notice of the traces of Roman civilization all around her. She had never seen such a city as this one in the colder climate back home. Everything was built to accommodate life in the sun, creating an atmosphere of relaxation and ease. Giant tropical plants stood out like creatures from another world. They were the heralds of even stranger beings awaiting her across the ocean.

Adela headed for the stables with a song in her heart. Today she would embark for the Holy Land and search for her beloved father. How often had she dreamed of this moment! There was no greater desire in her life and she now stood on the threshold of its fulfillment.

As she approached the stables, she pulled an apple from her tunic pocket and polished it merrily for her favorite horse. Walking into the alley, she noticed several stable boys standing near Tancred's stall.

"Have you fed my horse yet?" she asked. The boys turned to her. She smiled at the soiled faces and hardly noticed that they did not respond. Then she saw Tancred. The beautiful beast was lying on his side on the edge of death.

"No!" she shrieked as she hurried to him.

"He's been like this all night long, Mylady," one of the boys said. "We've tried to feed him and give him water, but the horse master says he's done for."

Adela could plainly see that the horse had only moments to live. All the joy and optimism of the moments before evaporated as she caressed his head. She placed the apple by his lips. The stallion licked it once, as a sign of affection for his mistress rather than in an effort to eat it.

"What's wrong with him?" she cried out.

"The horse master says his heart gave out. Even these eastern stallions have limits to their strength."

Adela saw the glaze of death appear in her horse's pupils. She choked back her tears and kissed him on his nose. The stable boys moved out quietly, leaving her alone with her dying friend.

"Oh, Tancred, you were so wonderful. You were Lord Reynald's last gift to me. What is he going to say when he learns that you have left us? Who will ever carry me across the fields the way you did?"

The horse lifted his head one last time and touched her face with his muzzle. Adela burst into tears as Tancred laid his head back and expired with noble serenity. The stable boys hurried away at the sound of her moans which rose in a doleful crescendo and filled the barn with her grief.

After a time, silence fell over the stables. The saddened, bewildered boys watched from a far corner as Adela came out of the stall. She had regained her composure but the fresh beauty with which she had greeted the day was gone. She seemed to have aged while kneeling in the humid hay beside her dead horse.

She returned to the inn, carrying the reins of her loyal animal like precious relics. As she rounded the corner, she saw a silhouette blocking her path. She didn't recognize him at first for there was something different in his presence, something detached and peaceful. But it was still her Bertran, the one person on this earth who was there for her when she felt her loneliness most intensely.

She walked up to him and quietly laid her head on his chest. He stood straight and tall like a marble statue. "Please hold me...." she whispered. His arms slowly rose around her and gently pressed her against his solid frame.

They both felt a glowing heat pass between them. He leaned his face into her silky hair and breathed in the sweet aroma as he kissed her tenderly on the forehead. It was a sign of forgiveness. For the first time, she put her arms around him and hugged him tightly. Their souls merged in that unbreakable bond of love that had blessed their lives for so long.

11

The Mediterranean Sea did not part as its sister, the Red Sea, was said to have done in the days of the Pharaohs. The children's joy turned to disappointment and finally to rage as they returned day after day to the shores and waited for the promised miracle to take place.

Stephen began to lose face. Even his loyal entourage could be heard muttering rebellious words to each other. The shepherd boy remained in the secure chambers of a wealthy citizen, hiding from the world that he had deceived and that had also fooled him. Perhaps that stranger on the hillside who had charged him with his mission was not the Christ after all.

Bertran and Adela spoke with the ship owners of Marseilles, seeking for a way to cross the ocean. They had never expected the prophet's words to come true and knew that they would have to leave the naive crusaders behind at some point on the journey. But now Adela could not bear the thought of abandoning the children she had come to care for to such desperate circumstances.

All that was left to them was to return along the road they had traveled and, if not taken by death on the way, face utter ridicule back home.

On their third day in the seaport, Bertran and Adela were introduced to two of the city's wealthiest merchants, Hugo Ferreus and William Porcus. Adela had sold a gold bracelet belonging to her mother in order to purchase new clothes for herself and her companion. She knew they could not do business with worshippers of money if they looked like beggars. Bertran had never worn such soft garments. He felt silly at first in the new fashion of the day, dressed in stockings and a leather tunic. But he loved the thick belt which now held his precious sword. Once again, he felt his heart soar as he came another step closer to the fulfillment of his most cherished dreams.

For he was no longer a peasant boy with the smell of manure upon him and the rough, stained rags of those who labor from dawn till dusk. His new outfit made him feel like a member of the nobility and he spent the first hours after putting them on learning how to walk like a man of means and education.

Adela laughed at his antics and showed him the proper behavior of one who courts the mighty of the land. Bertran's
big limbs were awkward in their fine linen and he felt for
awhile like a boy in girl's clothing. But then they entered
another shop and bought him a shirt of steel chain which
the knights' squires wore in battle. That was more to his
liking.

"All you need now, Sir Bertan, is to have your hair
trimmed," Adela told him playfully. "Your lengthy locks are
no longer in fashion."

"I don't want to look like a townsman who spends his days
sitting in a chair counting his silver!"

"So you'd rather have the appearance of a Visigoth from
the last century?"

"Why not? They were great warriors."

"They were also barbarians."

Bertran swaggered into the city square, heading for the
Roman fountain. Adela laughed. He swirled around and
drew his sword, testing the position of his belt and scabbard.

"No one laughs at me and lives!" he said with a dramatic
grimace.

"Well now, Lord Bertran of the hills and fields, you do
draw that sword of yours with speed and assurance!"

"I had a good teacher," Bertran said with a smile as he

struggled to insert the sword into its sheath.

"Replacing your weapon is a bit more difficult, noble knight of the Realm," Adela observed as she came to his side and helped him find a more graceful way to position it. "I would recommend that you not hold the blade with your fingers. Unless you want to be known as the infamous fingerless knight."

Bertran raised his leg and wiggled his toes.

"I'll fight with my feet!"

She laughed loudly. Bertran rejoiced at her gaiety. It had been so long since he had seen her so full of fun and playfulness.

"Are you ready to meet the merchants?" she asked after catching her breath. Bertran's mirth disappeared. He knew this was a crucial meeting, perhaps their last chance to find passage to the Holy Land.

"I'm ready, Adela."

"Let me do the talking. You just stand there and look like you stem from noble blood."

"But I did, Mylady, I did," Bertran insisted. "I've told you many times that my ancestors were..."

"Viking chieftains and Norman warriors, I know. They raped and pillaged and that's how you came about."

She laughed again but stopped short, noticing that Bertran was hurt.

"Come now, I know that you're of noble character. You even look like it, in spite of your big feet."

She sat on the edge of the fountain and cupped her hands in the cool water. Bertran watched her drink. She was irrepressible, untamable like a beautiful jungle creature. He was proud to be her companion, despite the abuse he had to endure.

They headed for the merchants' offices which overlooked a vast shipyard. A great variety of ships were under construction and the sound of hammers and saws filled the air. There were gigantic gulafres used for commerce across the oceans of the world; graceful galleons designed for speed and warfare; huge dromons with three masts and mighty bows to break through turbulent waves. Adela felt reassured about traveling the seas in such colossal structures. Surely, they would conquer the storms and treacherous rocks awaiting them. Bertran was less certain. The ships looked minuscule to him as he recalled the infinity of water he had observed a few nights before. But he knew that his life was no longer his alone and that he would follow his beloved into the depths of Hell itself. The two merchants sat in huge armchairs, their large bellies protruding like sacks of potatoes hidden under embroidered draperies. Bertran took an instant dislike to them. There was something inhuman about the look in their eyes, perhaps a result of so many years of scheming to fill their pockets.

Adela, however, charmed them with her manners. The moment she addressed them, their bulldog faces lit up with pleasant expressions like men drunk on cheap ale. Bertran had to restrain his disgust, realizing that, without their help, Marseilles could be the end of their journey. He was dizzied by the treasury of precious objects from all parts of the earth decorating the merchants' office. Few cathedrals were so filled with gold and gaudy decor. The vast room, lit by giant windows overlooking the ocean, and filled with this sprawling display of wealth, gave the impression of being a sort of perverse sanctuary, a temple to Mammon, the god of greed.

The two merchants were dressed in gold-trimmed velvet robes from Venice, the trade capital of the world. They hardly moved from their chairs as though their excessive weight from a life of lavish indulgence held them down like walruses resting on a beach. Adela knew this kind of creature for she had seen them at the King's court where her father had taken her on several occasions. They were the new pillars of the land's economy, making huge profits from death and destruction. Such men financed the King's wars and supplied the ships and weapons to fight them. The armies then protected their trade ships and served as guardians for the markets of silk and spice from the East.

The noble families of France, living in splendid isolation on their inherited lands, were paupers compared to the sea merchants. King Philip Augustus himself could not hope to rival the gold in their coffers. His wealth came only from increased taxation which further crushed the serfs who had nothing to begin with. Adela knew that there was no chivalry among this breed of men, no code of honor like the armored warriors whose depravity was generally confined to the battlefield. Even as a child, she had understood that such men lusted for the sound of jingling silver as mercenary soldiers did for harlots on their way back from bloody campaigns.

"I speak for the children crusaders who have come to your fair city with the hope of crossing over to the Holy Land," Adela stated with her usual directness.

"We've seen them sleeping in our streets," retorted William Porcus, sounding much like the name he bore. "They're an embarrassment to our citizens. We're used to visiting Kings, not dirty urchins."

Adela took a breath to keep her adrenalins from taking charge.

"The Pope himself has blessed their mission."

"I've heard that you have a child prophet leading you," stated Hugo Ferreus. "Why is he not here to speak with us?"

203

Bertran smiled to himself. Stephen and the merchants would understand each other quite well. He knew that barnyard animals seek their own and he had no doubt that the shepherd's depravity was matched by the lifestyles of these two lovers of pleasure.

"It is not for him to deal with practical affairs," Adela lied skillfully. "He is occupied with more...spiritual matters." Bertran cringed, but he knew that those words were fire to Adela's mouth as well.

"Ah, yes," Ferreus exclaimed. "Matters from on high! They are left to those who are too pure for the affairs of men. That is how the Archbishop of our city deals with his diocese. We fill the Church and his home with gold and he blesses us for doing so!"

He let out a loud, raucous laugh which shook his belly up and down like a bouncing ball. Porcus joined in the merriment until a hacking cough turned his face violet. Bertran and Adela watched their grotesque behavior with curiosity.

"So!" Ferreus cried out. "You are here to transport what...ten thousand children to the land of the caliphs?"

"Half that number, Sire," Adela replied. "Many have left for home."

"That's where they belong if you ask me," Porcus interjected. "I cannot understand how their parents let them leave on such a ridiculous adventure!"

"Their parents had no choice, " Adela stated coldly. "These children are sacrificing themselves for their faith."

Porcus leaned forward in his chair.

"Have you been to the Holy Land, dear girl?"

"No, I have not."

"It is not a world like our own. Those brown-skinned peoples are savages, I tell you. Life has no value for them. And their religion! They cut a man's hand off for stealing bread!"

Bertran wondered what they would cut off merchants who stole boat loads of goods.

"I will say for them that they do know how to keep order among their people. Their holy men are much more respected than our priests," Ferreus added.

Adela was getting angry. Not only were they keeping them standing like servants before their king, but she expected more from them since they had agreed to this meeting with enthusiasm and seemed eager to help the children in some way.

Despite his boorish look, Ferreus was astute and quick-witted. He could see that his beautiful visitor was losing her patience. He motioned for them to be seated in smaller chairs by the windows.

"We understand that your crusade had intended to cross the Mediterranean without ships," he stated with no effort to veil his sarcasm.

"That's what the prophet assured us would happen," Adela answered, humiliated by the pretence that she too had believed in such a miracle.

"Yes, well, the Almighty works in mysterious ways, does he not? Perhaps He was kept too busy by the Saracen hordes, eh?"

Ferreus chuckled. Porcus poured wine from a crystal flagon into a silver goblet and guzzled it gleefully.

Bertran thought of the hermit back home. The grotesque men before him were undoubtedly considered good Christians, loyal to all the requirements of Rome. Such material success and lofty standing among the wealthy of the city could only come to those who followed the accepted paths of the culture. It made Bertran sick to his stomach to think of the thousands of martyred believers of the Cathar faith. They were dying because they refused to be of this world, the world of greedy merchants and power-seeking Popes and depraved prophets.

"The children dream of liberating the Holy Sepulcher and the True Cross from the heathen by peaceful means," Adela said.

"Peaceful means?" Porcus spat wine on his robe as he guffawed.

"There will never be peace as long as a single follower of

Muhammad can hold a saber. They take their beliefs very seriously and would rather die a horrible death than give up their Jihad." "You seem to come from a good family, young lady," Ferreus added. "Why would you want to take such absurd risks?"

"We came to you because we thought you had an interest in helping our crusade," Adela said as calmly as she could. Bertran felt uneasy. He knew there was only so much she would put up with before exploding, even though it might cost them everything.

"Mylords," he stated with as noble a voice as he could muster, "we are the advance guard of another glorious crusade which the Holy Father is calling for at this very moment. After us will come the finest knights of three kingdoms and Jerusalem will be in Christian hands once again."

Adela looked at Bertran, impressed. She had never seen him put on such a good act before. Bertran was rather pleased with himself as well.

"Young sir," said Porcus, " we would be honored to be part of your worthy efforts. We are pleased to see that the children are not merely peasants and riffraff from the fields."

"Many of us are from the finest families in France," Bertran continued, carried away with his own bravado. Adela could barely repress a smile. Ferreus stood and pointed out the window.

"You see those ships moored at the dock?"

Adela and Bertran looked out and saw a flotilla of seven galleys anchored nearby.

"They are some of the most seaworthy vessels in our fleet. They will take you to Medina. We have caravans there which will guide you to the Holy Land."

Adela and Bertran were stupefied. They had not dared to hope for such generosity.

"How much will you require for this?" Bertran asked, knowing that they were not charitable types.

"Only that you offer prayers for our health when you reach the land where our Lord was born to the Virgin."

Bertran looked at them suspiciously.

"Don't be so surprised, young sir," Porcus stated with a grin. "We are good Christians and believe in the cause of your crusade. We know that our reward awaits us in Heaven."

"Not everything need yield profits in gold," Ferreus added.

"May the Good Lord bless you for your kindness, Sires," Adela responded with sincerity. She reached for Ferreus' hand and kissed his ring as though he were royalty. Porcus held out his bejeweled hand as well to receive her lips. Bertran winced at her exuberance.

His intuition told him that something was not right. "When will the ships be ready to set sail?" he asked.

"Can your companions be ready by dawn tomorrow?"
Porcus retorted.

"Of course!" Adela cried out. "We have been ready for days now."

The merchants accompanied them to the door.

"Tell your prophet that we will give orders to the ship captains to obey his word and make all provisions possible for a comfortable voyage. Your journey will be difficult enough when you arrive."

Ferreus handed Adela a small leather purse filled with silver coins.

"Please accept this humble gift for your journey. It isn't much but it will buy you the necessities for crossing the desert lands."

Adela was deeply touched by this last gesture of generosity.

"I cannot thank you enough."

"We wish you great success on your holy mission," Porcus stated with as sweet a tone as his raucous voice could produce. Adela and Bertran left the merchants' building and stepped out into the bright sunlight. Adela was bursting with joy.

"Isn't this the most amazing blessing? I know I will find my father. I can feel it!"

"There are still great dangers ahead," Bertran pointed out.

"How can you be gloomy at a moment like this? If you're

not hopeful now, you will never be!"

"I don't trust those merchants."

Adela stopped abruptly.

"What do you mean? Didn't you see what happened in there? They've just spent a fortune to provide us with a free trip! What's wrong with you?"

The last thing Bertran wanted was another argument. He chose not to share his bad feelings.

"You're right, that is a very...noble act."

"You should be on your knees thanking them. Without this blessed gift, we would be beggars!"

"We'll never be beggars, Adela, you have my word on that."

"Well, I want nothing less than my rightful title. And you can't give me that."

Bertran sighed. There was no way to alter Adela's mind. She was as stubborn as a bull. But he loved her for it. They headed for Stephen's headquarters at the home of one of the great lords of the city. They had to walk through street after street jammed with children waiting for a sign. Adela could barely repress her desire to shout the news to them all.

It took some convincing for the guards to escort them to Stephen's chambers. The boy still hated Bertran for having seen through his pretense.

They found the prophet of Cloyes lounging in a luxurious

room, dressed in the finest cloth. He looked like one of those child emperors of Rome whose every wish was deemed sacred. Bertran had to harness his disgust. If there ever was a person he could kill without remorse, it was the fraudulent shepherd.

"What is it you want?" he asked in a haughty voice.

It was obvious that he was in a terrible mood, for his position as prophet of the Almighty was sinking with every passing day. Perhaps he too was coming to doubt the words of the stranger who had put him on this extraordinary path. Even his devoted guards, who had found such glee in becoming the privileged servants of the sacrosanct leader and had carried out his every order with the greatest zeal, were now grim and tense. If the Mediterranean did not open soon, there would be mutiny among the prophet's followers.

"We have found a way to cross the sea," Adela stated as calmly as she could. She was too proud to reveal her excitement to the little monster who had fooled the entire Holy Roman Empire. Stephen sat up on his cushions.

"What do you mean?" he shouted out with disbelief.

"There are seven ships ready to depart tomorrow for the Holy Land."

Stephen jump to his feet and hurried to Adela.

"Is this true?" he asked, revealing a last ember of childhood wonderment.

"Two of Marseilles' leading merchants are financing the voyage."

Stephen ran across the room to his guards, wild with joy.

"I told you! I told you it would happen. This is the miracle of the parting sea! My prophecy has come true!"

The guards hugged him with great enthusiasm as Adela and Bertran looked on, revolted. They could already see the moment when Stephen would announce to the multitudes that his detractors were demons in disguise and that he was indeed a messenger of the Most High. The crowds would cheer and idolize him more than ever and he would triumphantly lead them onto the vessels.

Adela didn't particularly care that he would be credited with the results of her efforts. All she wanted was to reach the distant shores where her father had vanished. With each heartbeat, she felt closer to the moment when he would hold her in his mighty arms and everything would be set right.

Bertran, on the other hand, braced himself for great trials to come. He knew that the worst was still ahead. But he also knew that he had been blessed with a vision of the true life and that nothing here below could destroy that awareness. Nothing except the loss of his beloved.

12

Aimery sat on his black stallion, looking out at the tempestuous horizon. His coat of mail was stained with mud and his black and gold tunic worn by the wind. Anger tensed the square features of his darkly handsome face. He had ridden some three hundred miles to the shores of the Mediterranean only to learn that the goddess of his desire had been at sea for three days.

He strained to focus on the furthest point along the straight edge between the ocean and the sky. A storm was brewing where the two met, somewhere near the isle of Corsica.

Aimery had been informed about her departure weeks after she had left Vendome. He returned to Lord Reynald's castle after sending several messengers to Lady Beatrice, seeking news of her niece. It was only when he could bear it no longer that he went to find out for himself. Adela had haunted his nights relentlessly since the fateful day of their first encounter. Never had he seen such character in a woman before. There was more power in her presence than in many of the knights he faced at the tournaments. He knew he would never find her equal.

The young Duke understood immediately what her true plans were when he learned that she had joined the children's crusade. In their few hours together, he saw enough to conclude that she was not the sort to be fooled by the gibberish of superstition. Only the deluded, the mentally weak, and innocent children could hope that such an undertaking would end in anything but catastrophe. Aimery realized that Adela had left her lands in a desperate effort to find Lord Reynald. Her father was the only man who could save her from a world where women were reduced to servitude.

That tumultuous day taught him a painful lesson. He now recognized that the arrangements he made with Lady Beatrice were an insult to Adela's dignity. He cursed himself many times for falling victim to the conventions of the day and bartering for her hand. Aimery was convinced that if he had come to court her with the gentility of the southern nobles, he would have won her heart in a day. He could not stand the thought of watching her disappear in a foreign land where she was sure to be butchered. He had therefore chosen to rescue her both from the Saracens as well as from herself, and if she refused, to protect her with his life.

But when Aimery learned that the peasant boy was her traveling companion, he nearly lost his mind with rage. His heritage of royal pride boiled at the thought that his rival was a common serf. He, Aimery, viscount of Tours, champion of the King's tournaments, was considered the premiere knight of his generation. No other man could approach his prowess and aggressive courage. He had undergone the finest education in the world and was destined to be one of the great men of his epoch. But at the very dawn of this promising future he was faced with the humiliation of loving a woman who had chosen a boorish peasant over him.

Aimery prepared for the journey as he would for war. He took only his faithful squire and they traveled light with great speed. The saddlebags were packed with weapons of war as much as with necessities for the long voyage. With every beat of his horse's hooves, Aimery swore death to Bertran. His mind invented lurid reasons for the unnatural relationship between the serf and the baroness. Surely, he had made a pact with the demons and been initiated into the black arts to have enticed Adela of Vendome to share her life with a common man of the fields. No nobly born woman would ever make such a choice, especially one endowed with the intelligence and willpower of the Baron's daughter.

Aimery dismounted and walked along the very sands which that received Bertran in prayer a short time before. Once again, he was watching Adela escape from his grasp. Not having his way was a new experience for him. And he had never wanted anything as much as he wanted Adela. His mind was obsessed with her day and night, implacably insisting that his glorious future would not be complete without that unique woman as this side. He trained with less concentration and found no joy in any of his favorite occupations. To be with her was all that mattered now. He would give his lands and titles, his very life to hold her in his arms. Nothing would get in the way of finding the woman of his dreams and asking for her hand, not the ocean, not the Saracens, not the Devil himself.

"Find me a ship that will sail southward this very day!" Thomas the squire, a young man eager to please his master, kicked his horse's flanks and galloped off toward the city walls.

"Tell them I'll pay any price!" Aimery shouted.

His cry echoed down along the seashore over the melody

of the splashing waves. Aimery listened to his own voice ringing in the distance as though it were speaking to him. Yes, he would pay any price to have Adela as his betrothed. A strange sadness enveloped him. He was not one to dwell in melancholia for his feelings were most often confined to the physical thrills of battle. He had no time for introspection and wasted even less on spiritual reflection. Aimery was knighthood incarnate in an age that had lifted those skills to the heights of religious mystery. Chivalry was linked with mystic legends that haunted the noble spirits of every age since the tales of Arthur and the Holy Grail. Young men like the Duke of Tours found their natural vigor and beastly heritage for combat blessed as salvific to their souls. He had therefore no need to restrain the killing instincts lurking in the primeval shadows of his being. He had been taught that the worship of courage in battle was the true worship. All the rest was a show, a mystery play for the masses who needed something to help them forget the oppression of their daily labors.

Yet, in this moment, standing at the meeting point of water and land, he recognized that something was missing in all that he had learned and become. Adela had awakened new desires in him, new longings that he had not known before. They were not merely physical needs, but rather pointed toward an inner wasteland emotion that had to be conquered. Somehow, this vague new world was related to the brash young woman who had stolen his heart. Fearlessness and the thrill of battle could not fill the abyss of dissatisfaction that had opened within him. Where once a hard practice of swordplay with his friends would have healed any ill feeling, there was now no remedy for his anguish. Adela alone, Adela by his side would break this spell which had captured his valiant spirit.

* * *

The Greeks called the isle "Hierakon," the Island of the Falcons, because fishermen of old had seen flocks of falcons gather on its rocky shores. It rose higher than the other jagged peaks against which the giant waves of the deep warred relentlessly. A great boulder lay at the feet of the cliffs known as the Hermit's Rock. In ages long past, men of the sea had noticed a solitary figure watching them from that rock. The people of neighboring Sardinia handed down to their children's children tales of this refugee from the world of humanity. It was said that he had supernatural powers and could still the storms. Other legends spoke of the eerie vision of a lonely man walking on the foam of the ocean waves.

The hermit vanished as strangely as he had appeared and the rocks on which he lived his fierce asceticism came to be looked upon as full of mysterious tragedy. Many mariners swore the desolate isle was haunted by the hermit's ghost and some called to him for help when the winds threw their skiffs toward his desolate home.

Packed with children, the seven ships sailed side by side, slowly crossing the vast expanse of waters. They had remained far from land for days and the Island of the Falcons was the first sign of earth on their path. Over five thousand youths had chosen to cross the sea and fulfill their mission. The others remained behind, shamed by their cowardice. They had hoped to cross the Mediterranean on foot but to brave its treacherous waves was another matter altogether. Even those who no longer believed in sea monsters still dreaded the mighty waters which, when angered, could rise as high as the tallest turret of any king's castle.

Before the first night had passed, the priests who accompanied the children were reminding them that eternal salvation awaited those who died on a crusade for the Cross. Strong winds quickly revealed how frail the inventions of men were in the face of nature. The planks which kept the waters from engulfing them and the creatures of the deep from eating them cracked and shook under the assault of the elements.

By the second night of the voyage, a savage storm descended upon the seven ships and their precious cargo.
There was no controlling the panic
of the seasick children. The boats rose and fell with great
moans as waves the size of city walls crashed upon them.
Even the sailors who had seen every trick of the ocean
were crossing themselves and praying for their lives.
Bertran and Adela held each other tightly below the decks.
They had tied themselves to one of the beams of the ship
to avoid being thrown about as were so many of the children. The screams of terror were deafening even in the
midst of the thunderous storm.

"Don't let me go, Bertran!" Adela shouted out as they were
turned almost upside down by the colossal waves.

"Never! Never!" Bertran promised her as he wrapped his
arms tighter around her.

If he were to die now, he would die a happy man. Adela
clung to him as she had never done before, discovering real
fear for the first time in her life. She kept repeating a prayer
to Saint Christopher, the patron saint of travelers, that she
might be saved to look into the eyes of her father once
again. But the raging ocean seemed deaf to the cries of
both children and saints.

As night began to fade away, the storm abated. The sea was

still violent, but the tidal waves had disappeared. Bertran told Adela to stay below as he hurried onto the deck to assess the situation. Debris floated everywhere and torn sails dipped into the murky waters that had stayed on board. The captain and his sailors were working furiously to maintain their course and organize vital repairs.

Bertran looked out at the angry sea. The seven ships had been scattered by the wild winds. He strained to see through the rain and mist. He counted five vessels. He ran from the bow to the stern to find the other two.

That's when he saw the Island of the Falcons.

"Lord in Heaven, save them!" he yelled involuntarily.

The winds of the storm were leading the two tattered ships directly toward the rocks. Bertran ran back to the captain who was commandeering the wheel.

"Captain, those ships are going to wreck on the island!"

The crusty seaman looked in the direction which Bertran was pointing toward.

"Give thanks that you're on my ship, boy," he stated, unmoved.

"Can't we rescue them?" Bertran asked in a horrified voice.

"Get this lad away from me!" the captain barked.

Two sailors hurried toward Bertran.

"But sir, is there nothing that can be done for them?" Bertran cried out desperately.

"Do you want to go down with them? We're not out of the storm yet and if we don't tend to our needs, we'll be joining them on the Hermit's Rock!"

The sailors threw Bertran across the deck and assisted the captain in controlling the ship's rudder. Bertran jumped to his feet but slipped on the wet wood. He fell and hit his head on broken rigging lying nearby. The blow almost knocked him unconscious. He felt his body floating in the waters splashing across the deck. He reached for something to hold onto but his hand was too weakened to grip tightly. His body slammed against the edge of the ship. He struggled to regain consciousness, knowing that he would be thrown overboard with one tip of the vessel.

He thought of Adela below him and how terrified she would be if he were no longer there to accompany her on their desperate journey. With all the will power he could gather, he sent his last bit of strength shooting through his arms. They grabbed onto an iron spoke on which was tied one of the ropes of the main sail. At that very moment, a massive wave lifted the ship and nearly turned it on its side. Bertran felt his legs fly over the side. But his grip held and he swung himself back to safety. For an instant, he had been dipped into the sea and felt the tug of its waters. He spat out the salty liquid and looked down at his hands. They were bloodied from twisting around the iron stem.

Bertran marveled at how he had managed to hold on. He knew it was a strength that had come from a place beyond his physical capacity.

Painfully, he loosened his fingers and found that they were not under his command. The power that had taken over and held them in place was still there, separate from Bertran's will. It struck him that this foreign presence was of the same mysterious might as the force which had almost pulled him into a watery grave. How was it that such a strange power could enter into him and take over when he was no longer able to care for himself?

Still dizzy from the wound to his head, he wondered whether his thoughts were dreams leaking from some unknown corner of his mind. He vaguely remembered that this power had come to him after he had let go!

Bertran sat up and shook his head. He would ponder these things some other time. Adela suddenly appeared before him, like a vision from a seafarer's fantasy.

"Are you all right?" he heard her say.

"I told you to stay below!" Bertran stammered, attempting to stand.

Adela caught him as his knees wobbled and saved him from yet another fall.

"It seems to me that you could use my help," she said breathlessly.

"But I told you to stay below!" Bertran repeated with irritation.

"Since when do you give me orders?"

"It's very dangerous up here, Adela! I almost went overboard."

"Then you should be the one to stay below!"

Bertran grimaced both from pain and aggravation. There was simply no controlling this woman.

"Holy Mother of God!" Adela cried out.

Bertran looked up in time to see the first of the two ships crash upon the rocks. A swarm of falcons rose from the eerie cliffs.

Numb with horror, they watched as the mighty waves threw the

ship again and again against the rocks. With each impact, the vessel shattered and the screams of children rose into the somber sky. Adela covered her eyes as Bertran held her close. There was nothing to be done but witness the drowning of a thousand little pilgrims.

As the first boat splintered into fragments, the second ship was heaved upon the fatal rocks. A wailing echo spread across the merciless horizon. Bertran crossed himself and offered a prayer for the doomed souls of their companions. Adela faltered and fell back on his chest. She had reached the limits of her endurance.

Bertran struggled to take her below as the ship tossed to
and fro over the angry sea. He lifted her in his powerful
arms and looked back a final time before descending the
stairs. He saw the second ship rise into the air and explode
over the Hermit's Rock, releasing its precious cargo into
the deadly foam. He knew that as long as he remained alive
in this dark and agonizing world, he would remember the
terrible sight. A shudder of bitterness and anguish took
hold of him and he rushed Adela to the relative safety of
the lower decks.

He kept her in her hammock for the rest of the day
until they had sailed beyond the Island of the Falcons and
left the vast expanse of floating bodies far behind. Adela
would come to consciousness and weep hysterically, then
faint again. Her entire being was afflicted by the ghastly
sight. Bertran began to fear for her life as her fever soared.
He hurried through the bowels of the overcrowded ship,
searching for help. He came upon Peter, the good priest
who had helped him during the journey from Vendome.
The man was surrounded with sick and wounded children.

"I'm sorry, I cannot help you, Bertran. There's no one here
to care for all these children."

"But she may be dying, father! Please, in the name of all
that is holy, come and heal her!"

Peter wiped the sweat from his brow. Bertran could see

that

he was on the edge of complete exhaustion.

"Father, remember all that she has done for them! She deserves to be cared for in turn!"

"You say she is burning with fever?"

"Yes! I've never seen such an illness! She shakes and comes in and out of consciousness. Don't let her die, father. It would be the end of my life as well!"

Peter looked up at the desperate young man. He knew that Bertran spoke the truth.

"We've come too far to fail now!" Bertran cried out.

"My boy," Peter said as he rose to his feet and handed the child who laid on his lap to one of his helpers, "you're only saving yourselves for greater suffering."

They walked quickly through the shivering heaps of youths huddled in every corner.

"If we reach the Holy Land, we'll have a good chance to find Lord Reynald."

"You deceive yourself, Bertran. The storms of the sea are safer than the savagery you'll encounter there."

"But I thought you said that many of the Saracens were of noble character!"

"There is very little nobility left anywhere in the world, Bertran. We live in an age in which the Devil has conquered the souls of men. There has been too much killing to hope for mercy from anyone."

Bertran clenched his fists, refusing to accept the priest's gloomy predictions.

"Finding Lord Reynald is our only hope and by God we will find him! The world can't be so vile as to have lost all hope for happiness and justice!"

"Strange words to speak in such a place as this. These poor children will never see their mothers and fathers again. Death is the only place they'll find relief from torment."

Bertran stopped and grabbed Peter by the shoulders.

"I don't need your prophecies of hopelessness, priest! I've just begun to live! I've been freed from the slavery of the fields and a great destiny awaits me! Don't tell me that death is the best I can hope for!"

Peter smiled sadly and placed his hands on Bertran's arms.

"Forgive me, Bertran. Maybe I've seen too much suffering and have lost the joy of living. You're right! Don't ever give up, whatever may come your way. Perhaps when you have reached my age, the world will be a better place. I've seen too much and I'm too tired. But you, you must keep your hope and your joy in life! Come, let's bring Adela back to health."

Standing in the darkness of the ship's bowels, surrounded by

the sound of sick and frightened children, Bertran felt a
new strength surge through his being. He knew that, in
spite of all the evidence around him, life had to be good,
was good, and that his work must be to keep the fire of
such a belief alive against the forces of darkness that would
blow it out and bring eternal night into the souls of human
beings.

As he hurried to Adela's side, he realized that the Cathars
might be wrong after all. He had no desire to leave this
world, in spite of its misery, for a new life in the realm of
spirit. He had a great urge to fight off death with all his
might so that he could taste in this moment the blessing of
happiness in body and soul. The very presence of death all
around him revealed that life was worth living!

With the careful attention of the priest, Adela overcame
her illness. Bertran held her for many hours as she shook
from the shock she had undergone. By mid-afternoon she
had recovered enough to be taken up on deck for fresh air.
They looked out over the now peaceful ocean, breathing in
a fresh salty breeze.

"I didn't think I could be so weak," Adela murmured, more
to herself than to Bertran.

"There's no weakness in suffering for these poor children."

"What a terrible thing to witness. And to be so helpless!"
She suddenly turned to Bertran with fire in her eyes.

"If God is good and just, how could he let this happen?"
Bertran shook his head, studying the boundless spaces before him.

"I have no answer for such questions, Adela. I have only begun to ask them myself. It's all very mysterious and disturbing. The Perfect One who rejects this world as evil lives each moment in joy and the priest who accepts the goodness of Creation can't wait to leave it."

Adela looked up at a glorious mountain of clouds passing overhead. A ray of sunshine shot through as from a cathedral window, spreading a golden mist upon the blue-green shades of the sea.

"There are people who live these answers...Like the good man from Assisi. He loves all things, yet he lives as though he is no longer of this world. I'll never forget the look in his eyes. It was...it was like this!"

She waved her arm at the peaceful infinity before them. For a time, they stood in silence, losing themselves in the magnificent view. The song of the waves and the caress of the sea breeze lulled them into a quiet joy they had not tasted since leaving their home. Adela found great regeneration from the soothing moment, as though it were replenishing her for the trials ahead. Bertran felt that mysterious gratitude rise in his soul which called him to give thanks to forces greater than the mighty ocean and its sister the sky.

He looked at Adela. Her hair curled around her like a veil protecting a sacred object. The sun and wind had brought colors to her features and a sparkle to her eyes. Bertran turned his gaze upon the horizon, as though he feared that looking at her too long would melt him with ecstasy.

On the far side of the ocean, he saw a tiny black spot. It was soon followed by another, then another. He instinctively turned to the captain who was on the bridge, manning the wheel. He too was watching the horizon with his seafarer's eagle eyes. The sweet moment suddenly felt like the menacing silence before a devastating storm.

Bertran moved closer to Adela and put his arm around her. She looked up at him and noticed his worried expression. "What is it?" she asked.

"I believe we have visitors..."

13

It was too late to maneuver the boats by the time a sailor on watch shouted his terrifying cry: "Saracen ships starboard!" There would have been no time to change course anyway, for the enemy warships were the fastest vessels on the seven seas. Ten of them appeared on the horizon, their bows aimed at the merchants' ships.

"Get below!" Bertran cried out to Adela.

"No! That won't be any safer than being up here!"

"It will be when they attack!"

Bertran turned to the captain to find out what measures must be taken. To his utter astonishment, the old sailor was tugging at the wheel and barking out orders, setting his course directly toward the enemy ships. Bertran ran to the other side of the deck and saw the four other galleys doing the same. A frightful thought turned his blood cold as he hurried to the captain's side.

"Didn't I tell you once before to get away from me, boy?"

"You knew they were coming, didn't you?"

The captain looked over at Bertran. For an instant his weather-worn features drooped with guilt. But he caught himself and called for his sailors. Bertran drew his sword.

"They won't put their hands on me this time!" he yelled menacingly. He aimed his blade at the captain's chest and cut through his cloak. The cold sharp point made its way to the man's skin and impressed upon him Bertran's earnest intent. Three sailors appeared from the rigging on the mast and froze at the sight.

"How dare you threaten the ship's captain!" the man yelled, trying to back away from the sword.

Bertran pressed harder.

"Tell me what treachery is afoot or they'll be no more captain of this ship!"

One of the sailors lunged forward.

Bertran drew blood from the man's chest.

"Stop, you fool!" the captain cried out. "This boy means what he says!"

Adela appeared before them, having heard the shouting.

"What in God's name...!"

"Speak, old man, or you'll be bate for sea monsters!"

The captain bowed his head in shame and waved the sailors back.

"This is not my doing, boy, I swear before the Almighty it isn't. I am a servant of the ship's owners and either follow their orders or retire from the sea."

"What are you saying?" Adela questioned as she came to stand by Bertran.

The captain glanced at her sheepishly. This was perhaps the first time in his life that he was not master over all who boarded his domain.

"The Good Lord forgive me," he said as he crossed himself. "My orders were to deliver the cargo to the slave traders..."

"What cargo?" Adela shouted, her mind unwilling to understand what he had said.

"The children, Mylady...You have been sold by Masters Ferreus and Porcus to the Mohammedan slavers."

Adela let out a shrill scream that pierced the ears of all who stood nearby.

"Kill him!" she yelled at Bertran in an uncontrolled rage. "Run the traitor through!"

Bertran lowered his sword. Several sailors hurried toward him, raising their weapons.

"Leave him be!" the captain shouted hoarsely.

He watched Bertran walk away, dragging his sword along the planks.

"If it hadn't been me, it would have been another!" he cried out remorsefully. "Did you really think they would give you a free trip to the East? You should never have trusted such men! They always get their money's worth!"

Adela approached the captain, venom boiling in her eyes.

"Where will they take us?"

"Most probably to Bujeiah and then on to Alexandria. Some may be taken to Baghdad, across the deserts of Palestine."

"Will they hurt us?" she asked, trembling with emotion.

"No, they'll not damage their prize possessions. They understand the meaning of investment and they've paid too high a price to lose a single one of you. And if you're bought by a good master, you may live a comfortable life."

"There is no comfort without freedom, you swine!"

Adela cursed him for trying to justify the most dreadful commerce of all. "I'll see you chained for this, you mark my words! You've betrayed your own people and your God!"

The captain's guilt had receded and he was no longer willing to be abused on his ship.

"You'll never be coming back this way. Not one of you. There is no return from slavery. Now begone before I have

234

you tied to the mast!"

Adela rushed back to Bertran who was helplessly observing the warships approaching at full speed.

"What can we do?" she asked in a trembling voice.

"Those who were shipwrecked may be the lucky ones..." he said

hopelessly.

Adela shook Bertran violently.

"No! We can't let this happen! There must be a way of escape!"

"Would you care to swim across the Mediterranean?"

Adela slapped him across the face. Bertran hardly noticed.

"Don't give up now, Bertran! We've come too far!"

Swarms of children were coming up onto the deck, having seen the sun break through the storm clouds. Adela turned to them and saw their happy faces giving thanks for being spared.

"What are we going to tell them?"

"Nothing!" Bertran retorted, "unless you want to create panic. They'll know soon enough."

Adela grabbed Bertran's arm as he leaned back against the rigging, despondent.

"We can fight them! We must outnumber them by far!"

"That's one of your most wonderful traits, Adela. You never give up. But sometimes you have to recognize the reality of the situation. Surely, you don't want a massacre on your hands. Those warriors out there have won victories over the greatest knights of the kingdom. It would be a bloodbath."

"We must come up with a plan! I cannot believe that Providence would have me escape the tyranny of my aunt in order to make me a slave to the heathens!"

Bertran saw that she was beginning to lose control of her emotions again. He took her by the shoulders.

"Listen carefully, Adela. Father Peter has told me that many of these Saracens are devout and compassionate people. It wasn't until the Crusaders invaded their strongholds and slaughtered their families that they turned their wrath on all Christians. He also told me that they respect noble birth. If you remain calm and keep your head up, you will be recognized as high born and they will sell you to..."

"Sell me?" Adela cried out. "I'll kill myself before they make me a slave!"

She grabbed a small dagger which she kept in her belt. Bertran caught her hand and struggled with her. He tore the weapon from her fingers and threw it into the ocean.

"Calm yourself, Adela!"

She fought him like a wild beast as madness took hold of her.

"Stop, Adela, the children are watching!"

"You want to lie to them until the Saracens board the
ship?" she screamed.

Bertran covered her mouth and trapped her flailing limbs,
pressing her against him and wrapping his arm around her.
She struggled in vain. Her rage finally turned to tears and
she slumped against him, weeping bitterly.

He caressed her hair and gently rocked her back and forth
as a parent would an infant.

"I swear by all that is holy that we will find your father!" he
whispered. "I have seen it in a dream."

Adela looked up at him through her tears.

"I have..." he repeated softly.

"Do your dreams ever come true?" she asked with the innocence of a child.

Bertran's face beamed with a knowing smile. This very
moment, with his beloved pressed against him in need of
his strength, was a vision he had pictured a thousand times
when the sun had gone down over a world that made such
dreams impossible.

He nodded to her as though revealing his deepest secret.
Even now, as the slave traders relentlessly approached,
waiting helplessly in the middle of an unfriendly ocean, he
felt certain that they would bask in their love for a lifetime.
Adela smiled in spite of herself, as though she could read
the assurance of his thoughts. Somehow, she felt safe in his

arms and for the first time was conscious of a bottomless feeling for her loyal companion.

Screams suddenly tore them from their oasis of joy. Some of the older children had recognized the crescent embroidered on the flags of the warships.

From the other five galleys came the cries of terrified children. The swarthy faces of Saracen warriors could now be seen on the decks, along with the glitter of drawn sabers. Like giant hungry sharks, the ships prowled around their prey and soon circled their helpless victims.

Adela had regained her composure and was now staring defiantly at the foreign men as they hurled ropes onto the vessels.

"Throw down your sword!" she said to Bertran, recognizing that any resistance would result in a swift death.

Bertran hesitated. The weapon had become a part of his new identity has a free man.

"Will you please follow your own advice!" she cried out. "I need you to stay alive!"

Bertran unbuckled his belt and let the broadsword drop to the deck. He stood by Adela and grimly watched the Saracens leap onto the ship.

Mayhem erupted as the children ran in uncontrolled terror from their captors. These were the creatures of their nightmares and of the most horrific tales in Christendom.

Their turbans and strange, loose clothing suited for the desert sun, along with the razor-sharp blades of their curved swords were the ultimate vision of evil and dread for these children of the North. Most of them had never seen brown-skinned peoples before and that only added to the demonic mystery of this alien race.

The captain and his sailors gathered together on the bridge and watched sullenly as the invaders swarmed onto the decks. They shouted orders in an odd foreign tongue which made them all the more terrifying. They threw the children flat on the decks and forced everyone to lie down.

Adela and Bertran felt their pride trampled and resisted the humiliation. A giant of a man came up to them and brandished his saber. This was their first close-up look at the dreaded followers of the Prophet who had captured Christian holy places. They studied him with curiosity rather than fear. He was an exotic sight with his strangely shaped beard and eastern emblems.

The man let out a yell, the kind which precedes a fatal blow, and the two young people sat down before him. Soon all the children and priests were lying down at the feet of their captors. Even their moans were silenced by the roar of orders bellowed in the strangest language they had ever heard. A macabre silence fell over the sea.

Adela and Bertran lay face down on the wet planks like the

others. They watched the bizarre slipper-like shoes walk by them and listened to the odd sound of Arabic, trying to make out what was going on. But whenever they raised their heads to see, a foot struck them and forced them down.

Bertran reached over and found Adela's hand. He held it tight as she squeezed it in search of courage. They would spend the rest of the day in that position, feeling only the movement of the waves beneath them and the heat of their hands giving them hope in the midst of terror.

Near sunset, the ships came into the port of Bujeiah. The trembling children were allowed to sit up and see the first palm trees of the world which would engulf them forever. For a brief time, the wonder of exotic plants, and peculiar architecture stole their attention away from the fate awaiting them. The towering domes and minarets of the mosques were the materialization of fantasies and legends that had filled the imagination of these northern children from earliest infancy.

The city was one of the most beautiful harbors on the African coast. It was known as "Little Mecca" and built on terraces along the slopes of a great hill rising some two thousand feet above the ocean. Surrounding Bujeiah were mountains and valleys bursting with the summer colors of barley fields, olive groves, and vineyards pregnant with purple grapes. Brilliant white homes were nestled in lavish foliage and fruit-laden orchards.

As the ships docked, camels came into view, and veiled women, and giant tropical gardens. Lit by the golden light and long shadows of the fading sun, these sights mesmerized the boys and girls who had known only their village huts and the rugged fortress walls of their masters. Here was a world of grace and beauty, color and light. It seemed utterly disconnected from the gory sagas brought back by the Crusaders.

Suddenly, the splendid fairy-tale scene rang out with the soul- stirring cry of the muezzin, calling all Moslems to prayer. The undulating sound echoed across the city. The children were struck by its mystical power over the human heart. It seemed to awaken a longing for something unattainable yet very near. It shattered the painful realities of the present and revealed the cosmic Presence beneath it all. Some of the children crossed themselves, reacting instinctively to the call to remembrance of the Creator.

They were all the more stunned when they saw their fierce guardians prostrate themselves in an attitude of prayer. The children sat in astonished silence as they witnessed the solemn ritual of Salah, the daily prayer of the Muslims. There was such humility in these fierce pirates as they placed their foreheads on the decks and responded to the one who led them in their devotions.

The prayer lasted for what seemed like an eternity. Many of the older children, including Adela and Bertran, were forced to ask themselves how such believers in the Almighty could be the servants of the Antichrist as the Pope branded them, or the disciples of the Devil as they were portrayed in the lurid stories which haunted the minds of the peoples of the West.

Adela remembered hearing her father say that Eastern Christians from the dying empire of Byzantium had lived side by side with Muslims for generations. Their religious differences were merely debates, not the butchery which the West had indulged in. The great submission to Allah, the surrendering of pride and arrogance to the Holy One which was the very meaning of the word Islam, was more evident on the decks of the ships than in many a Mass celebrated in gaudy cathedrals.

The Saracens rose and quickly returned to their duties. The enchanted moment was shattered as they barked orders in their guttural yet lyrical language. The hordes of children began to move under their brutal shoves. It soon became obvious that some were being taken off the ships while others remained to travel to another port.

Bertran and Adela held each other tightly as they were

pushed forward with the others. They both feared the same thing: being separated. Being taller than most of the children, they tried to move along as inconspicuously as possible, hoping that they would make it off the ship without drawing attention.

Just as they reached the stairway, a Saracen wrapped in colorful dress denoting his rank, stopped them with the edge of his saber. He shouted at them angrily. Bertran and Adela froze like statues. The warlord shouted again and threatened them with his weapon. They looked at him helplessly, not understanding what he wanted.

Several Muslim soldiers came forward and violently separated them. Adela let out an uncontrollable cry as she clung to Bertran. His first impulse was to fight back but he quickly realized that he would be no good to his beloved as a dead man. An evil-looking Arabic knife appeared before him, sharper than any weapon he had ever seen. He let himself be pushed backwards out of the ship as he locked his gaze upon Adela. She called out his name in a fit of panic while the soldiers held her back. Bertran felt himself ready to explode.

"I'll come for you, Adela!" he yelled. "I swear by the power of the Almighty, I'll find you and take you home!"

The soldiers threw him down the ship's stairway onto the dock. He could no longer see Adela, but could hear her ter-

rible screams. He jumped to his feet and shouted with all
his strength.

"Be brave, Adela! I'll free you from the Devil himself!"

A Saracen struck him on the head with the hilt of his
sword. The young man fell to his knees and was dragged
away.

* * *

When Bertran came to his senses, he found himself in the
center of a busy marketplace. For a time, the foreign surroundings and the dizziness in his head kept him in a state
of confusion. He thought at first that he was dreaming.
Such images had appeared to him in his sleep. They were
different from other dreams because they were accompanied by a bizarre physical sensation, as though he were
mentally reliving some experience he had not yet known.
These dreams often left him in a state of vertigo, disconnected with time and the reality of the moment. He had
always disregarded these queer sensations for they were
unpleasant and disconcerting. Going out into the fields for
a hard day's work was a quick cure for such mysterious
mental phenomenon.

But this time, his visions were accompanied by a nasty
headache which seemed all too real. He struggled to touch

the source of the pain, finding it hard to command his arm. His head was wet with blood and when he looked at his hand, he knew that he was not dreaming. He strained to focus his eyes which could only make out moving shapes and colors. Strange alien smells entered his consciousness and brought back the memory of what had taken place. He heard voices shouting all around him, reminding him of market day back in the town outside Lord Reynald's castle. It seemed that someone was selling fish or cloth.

Suddenly, he was grabbed by the arm and lifted to his feet. He stumbled and regained his balance as another hand squeezed his bicep and opened his mouth. Bertran jerked his head back and was about to swing his fist at the person who dared to touch him in such a way when his eyes finally focused. Before him stood a dark-skinned man with a long white beard. He looked like the incarnation of a wizard from a story-teller's fantasy. His eyes glistened like distant stars as he observed the young prisoner. He stroke his beard and muttered a few words in Arabic.

Bertran breathed deeply to regain his senses, eager to be back in control of himself. He saw coins exchange hands and heard the rattle of chains. Then he realized what was taking place. The mysterious person staring at him so intently had just bought him as his slave!

14

"La ilaha illallah Muhammad-ur-Rasulullah!"

Bertran stared at his host, astonished at his fiery energy.

The old mystic pointed his finger to the heavens in the luxurious atrium of his home.

"You not know what that means, young Frank. Must never forget! Will save your soul. It means: There is no God but Allah and Muhammad is His Prophet!"

The dark-skinned wise man curled the tip of his pointed beard around his little finger and searched for the right words.

"We call this the Kalimah. This heart of every true Muslim. This difference between them and kafirs, the unbelievers.

You will hear this chant many time in our country. But it is more than words. It comes from Tawhid, knowledge sent from Allah through all His Prophets, blessings of Allah and peace be upon them."

He circled Bertran who sat on a silk cushion in the middle of the inner court. A ray of morning sun shot through the glass dome and lit up the great plants that surrounded a little water fountain at the center of the atrium. Bertran was no longer in chains, nor in his Frankish clothing. He wore the thin white linen of the natives, and was fresh from his new master's bathhouse.

He sat patiently, fascinated by this odd skeleton of a man who seemed to burst with the energy of twenty warlords. He had bought himself a western slave to educate the youth in the ways of Islam. Bertran didn't care as long he could have time to think of a way to escape and find Adela.

"Islam come from two words. Salm mean peace and Silm mean submission. So Islam mean surrender your will to Will of Allah and be at peace with Him. To live in such harmony, must have faith, obedience, and knowledge. How you do this? We say Iman-bi'l-ghayb! That mean you get knowledge of unknown from one who knows."

The odd little man bent forward and peered into Bertran's eyes. Bertran recognized something familiar about them. They were bottomless, like those of the Cathar hermit.

"I one who knows! You one who not know. I teach you, you learn. Then I set you free and you share wisdom with others."

Bertran heard nothing but the word "free."

"How long will it take for me to learn?"

The old man let out a high-pitch laugh which caused Bertran to wonder about his sanity.

"Youth always impatient, yes? Maybe ten years."

"Ten years!"

The man's face suddenly darkened with anger.

"I buy you in slave market and save you from terrible masters who beat you and work you until dead. I buy you because you look... how you say...intelligent. I think maybe you the one who brings teaching of the Prophet, blessings of Allah and peace be upon him, to the West."

The young man's eyes widened in shock.

"One good heart better than mighty Caliph's army!" the old man screamed, outraged at Bertran's reaction.

The youth tried to regain his composure and ease the man's ferocious mood swings.

"Do you really believe that one Frank can turn Christendom to Islam?"

The wiry Arab sat cross-legged on a large cushion nearby.

"I believe one Frank die horrible death if not try."

"But I am not a learned man..."

"Muhammad, blessings of Allah and peace be upon him, was a Bedouin goat herder at the beginning. Allah chose him as the Khatam-an-Nabiyyin, the last of the true Prophets!"

They sat in silence. The Arab studied Bertran with a piercing gaze. Bertran looked back at his owner, realizing that Providence had just saved him from a ghastly fate. The man was clearly a bit deranged, but at least he was not evil. It was obvious to Bertran that, along with wanting to make him a messiah to the West, he also needed a companion. Perhaps he could play along for awhile, until the right opportunity came for his escape.

"My name is Hasan Ibn al-Hanafiyyah. And I not a crazy man, and you cannot escape so easily."

Hasan smiled as Bertran's jaw dropped. The man could read his mind!

"But you right about one thing. I need you like you need me. I believe you have good heart and are the one I wait for many years now. I see you in dream twenty years ago when Saladin was sultan and our people not divided like now."

Bertran suddenly felt helpless. He thought of Adela and his heart tightened as though it would explode any moment.

"Mylord, I beg of you!" he cried out, "I must save someone from..."

"Call me Hasan. I your friend now. Who you must save?"

"A young noblewoman...She has been taken captive."

Hasan curled his thin white beard.

"You love this woman?"

Bertran hesitated. No one had ever asked him such a question before. He had never dared to ask himself that question.

"Is that difficult question for you?"

"Yes, I do love her, " he blurted out. "I love her more than my life."

"Aaah...She is a part of you then."

"Yes!"

Bertran had never thought of it that way. But Hasan stated it perfectly. Adela was the missing half of his soul and without her he was not whole. Everyone of his dreams of the future was colored with her presence.

"You must indeed find her, or you will never find yourself and be of no use to me."

Hasan stood and circled the atrium, deep in thought.

Bertran felt a ray of hope break through his despair.

"In my country, we have many arts. One of them is the art of...how you say...bartering."

He abruptly stopped beneath the glass dome and turned to Bertran. "We make deal, you and I."

Silhouetted in the shaft of sunlight, Hasan seemed like

some heavenly visitor come to change human destiny.

"I must have your word, before Allah, His Prophets and Angels, peace be upon them all, that you will let me teach you the message you must take back to your world."

"But, Sire...Hasan...I believe in the God of Jesus Christ! I have known His Presence! You cannot ask me to reject that..."

A beatific smile softened the strange man's features.

"Oh, noble spirit, I know you have experienced the Holy One. That is why you with me now. I not ask you to reject but to come closer to Him, to become His child in every way."

He came to kneel by Bertran, moving with the grace of an angelic being. All signs of insanity or ferociousness were gone.

"Hazrat Isa ibn Maryam, the one you call Jesus, is my Murshid, my Master also. He has unfolded within my heart the asrar which were unknown even to the Sufis and Dervishes."

"What is asrar?"

"The heavenly secrets, the mysteries of ma'rifah. The White Ones call it gnosis, knowledge which allows direct experience of Nur-i-Allah, the Light of God."

Bertran felt that infinite longing for understanding seize his soul as it had in the ruins of the chapel by the hermit's fireplace and on the shores of the Mediterranean.

"Who are the White Ones?"

"The Hawaries, the first disciples of Hazrat Isa, blessings of Allah and peace be upon them all."

"They have been dead a thousand years, have they not?"

The old Arab's features warmed with joy as he witnessed Bertran's great hunger.

"You forget that you now in Holy Land, Terra Sancta. All the Prophets, peace be upon them, have walked on these sands. And they have left disciples and communities which carry on with...how you say...Shari'ah, the law of Allah...Truth."

Bertran sat up, overflowing with excitement.

"Are you saying that there is a lineage here which goes back to the first Apostles?"

"That what I say. Your Pope says that he is direct successor. But you know that not true. The true successor is one who lives the Ma'rifah-i-Allah, in the knowledge of Allah. Such a man knows that there is but one Truth and all the Murshid-i-Tariq, the Masters of the Way, teach it."

Bertran felt his heart pound through the walls of his chest. He sensed that he was suddenly on the verge of discovering the greatest treasure in the world.

"You mean...."

Hasan nodded, a profound serenity radiating from his eyes.

"Islam and Christianity arise from same root. The secret is to see beyond follies of men and differences of peoples. Truth that makes free is within, not outside in rituals and clothing. There is one al-Sirat al-Mustaqim! One Straight Path! The Prophet Jesus, blessings of Allah and peace be upon him, taught pure Islam and the Prophet Muhammad, blessings of Allah and peace be upon him, taught pure Christianity!"

Bertran swooned with a dizzy spell. Such thoughts were too formidable to absorb. His mind rejected them while his heart embraced them. And at the same time, he was struck by the demonic nightmare of the Crusades. Untold numbers of faithful followers of the One God had been and would be slaughtered by brothers claiming faith in that same Creator. It was all a grotesque misunderstanding! Hasan's eyes sparkled with tears.

"Now you understand why I a little crazy...."

He took Bertran by the arm and helped him to his feet.

"Come...Let us begin our work together. You help me bring peace to world and I help you find woman you love." He took him to a table near the fountain and bade him sit down. He sat across from Bertran and pulled a large deck of cards from one of the ivory drawers.

"We begin with a reading. It always prepare us for what must be done."

The cards were unlike any Bertran had ever seen. They were illustrated with extraordinary images full of strange figures and symbols. Hasan noticed his curious expression as he carefully laid the cards out.

"You not see such cards before, my young friend? I know great lords from your lands who have brought them to their courts."

"What sort of games do you play with them?"

Hasan let out his odd high-pitched laugh.

"Truly, I must start from beginning with you. This not game, my son. This reveal destinies to those who seek. Cards represent Egyptian hieroglyphic book, one of few saved from library of Alexandria."

He made a triangular shape with some of the cards and laid others in a square formation inside the geometric figure.

"This represent relationship between God, man, and the universe. Square is visible world. Imagine point at center of square. That soul of man. Visible world is created in soul and is only man's idea. Cards instruments for understand-ing what cannot be seen."

He turned over the first Tarot card.

"Describe what you see."

Bertran studied the card, fascinated by the mysterious im-age.

"A man...seated on a throne...surrounded by water."

"This card we call King of Cups. That is you. You are King
of Cups."

"I am no king, Hasan. I am not even a free man."

"You free man!" Hasan yelled out. "No master can chain
your soul! No matter how many chains put on your body.
Never forget that!"

He looked back down at the card. Bertran smiled at the
man's volcanic energy and profound wisdom.

"You see waters around you in card. Much emotion...Turn
next card!"

Bertran turned over another one of the large, colorful
cards.

"It's upside down."

"Turn around so you can read it."

"Another king. He holds a sword in his hand."

Hasan curled his beard, suddenly worried.

"King of Swords. This man your adversary."

Bertran looked up at him, concerned.

"There is evil intent in him...toward you."

"What do you mean?"

"Next card is intent of reversed King of Swords. Turn it
over."

Bertran slowly turned the card, as though some demon
would appear from beneath it.

"Five of swords. See how sky is torn. There has been injustice and cruelty against you. King of Swords is dangerous enemy."

Bertran's mind began to resist this strange science.

"Listen carefully. If King of Swords not reversed, then evil deed finished. But it continue around you."

"This is ridiculous..." Bertran protested.

"Silence! Tarot come from ancient Egyptians. They know more than peasant boy from barbaric civilization! Next card will tell of present. What is it?"

Bertran turned it over reluctantly.

"Another sword. It has a name under it."

"Can you read it?"

"Judgment...A man sits on a throne with a sword and scales."

"This very sacred card in Divine Book called Kabbalah. It is path of adjustment."

"What does that mean?"

"There will be meeting between two of you. Adjustment in your hands. Can deal with sword or scales. Power will be in your hands. Next card."

Bertran's hand shook as he turned the card over. He had never experienced such bizarre phenomenon before.

"Give attention to card!" the old man cried out.

"It has a number eight at the top. There are cups at the bottom. It looks like a sun...or a moon eclipsing the sun...

And a man with his back to me, wandering among rocks near a dark river between him and his destination."

"This journey you must take. You will be thrown in dark time where you not see light of sun. Beware! For you will have to see by light of moon which is full of...how you say... illusion. Your fears may take over as you journey to Truth and Light."

They sat in silence for a moment. The gentle song of the gurgling fountain seemed to turn melancholic. A cloud dimmed the sunray falling into the atrium.

"Next card most important. Will tell what is to happen." Bertran turned it over slowly.

"It has a number four at the top. There are three cups on the ground. A man is sitting under a tree with his eyes closed, and a cup is being offered to him from a strange hand protruding from a cloud."

Hasan leaned toward Bertran and touched his hand. The young man felt a familiar heat radiating from the man's fingers and penetrating his flesh.

"This man again you. Cups on ground symbol of what you know. You sit under tree of Life. Your eyes closed to world around by your ignorance. Hand from cloud offers solution. But you must choose. When you find what you seek, outcome is uncertain. Consider very carefully. I cannot tell you outcome. But there is much danger ahead." Bertran stared at the mysterious cards which spoke to him of things to come. Somehow, he knew they revealed the truth.

* * *

The vessel had crossed the ocean with great speed. It was one of the fastest skiffs on the seas, and had managed to avoid the storms which had sent so many of the children to a watery grave.

Aimery and his squire stepped onto the docks of Bujeiah. They were dressed in merchants' clothing, the surest way of safe passage in a city built on trade. The people of Bujeiah were less concerned with the Jihad, the Holy War which had dragged on for too many generations to be of interest to anyone, than they were with the amount of dinars they could make from their Western visitors. Business was business and the color of skin or the form of religion was highly irrelevant to the practical trading mind whose primary skill was discovering new ways to make money.

Aimery wiped the perspiration from his brow and loosened the belt which held his mighty sword. He took in the new sights with virtually no interest. His squire, on the other hand, was in utter fascination.

"Are these not the most beautiful women in the world, Mylord?"

"How can you tell with those veils, Thomas? They might not have any teeth for all you know."

"Beauty is in the eyes, Sire, is it not?"

Thomas turned to his master and jumped in terror. He was no longer beside him. He frantically looked about and finally saw the familiar swagger heading through the dense market place. Thomas threw a huge bag over his shoulder and hurried after him. As he passed by camels and men in turbans wearing daggers in the center of their belts, the squire did his best to keep from trembling. He was not a coward, but he still believed that they were walking into the lion's den. Even though there were no Crusades being waged at this time, the Saracens remained the ultimate enemy simply out of habit. The name of Genghis Khan had yet to reach to western edges of the known world and therefore left the Muslims as the only foreigners to fear.

Thomas caught up with his master as he entered an inn.

"How will you tell these people what we need?" he asked nervously.

Aimery pulled out a small leather sack stretched to its limits with coins.

"Everyone understands this language."

He opened the purse and spilled its contents on a table. The loud sound of jingling gold pieces made every head in the inn turn toward them.

"Who speaks Frankish here?" Aimery called out.

Four men immediately stood and came to his side. Aimery handed them each several coins.

"There's plenty more for you if you can answer my questions."

The young knight was in a hurry. He knew that he had several days to make up before he could reach Adela and take her back to his domain. He had no doubts, however, that he would find her for he always got what he sought for. Anyone who stood in his way was a dead man.

The suspicious faces surrounding him made no impression at all on his boundless self-confidence. Thomas stood as close to him as possible, expecting those infamous knives to appear at any moment.

"What you want to know, infidel?"

"There were seven ships which docked here some days ago. Where have they gone to?"

"What flag did they fly on the mast?"

"The Oriflamme of France."

The Saracen spat at his feet. Every muscle in Aimery's face tensed and his hand flew to the hilt of his sword.

"No, Sire, there are too many of them," Thomas begged.

The Saracen smiled sadistically and took a step back, ready to draw his saber.

"I fought with the glorious Saladin and killed many a Kafir

in the name of Allah!"

The entire inn exploded with cries of "Allah Akbar!", the war cry of the Jihad.

"Mylord," Thomas pleaded, "surely we did not travel all this way to die within an hour of arrival."

"Silence!" Aimery ordered. The fearless knight drew his sword.

The iron hiss whistled through the room as a warning to all. His adversary was a veteran warrior and had seen too many broadswords to let this one frighten him.

"No one insults the King of France before Aimery of Tours and lives!" the young chevalier cried out.

"Mylord! You came here to find the Baronness, not to duel..."

Aimery pushed him aside. When his blood boiled, there was no turning back.

"I have longed to spill Frankish blood for many years!" the Saracen shouted with glee as he drew his saber.

The men hurried away from them as they circled each other. Aimery eyed his adversary with the keen observation of one who has made battle his daily exercise. The thrill of danger was his greatest pleasure.

"Before you die, will you tell me where the ships have gone?"

The Muslim warrior laughed as he made his saber dance in

his hand with incredible speed.

"You will not live to go there!"

"I will have my answer if I have to kill every man in this room!"

The saber swung through the air and crashed against the sword with a frightful sound. Thomas began to pray as hard as he knew how. His greatest worry was not for his fool hearty master who had done this to him many times before, but for himself if he were left alone in this alien land.

Aimery sent his weapon flying over the man's head who ducked in time to feel the blade slice the top of his turban. The grin faded from his scarred face. He had not expected such power from his youthful adversary.

He swung again, but less sure of himself. Aimery blocked and forced the Saracen's arm away from him. The silver blade flew by the man's face and cut a red line along his shoulder. The man fell back with a grimace of pain. He realized that he was facing certain death now. Aimery approached for the kill like a relentless hunter. The Saracen dropped his saber.

"No more!" he cried out. "You mighty knight, oh nobly born!"

He fell to his knees in an attitude of submission.

The other Arabs were stunned by the soldier's fear, although they too were amazed at Aimery's skill. But they had never seen a Muslim warrior give up before.

Aimery stood over the man and lowered his sword.

"Answer me then!"

"The ships have gone to Alexandria."

"Why? Were they not destined for Messina?"

"They are delivering their cargo to the slave market."

Aimery turned scarlet.

"The slave market?"

"Some were sold here..."

Aimery replaced his sword in its scabbard.

"Where is the market in this city?"

"Near the mosque," another man answered.

Aimery grabbed a handful of coins and tossed them at the Saracen who was still on his knees and to the one who had just spoken. He motioned for Thomas to fill the purse back up and follow him. As he turned away, the Saracen jumped from his crouched position, drawing a knife from his belt. With lightning reflexes, Aimery grabbed his hand as it descended on him for a fatal strike. He threw the man over his shoulder and, twisting his arm, brought his boot down on his elbow. The man let out a shriek as the bones cracked. Aimery calmly picked up the knife and placed it in his belt. He looked at the crowd.

"Anyone else?"

The Arabs backed away from him as he stepped out into the street. Thomas raced after him, keeping an eye on the angry faces and wishing he had become a minstrel rather than squire to the most impetuous knight in the kingdom.

15

Bertran quickly learned to appreciate the odd little man who had bought him as his slave. It was clear that he had paid more for his freedom than for his servant hood. Hasan was not a wealthy man, having only one another servant to care for him and his modest home. He was a scholar and a mystic who, like the hermit Bertran had come to know, lived on the fringes of his religion. Or was it the summits?

He was a lonely man, rejected by his own people as a probable heretic because of his interest in other faiths. It was his openness to the Truth in all teachings that had set his mind off its axis. He had been present at too many massacres and seen too much human tragedy in the name of religion, a word ironically meaning "to bind together"!

Bertran attributed his host's plan to make him a messenger of some new expression of Divine Revelation to the pain that clouded his mind. Much of what the man said or did was incomprehensible to him, though he was constantly astounded by his mysterious powers. Hasan had been a member of various esoteric communities that were annihilated by Crusaders fighting under Richard the Lion-Hearted. He had wandered the Judean desert for months, coming across ancient brotherhoods who took him in due to that hospitality of the desert peoples which was almost as sacred as the sutras of Muhammad and the parables of Jesus.

The bizarre words spoken to him as the cards were turned face up sent chills through Bertran, but they were soon forgotten like a bad dream upon waking. He now turned his attention exclusively toward finding Adela.

Dressed in Arabic garments, he wandered the marketplaces freely, seeking information on the fate of the children brought in on the ships. Hasan accompanied him on a few outings to serve as translator, but there were enough Frankish speaking merchants for the young man to get around so his master let him wander as he pleased, believing that he would be true to his word and return to him.

A week passed since Bertran had last seen Adela. On this particular morning, he was walking along the docks looking for sailors who might have answers for him when his gaze fell on the one person he hoped never to see again.

Aimery noticed him at the same moment and immediately recognized him. Bertran considered running but something held him back. The image of the hand coming through the cloud offering him a choice kept him from moving. Aimery ran toward him, followed by his squire. As he approached, his hand reached for the hilt of his sword. But, seeing that Bertran stood calmly before him, he thought better of it and resisted the temptation.

"You're Lord Reynald's serf!" he shouted as though letting out a war cry.

"And you're the Duke of Tours," Bertran replied, visualizing the mysterious Egyptian cards. He sensed with some inner instrument of perception that the belligerent young man was the King of Swords whom Hasan had warned him about.

"I've come for Lady Adela! Where is she, knave?"

Bertran felt his heart leap with anger, but restrained himself.

"I'm searching for her myself."

Aimery's right hand went for his sword.

"I am here for two purposes: to take the Baronness of Vendome back home and to tear your insolent heart out for the pigs to eat!"

"Are you such a coward that you would draw your sword on an unarmed man?" Bertran asked defiantly. He had never before felt a greater desire to fight an adversary to the death as he did in this moment.

Aimery roared with monumental anger and struck Bertran's face with his fist. He fell back and brought his hand to his lips.

"What sort of demon are you that you speak to a noble in such a manner? Have you not tasted the whip enough to learn your place?"

Before he could finish his statement, Bertran flung himself on Aimery, sending a ferocious punch to his jaw. The knight grabbed onto his arm as he fell and they rolled in the dirt, wrestling like wild beasts.

Thomas stared wide-eyed, having never seen anyone so foolish as to attack his master with his bare hands. He pulled a sword from his sack and thought of hitting Bertran with it, but he remembered that the peasant had spared his life on that fateful day at Lord Reynald's castle.

Aimery kicked Bertran away from him and they jumped to their feet. Both had savage grimaces on their blood-splattered faces. Aimery pulled the dagger from his belt.

"Die, you miserable wretch!"

Bertran took hold of a wooden pole laying nearby in a heap of construction materials. He held it before him like a spear, waiting for the knight's assault. Thomas realized that someone was going to die in the next few moments.

"I beg of you to consider what you are doing! How will this help you find Adela?"

At the sound of that name, the two enemies froze as though a spell had just been cast upon them. Their hatred for each other was not greater than their love for her.

"Where is she?" Aimery muttered between clenched teeth.

"I told you, I'm looking for her myself. She has been taken captive to another seaport."

"Why are you dressed like a heathen? And why did you not die trying to save her?"

Bertran lowered his weapon.

"I was sold as a slave to a good man who has sworn to help me find her. I am of more use to her alive than dead."

"That's doubtful," Aimery exclaimed, still ready to strike with his dagger.

"He's right, Mylord," Thomas cried out. "What good is there in fighting each other? Why not join forces and seek her together?"

"Are you mad, squire?" Aimery raged. "This is the villain I have come to destroy!"

"He's right," Bertran said as calmly as he could. "If you truly want to find Adela, then you will need my help."

"I need no man's help, swine!"

Aimery charged at him, swinging the sharp knife at his face. Bertran jumped back and fell into the stack of disguarded lumber. He swung the pole and knocked the weapon from Aimery's hand. Before the knight could react, Bertran struck him in the temple with a shuddering blow that knocked him to his knees.

Bertran scrambled to his feet as Aimery shook his head and tried to keep from losing consciousness. The young peasant resisted the temptation to crack his skull while he was defenseless. Thomas raised his weapon to protect his master.

"I don't care for you any more than you do for me," Bertran stated coldly at the dazed knight. "But I would consort with the Devil himself if he could help me find Adela!"

Aimery stood on wobbly legs. His face was red with humiliation at having been struck down by a commoner. He stared at Bertran with a murderous look.

"The Saracens are selling her as a slave!" Bertran cried out, trying to break through his stubborn prejudice. "If you care for her at all, you will join me in finding her. It will take a miracle to save her!"

Aimery rubbed the side of his head as he bridled his emotions. He was hot-tempered but not a fool.

"Here is the bargain I'll make with you, serf. We will accept a truce until the time when she is found. But the moment Adela is freed, we'll face each other in mortal combat and one of us will die!"

Bertran knew that he could not win a duel against someone

with Aimery's training and experience. But his concern was only for his beloved.

"So be it," he said fearlessly.

It wasn't long before the two rivals had their answer. The ships had gone to the great port of Alexandria. They were told that the Governor of the ancient city, a cruel ruler by the name of Maschemuth, was especially interested in children of the Franks. The Arab merchants they spoke with assumed that other probable buyers included the Sultan of Egypt, who would have them brought to Cairo, and the Caliph of Baghdad whose palace lay beyond the Delta of the Nile on the other side of the deserts of Palestine. Bertran returned to Hasan and told him of their discovery.

"You will have to travel across lands where peace not seen for a hundred years. The strongholds of Knight Templars are on your route and they vowed to fight till every last man is in grave.

They not require Pope to tell them if time to fight believers. You will be in lands where men live to do battle."

Hasan put his hand on Bertran's shoulder with fatherly affection.

"In truth, is this woman worth such risk, Bertran?"

"I will go to the ends of the earth to find her."

"If she taken to Baghdad, that precisely what you will be doing. Great deserts in those regions, even Bedouins avoid. This no place for Frankish boy."

"If that is the way to Adela, then I will cross it!"

Hasan's wrinkled face darkened with sadness.

"How you keep your word to me if you die of thirst or from sabers of Caliph's men?"

Bertran smiled at his worried mentor.

"Have you not dreamed that I would fulfill the mission I am to be entrusted with?"

Hasan curled his beard with his fingers.

"Aaah...Dreams...Hard to say which fantasies and which messengers of the future."

"Hasan, if I don't find Adela, I'll be worthless to you. I'd become a walking corpse."

"She must be very special woman..."

"I told you, she is my life. I've always known that we were meant for each other."

The old man moved away, limping with age and sadness.

"I not save you from slavery to watch you kill yourself on crazy adventure!"

Bertran felt the man's pain. In these few days, he had come to love him for his goodness, and even for his strange ways.

"Hasan...It is Destiny that calls me to this. I have no

choice. I will be in the company of the King of Swords."

The wiry Arab suddenly turned around, eyes wide with astonishment.

"What madness is this?"

Bertran nodded calmly.

"He has come to kill me. After we find Adela."

Hasan hurried to him and grabbed him by the collar of his tunic.

"Did you not understand reading? He is your doom!"

"Or my fulfillment..."

Hasan walked to and fro through the atrium, highly agitated.

"You not understand...You my most precious...possession."

"You've taught me that I am no one's possession, Hasan."

The old man peered at him out of the corner of his eye.

"Spoken truly, my friend."

He continued his nervous pacing.

"But consider what will become of me and my many years of searching...studying...praying...They all die with me. I have seen things that people must know about."

Hasan hobbled over toward Bertran.

"I waited for you many years to come and carry this treasure to new generations."

Bertran hadn't thought the man was that mad.

"Consider what Crusades have done. Holy Land has

been...how you say...sacked! And this just beginning. There will be more Crusades and greater invaders!"

"Greater invaders?" Bertran asked sarcastically.

"The Mongols!" Hasan exclaimed, his eyes rounding in terror. Mongols will be upon us soon and make you Franks look like children at play!"

Hasan's wrinkled, weather-beaten face shriveled with despair.

"I have seen with these eyes scrolls of sacred writings in Sinai desert. Secret brotherhoods keep for thousand years words of one you call the Christ. And Christian lords use them to warm meals while they kill guardians of your Faith!"

The old mystic took Bertran's face in his hands.

"This dying age, Bertran. Dark times. Great light blown out like candle. Wisdom of Ibrahim, Moses, the Ancient Ones of Egypt, blessings of Allah and peace be upon them all...All gone in flames!"

Tears fell from his cavernous eyes as he mourned the devastation of humanity's spiritual treasures.

"What left for future? What light they live by? Only killing and greed and death! God the Compassionate, the Merciful has spoken through His Prophets, peace be upon them all. And children of darkness destroy true meaning and make words instrument of death!"

Bertran was shaken by the man's profound emotion and felt his resistance begin to break down.

"Understand, Bertran? Allah make well in desert and well now poisoned by human ignorance. Sandstorm soon come and all will disappear..."

Bertran was too young to be interested in the future of humanity. It was the present that held his attention.

"What can I do?" he asked to appease his unhappy host.

"You must be like animal that gather food for winter. Take knowledge I give, knowledge of others who also travel this path. Keep it alive in your soul. Let it grow and blossom. Then give to someone else when you old and dying like me."

Hasan's words struck him like a bolt of lightning. He suddenly remembered the Perfect One and the wisdom he had imparted to him. He knew even then that he was especially blessed to receive such hard-earned understanding of the mysteries of life.

"Why me?" Bertran blurted out, resenting the weight of such responsibility. "I've done nothing to deserve such...honor."

"No, you have not. But none of us have, my boy. This is mysterious goodness of all-knowing One. Perhaps no one else available so you must take this great and terrible gift."

"What if I don't want it?"

Hasan fell silent for a moment. A deep serenity came over his features as he observed the young man. It made Bertran strangely uncomfortable, as though he were betraying his dearest friend.

"That your choice. But, remember! This not only for salvation of others, but for yours. No happiness if reject Truth offered to you. Too many paid for it with their blood for you to let it die when you can help."

"But I traveled here to help Adela find her father, not to become involved in your madness!"

"Silence!" Hasan ordered. "You call me mad when you one who want to travel in land you know nothing about! A Bedouin child could survive in desert long after your bones bleached by sun!"

A misty light suddenly flashed in the old man's eyes. His anger dissipated and a wondrous smile softened his features.

"Allah be praised!" he cried out.

Bertran thought he had completely lost his mind.

"Now I understand! It is His Will that you go!"

He laughed like a child and slapped a bewildered Bertran on the shoulder.

"Great and mysterious are His ways! Yes, go on your journey!" He pulled a small medallion linked to a thin gold chain from around his neck.

"Wear this!"

Bertran looked at the round amulet. A strange geometric figure was etched in the bronze. He turned it over to find another design, that of a spiral-like wheel.

"When time comes, show this."

"How do I know when the time will come and who do I show it to?"

"You will know," Hasan said with a twinkle, "you will know..."

He place it around Bertran's neck.

"Keep hidden until then. Will cause death if wrong people see it."

Bertran grabbed his hand angrily.

"I will not wear this medallion, then! I told you, nothing will keep me from finding Adela!"

Hasan patted his hand gently.

"Now I know why you must find her. In finding her you fulfill my mission too. She bait and you fish!"

Hasan laughed merrily. Bertran moved away, enraged.

"Don't say that! I am here for her sake, not yours!"

"Remember," Hasan stated, oblivious of the young man's anger. "You must receive from all who know, even from most unexpected. Truth like light. In prism, break into many colors, but all from one source. So do not fear opposites. Remember the one true color."

Hasan placed his hand on Bertran's head and blessed him. Bertran had the feeling that he would never see the strange little man again.

"I decrease, you increase," Hasan stated with a bright smile. He walked over to his desk and took out several items from the drawers.

"I want you to have this," he told Bertran as he handed him a satchel full of dinars. Bertran tried to protest but Hasan put his fingers on his lips.

"You will need to pay for caravan. Franks must have great sums to travel through our lands. We only need good camel. These coins will open way to your destination."

He then held out an Arabian dagger. It was short and curved with a long hilt like those Bertran had seen in the belts of every wealthy man in the city. But this one was made of gold, ivory and pearls. It was a sultan's weapon, as much for show as for protection.

"This belong to my father and his father before him. It was once in possession of a great Iman and was given to my family because of our loyalty and devotion. It will remind you of our bargain."

"I cannot take such a treasure!" Bertran exclaimed. He had never held such a priceless object.

"You must be armed for your journey. Take it as I took it from my father. I only know you for few days, but you the son I never have."

Bertran was deeply moved. He regretted his harsh tone and disrespect for Hasan's wild ideas.

"I know you not use in dishonorable way. If you must shed blood with it, let it be for noble cause."

"I have no desire to shed blood," Bertran said. "I have never killed a man in my life."

"You do not know what awaits you and what you may have to do. I give you one last word of advice: if you must draw this dagger from its scabbard, use it!"

* * *

That very afternoon, the two rivals set off for the legendary city. A small fishing vessel took them along the coast of the continent, past the pillars of Pompey, Cleopatra's Needle and the remnants of the mighty Egyptian civilization. Aimery and Bertran stayed away from each other. Both knew that their fragile trust could break into deadly combat at the least word or glance. Thomas kept his master occupied with the concerns of the journey, doing his best to sooth the violent hatred which possessed him. He had never seen the noble knight in such a state, not even when he prepared for battle. It was true that he knew him to be a terribly aggressive adversary in the jousting tournaments.

But that was what made him the King's favorite. The squire had always assumed that it was the heat of competition which caused such a dangerous spirit to enter his lord, for it left him as soon as the fight was won. But the evil anger which now brewed within his breast and kept his face a dark red was a new manifestation. For the first time in his five years of service to the young Duke, Thomas feared him and felt that some uncontrollable demon had taken hold of him.

Bertran paid no attention to his nemesis. His only thought was for Adela, and all the rest - duels and mysterious missions - be damned. He couldn't wait to feel her next to him, to look into her eyes and smell her hair. Their journey together had only intensified his love for her in a way he had not thought possible. He knew that such feelings were greater than both of them, for they had opened a bottomless abyss in his soul and revealed a glimpse of the Unknown. He knew now that Love, human love, was the key to all the religious mysteries of the world. The man from Nazareth had said it plainly and his disciples had written the divine revelation for everyone to hear until the end of time. Bertran understood that when the sun faded for the last time over the earth's horizon, the words of Holy Scripture would still hold true: "Every one that loves is born of God and knows God."

As the young man looked out at the passing ruins of an ancient civilization, he understood that this love burning in his breast spread from the sweet affection for another person to the beatific vision of Eternal Life. It was all one and the same. No rituals or sacraments could enhance it or transform it. For that infinite ocean within transcended concern for self and reached out to all things. This was the very presence of the Holy Spirit!

Here lay the great mystery which the priests of all civilizations searched for or sought to veil from those who would expose their emptiness. This was the heart of esoteric mystery schools and great philosophies.

The monster silhouettes of three pyramids appeared in the distance as though claiming to hold secrets unavailable to the uninitiated. Without education or power of any kind, Bertran knew that he had received the greatest knowledge of all, that which the Christ had died for and which was within reach of every human being.

As the boat floated passed colossal statues of long dead Pharaohs and majestic temples left to scorpions and snakes, the young man felt a new light dawn within him. Before the carcasses of former glory, he saw clearly that the simple things of life had more grandeur than any monument or wealth. All that already belonged to him in his poverty and ignorance, a bird song and the aroma of a summer meadow, were the only true wealth and joy.

In that moment, Bertran realized that even the Perfect One was mistaken. Despite his purity and rare spiritual powers, he was wrong. Creation was good, life in the flesh was sacred! There was nothing man could do to destroy that reality. No matter how depraved, how barbaric, how godless he made himself, man could not dim the glory of life! Death itself could not conquer it for, to those who had eyes to see, it was the temporal sanctuary of the Holy and human beings were witnesses of its constant revelations.

Out of the corner of his eye, Bertran noticed that Aimery had crossed the deck and was also gazing at the splendid sights of a fallen empire. He too was caught by the timelessness of the moment and lifted out of the turbulent seas of passing time. The two witnesses watched in silence as five thousand years looked back at them, speaking to the deepest recesses of their souls, reminding them of things mortal and immortal.

In that instant, Bertran lost his hatred for his rival. He saw him as a brother on the journey of life, confused and lost, but still a seeker of that which all are meant to find. It no longer mattered to him that Aimery intended to kill him. He had the odd sensation that this bloodthirsty opponent had been sent to help him find his beloved and that, behind what seemed like opposites and paradoxes, there lay the single-minded purpose of the Good.

Bertran smiled to himself. Crazy Hasan was right after all! All the variety of color and people and religions were merely the reflection of a divine unity so simple as to be incomprehensible.

The boat drifted by the great pyramids. Their sharp triangular edges rose into the sky like sacred instruments seeking contact with Eternity. As scarlet colors emanated from the eastern sun's descent, the stoic tombstones seemed to resonate with a cosmic vibration, as though reflecting the voice of the stars.

Bertran strained to identify the low hum. He wondered whether his mind was playing tricks on him. Suddenly the echo of a distant muezzin's chant blended with the sound. Bertran had the queer impression that he was hearing back into the past and far into the future. The splashing waves of the Mediterranean added a soothing rhythm to the eerie melodies.

"Do you hear that?"

Bertran was surprised to hear himself question his enemy, but it seemed so natural to break through the ice that had formed between them. He looked over at Aimery.

The handsome knight was listening intensely to the sounds of the Egyptian dusk. His raven hair fluttered about in the sea breeze like grass on the edge of a rugged cliff. Bertran had the distinct impression that this was a man who would not let himself be penetrated by such fleeting, vaporous sensations. He seemed locked into himself as though a thick dungeon door had slammed over his soul.

Nevertheless, the awesome presence of the ancient stones had temporarily released him from the madness in his breast. Bertran realized that all people carried within them in some way the longing for a universal Power that transcended them all and yet cared for each individual. Even the blocks of granite and limestone sang of a vaster world than earth.

Aimery crossed himself.

"Demons!" he whispered hoarsely as the strange hum continued to resonate across the shoreline.

Bertran was stunned. While his soul contemplated the glories of Heaven, the educated nobleman feared the shadows of Hell. He felt a shiver of rapture race through his bloodstream as he understood that, in spite of the darkness of the human mind, the Creator was sending forth His blessing. "In this was love, not that we loved God, but that he loved us..." The words came back to him from some long-forgotten Mass. He felt himself filled with a new strength unlike any he had ever known as he realized that, from the watery depths below to the infinite space above, the world was overflowing with the glory of the Almighty.

"What are you smiling at?" Aimery asked in a harsh tone.

"Are you in league with the pagan gods?"

Bertran turned to him, beaming with unspeakable joy.

"Don't you see the beauty of the Almighty everywhere around you?"

Aimery was taken aback.

"What nonsense is this?"

Bertran could hardly feel his body anymore. He seemed as light as a feather as he sent his arm out into the air and pointed to the magnificent vision of mountainous clouds lined with gold and orange colors behind the incredible symmetry of the Egyptian religious symbols.

"I see pagan idols. Are you a pagan too, boy?"

Bertran turned a luminous, serene gaze upon his beloved enemy.

"I am your brother, Aimery of Tours!"

16

Maschemuth was a giant of a man. He could hardly move his huge body, weighed down by nearly five hundred pounds of bronze-colored fat. His heavy jowls kept his lower lip permanently open in a fish-like expression, but his eyes, spread unusually far from each other, glistened with cruelty.

He was Governor of Egypt, subject to Sultan Malek Kamel whose father had usurped the throne and divided the empire among his sons. Nothing was left of the mighty dominions of the great Saladin. The Islamic world was in chaos as power-hungry viziers and tribal chieftains fought among themselves over the corpse of the Holy Land. Many of the glorious cities of old were now in ruins and Alexandria was one of the saddest examples of faded splendor. It had been sinking into oblivion since the fall of the Roman Empire and the tragic destruction of its famed library had broken its pride forever.

Maschemuth was a petty tyrant ruling a squalid seaport. He was a Muslim in name only and gave attention to only the harshest tenets of the Prophet's teachings. He found perverse pleasure in dispensing savage punishment to those who were foolish enough to bring his displeasure upon themselves. The Governor's executioners were the busiest in the land and their monstrous sabers were hardly ever dry.

It was to the home of this beast of a man that many of the little crusaders were taken. Upon hearing of the precious cargo of young Frankish slaves, Maschemuth purchased a thousand of them on the spot, condemning every one of them to a wretched life of servitude and the certainty of an early death.

Among the ragged mobs of manacled youths were proud Adela and the now accursed boy prophet, Stephen. He was hardly recognizable for his loyal guards had turned on him in the belly of the ship and beaten him ferociously. He escaped death only through the interference of Saracen warriors who had first enjoyed the beating but then realized

that they were about to lose a good sale. Having identified
Stephen as the children's leader, they planned on selling
him at a higher price.

The boy was brought before Maschemuth and scornfully
introduced as the prophet who had guided the pilgrims into
slavery. Some fifty other children, among whom was Adela,
stood in the back of the vast palatial room as Stephen approached the Governor.

The giant sat on huge cushions on a marble platform rising
several feet above the magnificent oriental carpets that
covered the floor. The room was flooded with light and
seemed to the grime-covered children like a chamber in
Paradise. Many of them were barefoot and had never before felt such softness beneath their feet. The ceiling's
massive arches were lined with multi-colored drapes that
fell gracefully like angel wings from above.

But the exotic beauty around them was of no interest to
the children for their hearts were bursting with dread and
sorrow. Their eyes were focused on the huge turbaned man
who sat in the far end of the room. They could only see the
shimmering of his giant rings which he wore on every finger.

Stephen could barely stand. His face was a mass of swollen
bruises and his clothing was shredded, revealing cuts all
along his body. He wept quietly, wishing he had never left

his flock on the gentle slopes of Troyes.

The Governor shouted in Arabic with a coarse, gravelly voice. A scholarly man, with fear permanently etched on his face, approached Stephen.

"His Highness wants to know if you are the children's prophet?"

Stephen nodded in great shame.

Maschemuth took a handful of dates from a silver tray and popped them in his mouth as he studied the trembling boy. He muttered to his entourage of a dozen men and women standing around him. They all laughed at the tyrant's joke. The Governor impatiently gestured for his attendant to translate.

"His Highness gives you his thanks for bringing all these children to him."

Stephen began to shiver as tears rolled down his cheeks. Maschemuth barked out an order that caused all the children to jump. Though they could not understand the words, they knew something terrible had just been said.

"His Highness wants you to be an example to your followers. Convert to the true faith and you will live in luxury the remainder of your days."

Stephen raised his head for the first time and looked at the Governor. The grotesque suzerain smiled a crooked, evil smile. He stated something in Arabic to the translator.

"He will make you an honored member of his court and give you all you desire."

Stephen felt the dark side of his nature thrill at this opportunity to escape misery. But the events of the past weeks had taken away the allurement of selfish pleasures. He remembered the sad eyes of Cecilia and trembled with remorse at the thought that he had destroyed the young woman with his wantonness. He heard the rattling chains of the children behind him and the grim future awaiting them.

In a flash, he saw the stranger who had started him on this course and fooled him with ideas of grandeur. At first, he had preached out of genuine belief that he was on a divine mission. But all the attention and praise heaped upon him had quickly turned it into something else.

Now another stranger offered him a new temptation. The shepherd boy's soul longed for nobility and purity once again. He was sickened with the stain of his self-indulgence. "No!"

Maschemuth's little eyes rounded in shock. He didn't need the translator to explain the boy's reply. His massive face hardened in a grimace of rage and he shouted orders to his guards.

Several soldiers grabbed Stephen and, obeying their shrieking master, made him face the children. The translator was ordered to address them.

"His Highness says that all of you will be asked to convert to the true faith or he will kill you one by one. Witness what has become of your prophet and his god!"

A saber whistled through the air and the children screamed with horror. Hysteria caught hold of the group as they cried out in desperation. Several of the Governor's entourage could barely conceal their shock and disgust, especially his son Suleiman, a sensitive lad of eighteen. The boy was sickened at his father's brutality and turned his back on the bloody scene. He would have covered his ears had the captain of the guards, a scarred warrior with herculean muscles, not grabbed his arms and forced him to turn around. He knew the boy's weakness and felt it his duty to save him from his father's wrath. Cowardly rulers were short-lived in this land.

Suleiman caught sight of Adela standing among the children. She had closed her eyes, but kept her back straight in defiance of the tyrant's cruelty. The boy had never seen such courage in a woman before.

* * *

The grounds of the Governor's palace were not well guarded. Few people would ever dare enter the tyrant's gardens.

Royal palms stood as sentinels by the tall gates, their great leaves shivering in the ocean breeze. It was a quiet summer afternoon. The Saracens who paced at the edge of the luscious property were bleary-eyed with fatigue, having just filled themselves with their mid-day meal. Not one of them noticed the three young men leap from the palms into the gardens.

"Look for an entrance!" Aimery whispered as they rushed through the tall plants decorating the Governor's yard.

"Your master is crazy!" Bertran muttered to Thomas as they followed him in the shadows of the tropical growth. "We should wait until dark, I tell you!"

Aimery stopped abruptly and turned to Bertran.

"You heard what the merchant told us! This man is a monster. Who knows what Adela may be going through at this very moment."

"We surely won't know if they slaughter us before we get to her!"

"Are you a coward as well as pagan, serf?"

Bertran went for the sword Aimery had given him. Thomas caught his hand.

"Save it for the Saracens, Bertran! We have enough danger ahead of us as it is."

Aimery smiled cynically at the peasant's anger.

"We will face each other soon enough, 'brother'! "

Bertran pulled himself away from Thomas' grip, repressing his rage. He was astonished that his anger was still so uncontrollable, even after having experienced those extraor-extraordinary moments of spiritual bliss. How great the struggle was to live in the high place he had tasted so fleetingly.

Aimery managed to contain his murderous feelings toward Bertran, knowing that the time would come when he would satisfy himself with his rival's blood. He was living on the patience of a tiger eyeing its prey.

They hurried through the strange vegetation, losing sight of the palace in the dense flora.

"Over there!" Thomas murmured suddenly.

They crouched and peered through the bushes. Two Saracens were coming out of a small door at the side of the meticulously sculptured home. They carried a blood-splattered body.

"God in heaven!" Bertran whispered. "It's one of the children!"

"How can you tell?" Aimery questioned, moving the large leaves out of his way.

"It's a light-skinned child in northern clothing."

"Why would they kill them after paying such sums for them?" Thomas wondered, looking away from the grisly sight.

"If they've hurt Adela, I'll cut every throat in the palace!"
Aimery muttered through clenched teeth.

"You'll have to leave some for me!" Bertran added feeling
his anger return once again.

The Saracens entered through the little door and soon returned with another corpse, carrying it to a nearby wagon.
The young men strained to see the contents of the vehicle,
but were too far away.

"Those wounds are fresh!" Aimery exclaimed. "They are
killing them at this very moment!"

"Let's go in!" Bertran said as he rose to attack the guards.
Aimery grabbed his tunic and pulled him back down. The
two rivals came face to face and stared hatefully at each
other.

"You will follow my orders!"

"I'm not your squire!"

"Listen to him, Bertran, he knows more about these
things," Thomas said as he put his hand on his companion's shoulder. "Remember why you're here."

Bertran nodded in resignation. He had come to like the
squire whom he had almost killed back in Lord Reynald's
castle. They were of the same background, children of
peasants and innocent of the sin of haughtiness that so poisoned the minds of noble families. Thomas secretly
admired Bertran for his refusal to bow to the obligations of

his low birth. He recognized in him a free spirit, a herald of a new day for those who lived in misery under their feudal lords. If there ever arose a hero among the serfs to lead them toward a better life, it would be a man such as Bertran.

"When the Saracens return into the palace, we will run to the wagon and await them there," Aimery whispered.

Bertran felt his heart pound like a war drum. He knew he would soon have to kill another human being. He placed before his mind's eye the icon of his beloved and focused his attention on her desperate plight. That was all he need-ed for a thunderous energy to rush through his bloodstream and overcome any resistance. No one would stop him from saving Adela!

As soon as the warriors re-entered the Governor's home, the young men rushed from their hiding place and hurried to the wagon. Aimery was the first to see its cargo.

"There must be a dozen bodies in here!" he shouted with outrage.

"Be careful, Mylord, they'll hear you," Thomas stated fear-fully.

Aimery drew his sword with a firm grip.

"Not for long! Get behind the wagon!"

Bertran pulled out his sword, realizing that the knight was not to be held back. As he raced around the cart, he caught a glimpse of the corpses. They were piled on top of each other in a jangled mess of limbs and inert faces. Bertran recognized Stephen beneath the gruesome mound. To his surprise, he felt sadness for the dead boy. There was no more reason to hate him or wish him ill. His short life had come to a gory end far from his homeland and it was hard not to pity the unfortunate shepherd boy of Troyes.

The Saracens emerged from the doorway, carrying another body. But this time it was the cadaver of an adult. As the soldiers approached, Bertran recognized Peter, the kind priest who had befriended him on the ship. The cleric's words came back to him: "I am here to die with the children." He tightened his hand around the hilt of his weapon, feeling the madness of revenge swirl through his soul.

"Now!" Aimery whispered.

The three companions charged the Saracens, weapons raised. Before the men could drop the body to the ground, they were struck down with savage blows. Bertran hacked at them with all his strength, possessed with the fever of violent hatred.

"Enough!" Aimery cried out.

Bertran froze with his sword in mid-air as though coming out of some fit of insanity. He noticed that his clothes were splattered with blood. It also dripped from his sword in big drops that rolled down his arm.

"You can't kill them anymore. They're plenty dead, boy."

Bertran had a shudder of revulsion at what he had done.

He realized that he was as vulnerable to the demons of violence as any of those warriors whose deeds were cursed by the whole world.

"Come on! There'll be a lot more of that in there!"

Aimery ran toward the doorway. Bertran stood over the dead Saracens in shock. Thomas had to grab his arm and drag him along.

"Get a hold of yourself, Bertran. Adela may be in there!"

The magic name shook him out of his daze. They hurried into the palace and caught up with Aimery who was charging ahead down the narrow, vaulted corridor.

A servant appeared around the corner and was instantly cut down by the young knight. As he passed over the corpse, Bertran noticed that it was an old man carrying a jug of water who could not have hurt anyone. He had never expected battle to be so ignoble.

They raced up a mosaic-covered stairway, drops of blood falling from their weapons at every step. Aimery stopped at the top of the stairs and listened carefully. Shouting could be heard coming from one of the rooms. He ran to a door and peered through the keyhole.

He raised two fingers telling the others how many he could

see. Then he turned the handle and burst in.

Suleiman stood in the middle of the chamber confronting the captain of the guards. They had been shouting at each other over the fate of the children. The Governor's son wanted to stop the savagery regardless of the young crusaders' refusal to reject their faith. Even though they had failed miserably in their misguided efforts, they were choosing to face martyrdom in a final witness to their Lord.

The powerful captain jumped back and pulled out his great saber. Aimery charged him without hesitation and sparks flew in the air as the blades met. Bertran and Thomas grabbed Suleiman who had no weapons. The squire hurried back to the door and locked it as his master fought viciously with the bearlike warrior. Bertran held his sword against Suleiman and watched on. He noticed that Thomas had remained by the door, assuming that the King's champion needed no help.

Aimery's dexterity was astonishing. He blocked the saber's every blow and matched the Saracen's strength when the weapons crashed into each other at full force. The young Duke was utterly unimpressed by the size of his adversary and took control of the fight as he backed him into a corner. Bertran winced at every swing, having never seen such fierce swordplay up close. His heart sank as he realized that he would have to face the bold knight someday soon and fight for his own life.

The Saracen let out a grunt with every blow as he soon lost his breath in the lightning speed of the battle. Within moments, he also lost control of the flashing iron and was stabbed in the ribs and arms before crumpling foreword and sprawling, lifeless, on the marble floor.

Aimery whirled around. His face was covered with perspiration and radiated with a lust for blood. Though he seemed calm and controlled, his eyes shone with the fury of a hungry leopard and Bertran felt a chill rise up his spine at the thought of the mortal combat awaiting him.

"Where is she?" Aimery called out.

"He won't understand what we want," Bertran stated as he removed his sword from Suleiman's throat.

"He'll understand!" the knight exclaimed as he aimed his broadsword directly at the young Arab's stomach and walked swiftly toward him.

"You do not need to kill me!" Suleiman stated with amazing detachment, "What do you want from me?"

"You speak our language!" Bertran cried out. He shielded Suleiman with his body, concerned that Aimery would run him through anyway. "We are seeking a young woman who is with the children brought here as slaves."

"A woman?" Suleiman asked, knowing already who it must

be.

"A beautiful woman with long dark hair and magnificent brown eyes," Bertran added with great longing.

"Yes, I have seen her."

Aimery grabbed him by his shirt and raised him up with one hand.

"Where is she, heathen? Have you killed her, too?"

"No, she is alive," Suleiman stated calmly.

Bertran and Aimery both shouted out with joy.

"I saved her," Suleiman continued. "I begged my father not to have her put to death. Never have I seen such a spirit..."

"Yes, we know!" Aimery said as he shook his prey against the pillar. "So where is she?"

"My father decided to send her as a gift to the Caliph..."

"To the what?" Bertran asked, losing his patience.

"The great Caliph of Baghdad, leader of all Muslims. It was the only way to keep her alive..."

"Where do we find this caliph?" Aimery cried out with anger. "Answer or I'll spill your innards!"

"I told you," Suleiman stated with the unmatched fearlessness of the desert peoples. "He is in Baghdad!"

"What's in God's name is Baghdad?" Bertran asked, unable to stand still with excitement. He felt sure that he would see Adela soon.

"It's across the most barren wastelands in the world, the

deserts of Palestine!" Aimery stated bitterly.

"They've taken her into the desert?" Bertran shouted out.

"The caravan left this morning at dawn. They are entering the Sinai by now."

"How can we find them?" Aimery asked, threatening Suleiman with his bloody sword.

"You must have a guide..."

"We've got one. You!"

"No, Sire, I cannot..."

"Then die like a dog!"

Aimery drew back to plunge his sword into the Arab's chest. Bertran grabbed his arm.

"We need this boy. Let's take him with us into the city and find what we will need."

Aimery's eyes flared with outrage at Bertran's insolent hands. He turned his weapon on him.

"Mylord, I hear footsteps!" Thomas whispered frantically.

Aimery stared with piercing hatred into Bertran's eyes.

"Soon..." he murmured menacingly, "soon..."

* * *

An endless sea of sand stretched out to the horizon and beyond. Jagged rocks, barren mountains and deep gorges broke through the wasteland like scattered teeth of some

prehistoric colossus partially buried beneath the ground.
This land beyond the Delta of the great Nile River had
seen the exodus of the children of Israel and watched in
majestic silence as Moses encountered the God of Abra-
ham, Isaac, and Jacob.

Solitary monks and hermits now made their home in the
harsh terrain for the very reason that it was unfriendly to
humans. Ancient temples crouched among the rugged
stones, hidden from those who were not willing to risk everything in their search for meaning. It was a country of
scorpions, skeletons and the relics of long forgotten civilizations.

Suleiman was no coward when it came to leading a camel
into the desert. He had not only helped the Franks purchase the necessities for their wild chase, but voluntarily
guided them on the unmarked road toward the land of ancient Babylon. The Governor's son saw this adventure as
his opportunity to escape his evil father and to do penance
for all the cruelty he had witnessed in his young life without
a word of outrage. He had been as much a prisoner in the
palace as the children were now.

Suleiman knew that he was headed toward certain death.
For if the Bedouin nomads, the Touareg warriors or the
roaming Knights Templar did not cut him to pieces, then
Maschemuth would. But he rejoiced at this freedom for his

life had been one long, fearful nightmare under his father's rule, punctuated by trips to the Caliph's lavish home across the desert. He knew the journey well and prided himself with the little bit of knowledge he had learned from his guides.

Aimery, however, did not trust anyone who was not light-skinned, of the same religion, or even of the same region of France. He would listen to none of Suleiman's suggestions despite the vital rules of survival in the desert. The brazen knight had no intention of being in the wilderness very long. It was all very simple for him. They would race after the caravan, rescue Adela, and return to Alexandria to board the first vessel they could find back to their homeland.

He therefore refused to listen to the Arab prince and insisted that they whip their camels into a fast trot across the wasteland. He would not even wear the clothing of a desert traveler, being too proud to dress like the hated Saracens. Within three hours, they had reached the first well. Bertran and Thomas were agonizing with thirst and had refrained from drinking out of their water sacks, following Suleiman's directions to the letter. They did not have to be convinced that they were like helpless children in a savage and deadly foreign land. Upon seeing the desolate expanse of sand and rock for the first time, their hearts sank. It felt

as though they were going to leap into a void that would
surely swallow them up forever. But the thought that Adela
was out there somewhere gave them all courage to move
on and brave the great unknown.

They dismounted painfully from the strange beasts. Suleiman pointed out the tracks and debris left by the caravan
and calculated that it was only hours away, moving at a
much slower pace than they were.

"We must keep moving then," Aimery insisted.

"No! We will have to set up camp before the sun sets or..."

"I'll leave you here to be eaten by the creatures of this
God-forsaken place if you disobey me, heathen!"

Aimery threatened to pull out his sword.

Bertran tried to ease the tension. He knew that Aimery was
fool hearty enough to kill their only hope for getting out of
this infinite cemetery.

"How much more can we push the camels before they
fall?" he asked Suleiman.

"They can maintain a fast stride for a hundred miles, but
then they must rest and replenish themselves."

"We will have caught up to the caravan by then!" Aimery
exclaimed. "We'll worry about the return after that."

He mounted the strange beast and tried to make it rise. Suleiman hurried over to him to keep him from striking the
animal.

"No, use it gently, like this."

The camel rose gracefully and Aimery headed it off toward the distant rocks silhouetted on the horizon.

"Hurry! The further off they get, the longer it will take us to get out of this hell."

Suleiman resigned himself to his fate and mounted his camel. He showed them how to get the animals to break into their long strides. For the first time since he had left his homeland, Bertran experienced a moment of sheer pleasure as he raced through the empty space of the desert atop the exotic creature. Thomas rode alongside him, laughing boyishly. Ahead of them, Aimery rode silently toward his goal.

It wasn't long before they spotted the column of dust rising from the slow-moving caravan. Suleiman pointed to a skull-like mound of bare stone rising between them and the travelers. They circled around it to remain out of sight.

From their higher vantage point, the young men observed the caravan below.

"It is a small caravan," Suleiman observed. "There are no more than a hundred travelers."

"How many armed men?" Aimery asked.

"Perhaps fifteen or twenty."

It took only moments for Aimery to come up with a plan.

"We'll wait until they camp for the night. Two of us will stage a raid and distract them while the others find Adela. We must locate her among the others before the sun goes down."

As a the vast sky filled with resplendent shades, the young men rode alongside the caravan, peering from behind the gigantic rocks. Bertran was the first to spot her. He knew the shape of her head and shoulders better than his own hand. She was walking among several dozen children, surrounded by mounted guards. They wore no chains as no one feared that they would dare run off into the nothingness which spread around them on all sides.

The boiling heat of the day gave way to a bone-chilling cold that forced even Aimery to wrap a cloak around himself. The long woolen tents were set up and the travelers settled in for a much needed rest. Campfires flickered in the blackness while countless stars lit up the night sky.

Bertran looked up and felt as though the heavens had opened up and revealed the portals of the celestial Kingdom. He almost lost his balance as his soul surged forth in a longing to leap into the cosmic spaces and swim amid the luminous orbs. Never had he seen such vast fields of starlight. His spirit soared as he found himself peering deep into the heart of Creation. The other worlds seemed close enough to reach out and touch.

"It's time!"

Aimery's harsh tone pulled him back to earthly reality. Bertran tightened his scabbard around his waist, restraining a shiver of anticipation at seeing Adela again. She was out there in the darkness and he could feel her presence. He wondered if she could sense that a friend was nearby in this forbidding place.

Bertran and Suleiman hurried quietly to one side of the camp while Aimery and Thomas circled toward the tent where Adela had been seen. Suleiman pointed the way to the camels. They slipped under the ropes surrounding the animals and untied their bridles as quickly as they could. Soon the camels were jumping up, snorting and running to and fro, panicked by the disturbance of their rest. Suleiman returned behind the rocks as Bertran rushed through the camp toward Adela's tent. He no longer cared if the Saracens saw him as he ran at full speed through the little city of hanging cloth. Two dead guards lay at the entrance of the tent. Aimery had already entered. A commotion now rose to a high pitch as the Saracens barked orders, fearing an attack from the fierce Bedouins. The children were rushing out of their tents like stampeding cattle. Bertran forced his way against the current of bodies pressing against him.

"Adela! Adela!"

His beloved stood in a corner of the tent, embraced in Aimery's powerful arms. Three more guards lay at the knight's feet. Bertran was struck by the sight with the force of a lightning rod. The flood of children pushed him back as his strength drained out of him. He watched on while Aimery received a kiss from the woman he had just saved.

Bertran suddenly came face to face with the insanity that had overcome him since their departure from Vendome. How could he have imagined that a baroness would share her life with a common serf? Adela was made for glory and royalty, and Aimery was a most fitting companion.

The young peasant turned away and let himself be shoved out of the tent. He wandered about like a man in a drunken stupor. A light had gone out in his soul and left him as empty as the desert that sprawled out before him far into the shadows of the night.

A strong hand suddenly fell on his shoulder. He turned around in a numb haze. Had a Saracen warrior stood before him, he would have gladly offered himself to his saber. But it was Aimery. There was fire in his eyes.

"Where's Adela?" Bertran mumbled in surprise.

Aimery pointed to two figures heading for the rocks where Suleiman awaited them.

"Thomas is taking her to safety. Our time has come, serf!"

The knight took a step back and drew his glittering sword.

"Here, in the Saracen camp?" Bertran asked in a daze.

Aimery gestured with his heavy blade toward the shadows a little ways from the tents. Bertran stared at him, unable to come out of the fog that was eclipsing his purpose for living.

"Draw your sword, villain!" Aimery shouted as he hurried into the dim starlight reflected by the ocean of sands. Bertran followed him and pulled out his sword. His heart was knotted in an agonizing cramp from the sudden loss of the only one who made his life worthwhile.

"Prepare to die!"

Aimery took a warrior stance and raised his weapon. Bertran looked at his rival, seeing in him everything that Adela would want. He was strikingly handsome, of noble bearing, and a greatly skilled knight of the Realm.

"She kissed you..." he whispered.

"What's wrong with you? Are you a coward after all? Raise your sword!"

"What's the use? I can't fight you. I have no training. Besides, you've already killed me."

"Your mind's disturbed, peasant, just as I suspected from the first moment I saw you. Either you fight me with honor or you die like a rat!"

Bertran hesitated, trying to regain his senses and his strength. He had never been struck with such emotional agony before. He had always dreamed that he would be the one embracing Adela as he saved her from danger. Now he witnessed his dream coming true, but with someone else in his place! No nightmare could ever be more horrible.

Aimery swung his sword. Bertran reacted instinctively and blocked the blow which nearly knocked him off his feet. The knight swung again and again. Bertran tried desperately to fend off the attack, but couldn't keep up with the speed and tactics of one of France's finest swordsmen. The sharp iron cut into his left arm, then sliced across his chest. Bertran fell back, dropping his weapon. Aimery lunged at him mercilessly and ran the sword into his side. Bertran cried out and rolled in the sand, holding the bloody gash.

Aimery watched him contort in agony as the sand turned crimson.

"Adela is mine, serf. And you are the Devil's! I told you that I would teach you your place. Damn your insolence!"

The knight wiped his blade in the sand.

"Now you die alone in a place with no name. That is just punishment for your misguided ways. But I'll favor you for helping me find my future bride. I'll tell her that you died nobly while seeking to free her from her captors!"

The fiery knight swung his black cloak over his shoulders and disappeared into the night.

17

An icy desert wind whistled until dawn, raising up ghostlike swirls of sand that danced in the starlight.

The disturbance had greatly angered the Saracens and they whipped and beat the children back into their tents. But no one noticed that one of them was missing. The guards remained alert for the rest of the night, but saw nothing suspicious.

While the myriad stars still twinkled in the black immensity above, the tents were dismantled and the caravan prepared for another interminable day across the sea of sand and rock. They left behind the ashes of their campfires, bits of food and materials, and by the time the soft pastels of dawn veiled the wonders of the cosmos, the travelers had disappeared.

A man astride a camel appeared on the cliffs overlooking the abandoned encampment. He wore the flowing robes of a nomad of the desert, with only his eyes unprotected from the sandstorms. He observed the desolate valley with an eagle's gaze, as still as the rocks beneath him. His leather belt held a silver saber and several daggers. The Arab was no goat herder or tribesman of the wasteland. He was a warrior, independent and proud.

His expert eyes soon spotted the body. It was sprawled in the shade of a great stone several yards away from the camp's debris. After a moment, the man left his observation post and descended into the plain.

He approached cautiously and dismounted a short distance from the bloody corpse. The warrior pulled out his saber and approached with the grace of a tiger.

Bertran lay in the wet sand, unconscious but still alive. The Arab turned him over and studied his wounds. The sand had cauterized the deeper ones and kept him from bleeding to death. He pulled aside Bertran's soaked shirt. The cut across his chest had been slowed and halted right above the heart by the medallion Hasan had given him. The nomad lifted the amulet with the tip of his weapon and looked at it carefully. His eyes widened with amazement.

He quickly felt Bertran's pulse and untied his water sack from his side, pouring its life-giving contents on the young man's parched lips. Bertran convulsed for a moment as the cool, precious liquid revived him. He weakly opened his eyes and tried to focus on his savior.

The warrior asked him a question in Arabic. Bertran attempted to speak but began losing consciousness again. "Adela..." he murmured as he fainted.

The Arab thought he had said "Allah" and responded with great fervor "Allah Akbar!" He swiftly lifted Bertran in his arms and carried him to his camel. With a shrill cry, he whipped his camel into a rapid stride.

The castle of Alamut rose high above the desert on a sharp ridge atop a colossal mountain of sheer rock. It was surrounded on all sides by a barren salt desert and could only be approached by a steep, narrow path cut into the granite. The mountain on which it was perched could only be found after passing between the sheer, overhanging cliffs of a dry river gorge.

Legends from long ago had it that the remote castle was built by a king of ancient Daylam. One of his hunting eagles had landed on the ridge and revealed the impregnable spot to the suzerain who called it Aluh Amut, the Eagle's Teaching.

Seljuq sultans added to its awesome construction over the centuries until it was captured by Hasan-i-Sabbah, the revolutionary genius of the Ismaili sect. They were mystic followers of the divine Imam descended from the

Prophet's daughter and her murdered husband Ali who had given rise to the Fatimid Caliphs of Egypt in the golden age of the new Faith. Persian tales recorded that he stayed on the rock for the last thirty-five years of his life, devoting himself to the da'wa, the sacred mission of returning Islam to the spiritual purity of its origins.

Alamut was now the home of the dreaded Old Man of the Mountain whose loyal devotees, the fida'i, were the most feared killers in the world. These were the Hashishiyyn, Assassins as the Franks called them, who were skilled in the art of murder and disguise, cutting down princes and religious dignitaries of the Sunni Muslims with the certainty that eternal bliss would be their reward. Even the Crusaders had felt their lethal daggers when Conrad of Montferrat, King of Jerusalem, was killed by one of the Old Man's followers.

The devotion in which the Old Man of the Mountain was held by his people was the envy of every ruler. Count Henry of Champagne told of the time when he was granted a visit with the Shayk of the sect and witnessed his followers jump one after the other to their deaths from a high cliff to prove their loyalty and fearlessness. The Count had to beg the Old Man of the Mountain to stop the senseless show of devotion or it might have continued throughout the day.

Bertran awoke to find himself in a small room of white stone. A brilliant light came through the square window which overlooked a breath-taking view of mountains and gorges spreading out into infinity.

"Is this Heaven?" he wondered to himself.

Though confused, his consciousness seemed more vivid than ever before. His attention wandered over the gentle colors of the wall brought to life by shimmering sunrays, soaked in the quietness that rose from miles around. The smell of incense perfumed this unique moment of well-being.

A sense of euphoria took hold of him and he had the urge to laugh. Then he realized that he was still tied to his body. He tried to move, but found that his body was not responding. He looked down to find that he was lying in a bed and dressed in fresh white linen. Bandages covered his arm and chest.

A door opened and someone entered. Bertran tried to turn his head but was restricted by a painful stiffness. A woman appeared before him. She was dressed in white silk which covered her from head to foot. Large, dark eyes peered out at him between the shimmering folds of her clothing. Bertran wondered if he was looking at an angel.

She studied him and then left as quietly as she had appeared. He wanted to call after her but he had no control

over his mouth. He held up his right hand. It seemed to be
a foreign object, detached from both his will and his sensation. He felt as though he was only spirit looking with de-
detachment upon matter.

The door opened again and a man came to stand at his
bedside. He too was dressed in a white tunic. Bertran was
stunned by his dark-skinned face and black beard. He recognized him as an Arab. His ethereal state was suddenly
shattered. He was alive and still on this wretched earth!
The man motioned for someone to enter and stepped
back. Bertran saw him bow as another figure approached
and stood at the foot of the bed, silhouetted in the light.
Bertran could only make out the folds of his flowing gown
and the shape of a long grey beard. The figure was tall and
thin with an imposing presence. Bertran looked up at his
face. Out of the shadow came the light of two piercing eyes
observing him with stern intensity.

Before him stood Jalal al-Din, the Old Man of the Mountain, all-powerful ruler of the Assassins. The serene mystic
held up the medallion that Bertran had been given. It was
still stained with the blood of his wounds. Another man respectfully stepped forward, standing behind his master.
"Our mighty Shayk, Protector of the true Faith, Bearer of
the Qiyama, Lord and Qa'im of all believers, desires to
know how it is that you came into possession of this me-

dallion."

Bertran tried to gather his strength. The woman he had seen a moment before came to his side and gave him a bittersweet liquid to drink. His head cleared almost immediately and he realized that he had been under the effects of some drug that had kept him from feeling the pain of his wounds.

"It was given to me in Alexandria."

The man translated quickly and the Old Man whispered a few Arabic words in a deep, gravelly voice.

"Who gave it to you?"

"An elderly man by the name of Hasan..."

He heard the ruler's entourage gasp at the mention of the name. A heavy silence followed. Then the ruler whispered another sentence in the melodic cadence of the strange language.

"Our Lord wants to know how is Hasan's health?"

Bertran felt his heart leaped.

"He is known to you?"

"Do not question His Holiness, infidel!"

"He is well..." Bertran stated, realizing that his life was at stake with every word he uttered.

"Why did he give you the medallion?"

"To assist me on my mission."

Bertran remembered his eccentric friend's words concerning the amulet. It would either save his life or cause him death. He didn't know which it would be with these strange mountain dwellers.

The man held up the dagger Hasan had given the young Frank.

"Did he give you this also?"

Bertran nodded. Jala al-Din muttered a somber statement.

"Our holy Imam says that if any Arab blood had been found on this blade, you would be buried alive in the sands below with your head exposed for the beasts."

The stern Old Man whispered again.

"What is this mission of yours?"

"I seek Baron Reynald of Vendome," Bertran answered, unsure as to which mission they would dislike more. Besides, he could not bring himself to describe Hasan's fantasy that he would somehow bring transforming knowledge back to his homeland.

Silence again fell over the room.

The Old Man of the Mountain made another statement, running the chain of the medallion through his fingers as though reading some invisible energy it contained.

"The Lord of Alamut says that the valiant Crusader is his friend."

At first, Bertran thought he had misunderstood. The translator repeated himself.

"Are you speaking of Lord Reynald, the sovereign of...?"

"He has been a guest of His Highness for five years."

Bertran sat up with a jolt, hardly feeling the searing pain of his wounds.

"Is he here?" he cried out.

The Arabs looked at him with repugnance. Excitement was not part of their desert ways.

"It was his wish that he be taken to Jerusalem. Our compassionate Shayk gave his blessing to him and had him carried there nearly a year ago."

"He is in Jerusalem?"

Bertran felt new life flood his being.

"The noble Crusader has gone there to die. He desired to see the sacred places where the Prophet Hasrat, blessings and peace of Allah be upon him, gave his revelations."

A shudder shook Bertran's frame.

"He is dying?"

"He suffers from a terrible wound and can no longer use his legs. Through the compassion of Lord Jalal al-Din, he has been kept from death these many years."

"I have come to take him home! I must find him!"

The mighty Imam raised his hand and stated solemn words.

"Our wise and venerable Ruler says that he will not live much longer. He dies not only of old wounds, but of a broken heart."

Tears glistened in Bertran's eyes.

"I traveled here with his daughter whom he loves more than all else in the world! She can heal him!"

A gentle glow emanated from the Old Man as a smile broke through his impassive features.

"Adela..." the Old Man of the Mountain whispered.

Bertran nearly exploded with emotion. He couldn't believe his ears. To hear the enchanted name, which had held him in a spell his entire life, spoken affectionately by this desert lord was more than he could bear.

"Yes, Adela! Adela!" he exclaimed as he wept.

The Old Man of the Mountain, shadowy figure of myth and legend, nightmare of children and knights alike, placed his hand upon Bertran's head. The young man quieted down and sank down upon the cushions. The noble master motioned for his devotees to leave the room. He spoke to Bertran through the translator.

"Your soul is filled with grief, young man," he observed.

Bertran wept bitterly, unable to contain his sorrow. The loss of his beloved was breaking his spirit.

"Do you believe in Allah the Merciful?"

Bertran nodded through his tears, looking away from the paternal presence who spoke to him tenderly.

"Then you know that there is a greater life than this one

here below."

"I cannot live without Adela!" Bertran blurted out, gaining control over his anguish.

"My brother Hasan did not give you our medallion without purpose. He must know that you have the sight."

"Your brother?"

Bertran turned to him in astonishment.

Jalal al-Din nodded with melancholy.

"Hasan disappeared shortly before our father, Muhammad the Second, left us for the other shores. My brother hated our ways and did not understand the cycles of occultation and manifestation. He believed that the outward form was the only way of our teaching. So he rejected our creeds and the so-called heresies of the brotherhood. I have wanted him to know these many years that I am the Mahdi that our people have long awaited. I have come to announce that the Qiyama, the Time of Resurrection, is here and the holy laws are no longer necessary. In this cycle, it is our duty to hide the inner truths from the unbelievers for the sake of the Ta'wil al-Batin, the secret knowledge within the divine revelation. Hasan did not understand that what seems to be and what is are not the same."

Bertran's tears had stopped. He listened intently to the royal, soothing voice of the Imam.

"Hasan spoke to me of such knowledge, and told me to

find it wherever I might," Bertran whispered breathlessly.

A joyful glow irradiated from the dignified features of the mysterious sultan.

"Then perhaps he has come to understand after all. It was a terrible loss when he left us, for there is no returning once we have broken our vows."

Now Bertran understood why his strange friend had such a quality of inconsolable sadness about him. He had cut himself off from a world that fed his soul and was lost in the empty world of ordinary, blind men.

"Did he tell you of our great library?"

"No..."

"Then he has remained devoted to our oath of secrecy. May Allah forgive him. But I will tell you because he has sent you to me. You are a sign that perhaps he has come to understand my actions after all. We have in this desert a library containing the greatest treasures of the human spirit. Hasan was the keeper of our library."

Bertran could see that the loss of his brother was still an open wound in the man's heart.

"What is this time of Resurrection?" Bertran asked.

"We violate the holy laws of the sabah, our daily prayers, because we know that the Resurrection is here and we must now stand before God in our hearts always, not merely five times during the day. The face of our soul must be constantly turned toward the Divine Presence for that is indeed true prayer. This new dispensation frees all believers from ritual and religious obligations, for the law has served its purpose and now the secrets are revealed to all who contemplate the Divine Essence. Now is the time foretold by all religions when believers shall come to know God without intermediaries and the mysteries of Creation shall be revealed to those who seek."

A holy silence filled the room as a cool breeze swept through the window, carried high above the mountain chains and desert wastes to end in this little alcove of peacefulness.

The Imam peered deeply into his listener's soul, noticing that a seed had been planted in the eternal depths of the boy's spirit which would sprout like the mustard seed into a great tree of life.

Ravished by a sanctified peace that resonated throughout the recesses of his soul, Bertran felt himself lifted on the summits of a new consciousness, as though awakening to a reality he had never known before. An infinite abyss, greater than the desert expanses stretching out in all directions, opened within him and he was flooded with a tidal wave of joy so sweet that it made his head swirl. All the experiences of the sacred thath had broken through his dreary world since meeting the Cathar hermit came together in this instant of cognizance. Time melted away and eternity was present in his breast. The Divine Goodness appeared in everything that his eyes beheld.

He realized he had awakened to a new dimension of himself that had been dormant or buried under the monotonous rhythms of his life and the opaque ideas he had formed concerning the reality around him. High on this remote mountaintop, in this secret castle, he knew that he was a child of the Creator, a visitor to the realm of passing time whose true home was eternity. From his vast perception, he could see how the Cathar had sided with that higher realm where bliss was like a sun that never set. He could also see that they had mistakenly rejected Creation in favor of their first homeland. For the temporal world was bursting with the Divine Presence which called upon him, its awakened messenger, to enjoy it, care for it, and transform it into holy sacraments for the glory of its Maker.

Bertran understood that the Church had caged these spiritual truths and suffocated them with rules and rites that were no more than the coffin nails sealing in a life-giving wisdom.

A mighty force swept through his spirit, healing his physical and psychic wounds. He turned to the master and found himself asking him a bold question.

"Why do you kill for the sake of these revelations?"

A shadow fell across the features of the Old Man of the Mountain.

"I am the guardian of mysteries for the initiate and bearer of liberation from the law. It is my duty to free this age from the tyranny of false doctrines that murder the souls of Allah's children. My people have a saying: When the time of triumph comes, with good fortune from both worlds as our companion, then by one single warrior on foot a king may be stricken with terror, though he own more than a hundred thousand horsemen."

The noble spirit moved slowly to the window and looked out at the magnificent view. He seemed to be staring into the very eyes of God.

"The Imams before me believed that only terror could overcome the greed and ambition of idolatrous sultans and caliphs. Their purpose was to destroy the rule of the Sunni Muslims who turned our Faith into culture and pride instead of recognizing it as a path to the Holy One. They have been murdering true believers since the day of Ali's death, blessings and peace of Allah be upon him."

He turned back to Bertran, the burden of deep melancholia weighing down upon him. He was witnessing in his mind's eye an endless future of bloodshed, some day embroiling the whole world in flames. He already knew that this was

325

his legacy - terror and death - though his ultimate purpose had always been the very opposite.

"In truth, I tell you that I seek peace with our enemies. I have inherited the duty of the Mahdi, the rightly guided-one who is upon earth to destroy tyranny and establish justice. From the days of the Abbasid Caliphs, the Mahdi was to restore true Islam and fill the world with justice and equity as it is now filled with tyranny and oppression."

The somber leader shook his head with sadness.

"My loyal fida'i, the devoted ones, have gone through many stages of initiation as I have sought to show them the true da'wa, the true mission. Some of them continue to kill for the honor of their Imam. And the unbelievers spread lies about us to justify their persecutions. They say that I have absolute power over my people, but I know that someday I will be poisoned by my very own followers. We who preach a faith without boundaries or laws are imprisoned in our own traditions. And the great Imam Hasan-i Sabbah has set us on a course of violence which we can no longer escape."

The Old Man of the Mountain fell silent. He looked terribly exhausted. Whispering words to his translator, he kissed the medallion and placed it in Bertran's hands. Their eyes met and he smiled a sad smile, as though wishing the young man a better fate than his.

* * *

Bertran remained for a week in the great fortress high above the desert. The members of the Ismaili sect cared for him with much attention when they were informed of the regard with which their Imam held him. Not only had he filled the Imam's heart with gladness at having received a sign from his brother, but Bertran had also brought him great joy with the news that he was here to save Lord Reynald.

The sect's vizier explained to him, during the daily applications of medicine, that the Baron had also been left for dead in the desert after a fierce battle with the Caliph's army. He had led a motley troop of Templars, Hospitalers, and Teutonic knights in an attempt to enter Jerusalem. The foolish effort had resulted in dismal failure, leaving the sands covered with cadavers as far as the eye could see. Lord Reynald had been brought to the Old Man's lair and remained in a coma for many months. It took more than a year for him to recover and he did so only because of the special skills developed by the community to care for those who happened to survive their killing missions.

The Ismailis had at first assumed that he would bring a good ransom for it was evident that he was a man of high birth. But that was soon forgotten as the convalescent

327

knight entered into daily conversations with the Old Man. Bertran was told that they would sit together in the secret gardens hidden within the inner courts of the castle and talk for hours about the mysteries of Creation. The Baron never fully regained his strength and was not capable of traveling so he became a permanent guest, spending weeks in the ancient library which contained some of the finest esoteric parchments ever preserved. As time went by, his rigid mindset melted under the sun of Truth. He came to regret his hatred for Muslims and heretics and swore to spend the rest of his days in penance for his blind loyalty to Rome.

It was only when his health deteriorated and death seemed imminent that Lord Reynald insisted on traveling to Jerusalem. He wanted to complete his pilgrimage before leaving his body behind.

Now Bertran prepared to follow in his footsteps, hoping to find him in time. The Imam blessed him and ordered four of his best fida'i to accompany him to the sacred city. Before departing, Bertran was allowed to see the secret gardens of Alamut. A vision of Paradise had been created there and only those who prepared to sacrifice themselves for the sacred cause were allowed to enter and taste in time of the life that awaited them in eternity.

Here, at the top of a barren mountain in the middle of an

empty wasteland, flourished the most luscious flora imaginable. Rivers of milk, wine, and honey flowed along in the riverbeds and beautiful maidens played angelic melodies. Exquisite pavilions lined the banks of this enchanted miniature world.

But the dream world created after the Prophet's depiction of Paradise did not cause Bertran to linger. There was no Paradise for him without Adela. Besides, he was too eager to seek for his long lost sovereign. He bid farewell to the Old Man of the Mountain and thanked him for giving him an even greater vision of Paradise than the secret garden, an inner vision that he could call upon under any circumstance. The Imam watched him descend the slopes of the great mountain and remained at the window, a solitary figure misunderstood by both the outside world and his own people, until the small group was but a dot on the sea of sand.

They traveled most of the day in silence. Bertran's wounds bothered him little for his healing was virtually complete. Only the tear in his heart caused him serious pain for he could not escape the haunting image of what he had seen in the tent on the night they rescued Adela. Even if he found her father and brought him home, he felt that he had lost her forever to the ferocious knight who had taken her away from him.

The travelers stopped at an oasis and rested their camels. As they sat under the shades of the few palms lining the water, a cloud of dust appeared on the horizon. Bertran gave it no attention until his companions jumped to their feet and ran for their weapons. None of them spoke his language, so he was forced to guess at what was about to happen.

The men tried to mount their camels but the beasts were unwilling to turn away from the water. They began to beat them as the horsemen approached. In the haze of the desert heat, Bertran recognized the blood-red cross and white tunic of the Knight Templars, the warrior-monks vowed to the protection of Christian pilgrims.

Fifteen knights were upon them before they could escape. They looked like barbarians of old with their long hair and beards sprouting like wild jungles from under their helmets. The warriors didn't even stop to ask who the travelers were. Saracens were hated enemies of their Faith and they had been fighting them for over a century since the establishment of their Order following the First Crusade. When the knights saw Bertran's light skin, they assumed that he was a prisoner of the desert dwellers and began swinging their massive swords without mercy.

These were veteran fighters, always ready for war and as fearless as men could be. The Arabs never made prisoners of them for they knew that the Templars would endure anything rather than give up their Faith and that no one would ransom them. They would simply be replaced by another warrior sworn to poverty, obedience and chastity. The Templars had adapted many of the Saracens' ways and respected the culture of the land in which they had come to die. But war was their expression of worship and though they were on the very soil where Jesus of Nazareth had spoken the Beatitudes, they seemed unconcerned with the obvious contradictions.

In a few gory moments, the followers of the Imam lay scattered in the sand, their souls released to find the Garden of Bliss that had been promised to them. Bertran was backed against a palm tree, sword in hand, waiting for his turn to come.

"What's the matter with you, boy? We can see that you're not one of them!"

The rugged men laughed and surrounded him as they cleaned their weapons.

"What is your name and where are you from?"

"I am Bertran of Vendome," he said, still reeling from disgust at the slaughter that had just taken place at his feet.

"You're in luck, Bertran of Vendome. Your freedom has just been restored to you!"

Bertran tried to respond and tell the warriors of their error when one of them let out a fierce war cry.

"Look! Look at their insignias! We've just done away with Assassins! The Old Man should have known not to send them through our territories."

One of the knights jumped from his horse and walked up to Bertran.

"Why did they not kill you long ago, boy? Assassins never take prisoners. Unless you are worth a shipload of gold coins."

His companions laughed again. They could tell that Bertran was no prince. The knight grabbed him by his tunic disdainfully.

"And what are you doing in their burnoose?"

As he shook the clothing, he spotted the shining medallion around Bertran's neck.

"What have we hear? A gold chain? Maybe this boy is a prince after all."

He pulled it out and let out a cry of outrage. The knight drew his sword and readied to plunge it into Bertran's entrails.

"He wears the sign of the Ismailis!"

The other knights reacted with great shock. Several dismounted to examine the medallion. A red-haired monster of a man roared with rage and lunged at Bertran, going after him with his bare hands. The young man raised his sword, prepared to cut him down. The knights grabbed him before he could swing his weapon and wrestled him to the ground.

"Don't kill him! Let the Grand Master deal with this heretic!"

18

It was in the year 1118 that the Order of the Knights of the Temple of Solomon was formed. It began with seven knights who joined together for the purpose of defending the Holy Sepulcher and protecting pilgrims who might dare to cross through the lands of the Saracens. Jerusalem had just been conquered by the heroes of the First Crusade, and as most of the warriors were returning to their homelands, there was no one left to watch over the new empire. They first called themselves the Poor Fellow-Soldiers of Jesus-Christ and consecrated themselves to a stern life of prayer and military discipline. They wore white tunics decorated with red crosses over their mail in remembrance of the crucial siege of Antioch in which the first Crusaders were said to have been aided by Saint George and other angels who appeared among them in like dress on white horses. The miracle was enhanced by the discovery in one of the city's cathedrals of a spearhead believed to be from the lance that had pierced the side of Christ and that now led His armies to victory over the heathen.

The new Order was given the blessing of the greatest saint of the day, Bernard of Clairvaux, who gave them the Rule of Life by which their brotherhood lived. Above all the other harsh requirements, the brother knights were required to be obedient.

The Rule stated that "every brother who is professed in the holy service should, through fear of flames of Hell, give total obedience to the Master; for nothing is dearer to Jesus Christ than obedience, and if anything be commanded by the Master or by one to whom he has given this power, it should be done without demur as if it were a command from God, for you must give up your own free will." From those humble early days, the Order had grown into one of the wealthiest communities in the world. Thousands of noble chevaliers had joined them in hopes of finding salvation while leading a warrior's life. For the Templars were among the most feared fighters in the world. They were prepared for battle at all times and were known for their incredible courage. It was said that when they searched for their enemies, their question was not "how many are there?" but "where are they?"
Nobles turned their lands over to them and gifts were sent from all across Europe. Men from all northern countries

joined their ranks as they were the only way to reach
knighthood without being born in a family of means. Within a few decades the Order had more wealth than the
Kings of France and England combined.

In the year 1212, they had reached the zenith of their glory.
No one, except perhaps for a Nostradamus, could have
prophesied that one hundred years later the great heroes of
the Holy Land would be utterly destroyed, tortured and
burned at the stake by their own King.

It was to one of their mightiest strongholds, Castle Pilgrim,
that Bertran was taken.

William of Chartres, Grand Master of the Temple, studied
the medallion.

"What is a peasant boy from Vendome doing with the
Imam seal of the Assassins?"

"It was given to me, Sire."

"By whom?"

"By the brother of the Mahdi."

The knights gathered around the large oak table in the center of the great hall looked at each other in astonishment. A
tense silence, as heavy as the mighty columns of stone that
held up the giant vaulted ceiling, fell upon the group.

After a moment, the Grand Master turned to Bertran.

"Have you seen the Lord of Alamut, the Old Man of the

Mountain?"

"I have, Sire."

A shockwave rippled across the room of massive stone.

"Why would he have granted you an audience instead of cutting your throat?"

"Because he is a friend of the man I seek."

"What sort of peasant is this?" cried one of the knights.

"A courageous one," answered another.

"Do you know the way to the Imam's fortress?" the Grand Master asked.

"I do."

"Would you lead us to it?"

"I would not betray his trust."

William of Chartres approached him.

"You are a noble spirit, and Providence has smiled upon you. But do you realize that this man whose trust you would not betray is the enemy of all civilized peoples, Christians and Muslims alike?"

"I saw only a good man, a lonely man, a man of deep faith."

"Traitor!" cried one of the knights.

"Silence!" ordered the Master. "Bertran, this Imam and his predecessors have killed many of our brothers."

"Just as you've killed many of his."

"True enough," replied the Grand Master, admiring

Bertran's boldness.

"Why should we keep alive a friend of the Old Man?" shouted a knight. "Behead him I say!"

"Our brothers are valiant warriors consecrated to the Almighty, a bit zealous at times, but of noble intent," the Master said with a smile. "So you were on your way to Jerusalem under the protection of the Assassins?"

"Yes, Sire."

"How is this possible?"

"As I told you, Mylord, I've come to take an old crippled Crusader back to his home. He happens to have become a friend of the Imam."

"I like you Bertran of Vendome, and I admire your courage. What would you be willing to sacrifice for the life of your liege lord?"

"Everything!"

"You would give me your life for his?"

"I would," said Bertran straightening his back with resolve.

"You are a believer in the Christ are you not?"

"I am."

"Then here is the bargain I propose. I am in great need of men like you. I would have you join our sacred Order and become a Knight of the Temple, vowing your allegiance to us as long as you live. In return, we will accompany you to the Holy City and help you find your friend."

The promise of knighthood thrilled Bertran to the depths of his being. Though he had dreamed of such a moment many times in his life, it was more than he could ever have hoped for. The ways of the Templars attracted him: their stern discipline, their life of devotion, their courage and skills of warfare. But he knew it would mean that this vow would seal his life forever under the banner of the Order. Once again, the image of Aimery and Adela embracing hit him like a battering ram between the eyes. He had lost her! Perhaps she had never been his to begin with. But there was one final act of love he could do for her and that was to return her beloved father to their home. Then perhaps he could turn away from all that he ever cared for and die in peace for the sake of a higher cause.

His encounters with the Presence of the Holy had opened the cage doors of his soul and intoxicated him with the self- transcendent need to be Its instrument. If he could not give his love wholly to Adela, then he would offer it up to the Lord of the universe. He knew that he could endure any hardship now and would even find comfort in the self-sacrifice of the Templar's life. Besides, they were more than guardians of pilgrims and sacred places. The Order was steeped in esoteric lore and secret initiations which it had encountered in the underworld of eastern cultures. Upon entering Castle Pilgrim, Bertran had caught sight of ancient symbols similar to those he had seen in Hasan's home. More than the glory of knighthood, he longed for the knowledge of things unspoken and hidden from the uninitiated, from those who did not have the longing to seek for life's deeper meaning.

It took little time for Bertran to agree to the Grand Master's offer. Within three days, the solemn ceremony of entrance into the Order was prepared. Several hundred Knights, Seneschals, Marshals, and Sergeants gathered in the great hall under their banner, the Gonfalon Baucent, a giant black cross on a white standard.

Bertran was dressed in a plain mail suit of armor which was the finest outfit he had ever put on. He walked down the center aisle, passed the mightiest knights ever to wear a sword. At the far end of the great room, standing on a barren stone platform several steps above the floor, stood the Grand Master. On a table next to him lay a sword of the finest metal, waiting to be buckled at Bertran's side.

The Grand Master addressed the assembled knights.

"Good brother knights, you see well that most of you have agreed to make Bertran of Vendome a brother; if there is any one of you who knows any reason why he should not, in law, become a brother, let him say it, for it is better that such a thing should be said before rather than after this man has come among us."

The vast hall was silent. Bertran heard a voice in his breast cry out, but he kept it suffocated with his will.

The Grand Master looked down him.

"Bertran, you have stated your wish to join the brother-hood. Do you understand the charitable commandments and great hardness of the house?" Bertran nodded.

"Are you willing to undergo everything for God and be the servant and slave of the house for ever, for all the days of your life?"

Bertran strained to answer but his voice caught in his throat. Adela's image came before him. He relived in a flash all the precious moments they had lived together, from the walks in her father's fields to their embrace on the ship taking them to the Holy Land. He could smell her hair again and feel her heart beating against his chest.

Then the dark image of the desert tent returned and oblite-rated his sweet memories.

"I am," he stated with cold determination, as though con-demning himself to exile and death.

"Let us hear your formal request then."

Bertran took a deep breath.

"Sire, I have come before God, before you and the broth-ers, and I beg and require you in the name of God and of Our Lady to accord to me your company and the benefits of the house, as one who will henceforth always be its servant and slave."

The Master stepped forward and came closer to Bertran. He spoke sternly.

"Good brother, you are asking a great thing, for you see only the outer shell of our religion; you see that we have good horses, good harnesses, good food and drink and clothes, and it may seem to you that you will be at ease here. But you do not know the strong commandments which are within; for it is a difficult thing that you, who are lord of yourself, should make yourself the servant of another. You will hardly do anything that you wish: if you want to be in France, you may be sent beyond the seas; if you wish to be in Acre, you may be sent to Tripoli, or Antioch, or Armenia. If you wish to sleep, you may be awakened, and if you are wakeful you may be ordered to lie down. Good sweet brother, can you suffer well all these hardships?"

"Yes," Bertran said firmly, "I will suffer all that is pleasing to God."

The Master placed his hand on his shoulders.

"Good brother, in our company you must not seek lordship or riches, nor honor, nor bodily ease. You must seek three things: to renounce and reject the sins of this world; to do the service of Our Lord; and to be poor and penitent. Will you promise to God and to Our Lady that henceforth,

all the days of your life, you will obey the Master of the
Temple and any commander placed above you? That you
will uphold the good customs of the house? That you will
help, in so far as you are able, to conquer the Holy Land of
Jerusalem? That you will never leave this Order, neither
through strength nor weakness, neither in worse times nor
better?"

Bertran hesitated. Some strange intuition was holding back
his final vow. This last step would forever keep him away
from his homeland and the woman he would never cease
to love.

He took a deep breath and closed his eyes. An image
formed in his mind's eye, like a lightning flash in stormy
skies. He saw the face of the Perfect One blessing their
love. He could feel the warmth of her nearness and the
sweet ecstasy in his heart. He opened his eyes and was
shocked to find himself kneeling on the cold stone of the
Templars' hall.

Bertran looked up at the Grand Master who was studying
him, eyebrows knotted in a concerned expression. He
raised them as though saying "what will it be?" Bertran
could already hear the words of acceptance which they had
gone over the day before: "In the name of God, of Our
Lady, of Saint Peter and of our father the pope, we accord

to you, to your father, your mother and all those of your lineage whom you wish, the benefits of the house, as they have been from its beginning and will be until its end. And you, you accord to us all the benefits which you have and will have; and we promise you bread, and water, and hardship, and work, and the poor robe of the house."

Bertran was about to release his affirmative answer, when a great cry resonated through the hall.

"The Saracens have attacked a group of pilgrims near the well of Firan!"

A thunderous discord broke out in the ranks of the knights. The well was virtually within view of the fortress, on the mud- flats of their domain. Such an outrage was unbearable to their proud warrior-spirits.

The Grand Master called a halt to the ceremony and ordered everyone to run for their horses. Before Bertran rose from his kneeling position, the Master and his soldiers had left him all alone and raced out of the various doorways along the sides of the hall. He stood and stared in surprise at the vanishing crowd. A knight turned back and saw him. "What are you waiting for? Grab your sword and join us!"

Bertran leaped up the stairs onto the platform and took hold of the heavy broadsword that was meant for him. It had a huge hilt in the shape of a cross and a thick blade almost half his size. He held it up and balanced it in his hand, familiarizing himself with its weight and length. The sword fit perfectly in his grip as though it had been fashioned for his arm alone. Had Bertran been given a castle, he would have rejected it for this magnificent weapon, symbol of chivalry and independence.

He touched the blade. It was still warm from the black-smith's anvil. The mighty weapon had been forged for the new brother knight. Bertran slipped it in its plain scabbard and wrapped the leather belt around him. With new confidence, he rushed out of the hall.

* * *

A fierce battle was being waged on the desert plains. An army of Saracens had surrounded a caravan of some two hundred pilgrims heading for Jerusalem and were savagely hacking at the faithful.

The Knight Templars galloped into the skirmish with characteristic readiness for combat. By the time Bertran had secured a horse and left the fortress, the fight had escalated into an all out war. He drew his glittering new sword and galloped into the melee.

Swords and sabers clashed, horses reared, men yelled in anger and pain. The desert sand rose high into the sky as sworn enemies fought to the death. There were no prisoners between Saracen and Templar, only corpses.

Bertran found himself engulfed in the thick of the fight, releasing with every swing of his sword the pain he had been carrying in his breast. He never once considered that he had no training for this sort of thing. But in the heat of hand to hand combat, skills didn't matter much. Raw power, zeal, and luck were in command of the bloody chaos. The Templars greatly outnumbered their enemies for once and it wasn't long before the warriors of the Jihad littered the rocky soil. Bertran tore his way into the center of the battlefield where the pilgrims had gathered to face their assailants. Few of them were armed, and many lay in heaps on the edges of their desperate circle. Bertran's horse was struck in the neck and he was thrown to the ground, barely escaping being crushed by the falling animal. He rolled passed the stampeding hooves and found himself in the no man's land between the pilgrims and the fighting warriors. Leaping to his feet, he joined the terrified travelers and turned back to face the attackers.

Most of the Saracens were still on horseback fighting off the charging knights. Only a few continued to flay at the pilgrims who fought back with their staffs. Bertran hurried to one side of the circle where several Saracens were in deadly combat with one of the few armed men. He swung his sword savagely and cut down two of them, no longer concerned with any code of honor. In the madness of battle, it was kill or be killed and if the enemy could be struck in the back, so much the better.

Bertran flung himself beside the fighting pilgrim who stood alone defending his companions. They fought side by side against the unrelenting Saracens. The two broadswords whistled in the air and cut through the desert warriors as though clearing a path through a jungle terrain. Soon the two fighters stood over a mound of cadavers.

Breathing heavily, they turned to each other. Both cried out in surprise. Bertran and Aimery stood face to face.

"You!" Aimery cried out in shock. "What witchcraft is this?"

"Where's Adela?" Bertran shouted, suddenly filled with a wild hope.

He looked over toward the band of pilgrims pressing against each other. Adela pushed her way through the crowd, followed by Suleiman.

"Adela!"

Bertran was overcome. He rushed toward her and would have picked her up in his arms had her expression not stopped him dead in his tracks.

"I thought you were dead," she said awkwardly.

Aimery stepped between them.

"So did I!" he yelled. "And so you are!"

He raised his sword to strike Bertran but the Templar
weapon blocked it.

"I know where your father is!" Bertran shouted.

Adela stepped forward as Aimery lowered his sword.

"How is that possible?" she exclaimed, her eyes sparkling
with desperate expectancy.

"Everything is possible," Bertran cried out with great joy,
"I never thought I'd see you again."

"Neither did I. Aimery told me..."

The roar of battle interrupted them and the young men had
to rush against attackers who would not give up even
though they were being decimated by the Templars.

When the dust settled, there was not a single Saracen left
alive. The wailing pilgrims hurried away from the grisly battlefield, praising their God and thanking the brave knights
who had saved them from certain death. Among the dead,
Bertran found Thomas the squire and said a silent prayer
over the loyal young man's corpse.

William of Chartres, the Grand Master trotted over to
Bertran who was still traumatized by the encounter of his
beloved.

"I see you survived your first initiation, Bertran of Vendome," the Templar stated with a smile. "We can now
conclude our proceedings and make of you the knight you
already are in spirit."

Adela and Aimery turned to Bertran in great surprise.

"What do you mean, Sire?" Adela called out.

"This young man is our newest brother in the Order of the Knights of the Temple. He has already earned the sword which was to be his before his final vow was interrupted by this little skirmish."

"But he's a peasant boy, a common serf!" Aimery protested.

William of Chartres turned a cold eye on the arrogant noble.

"The Templars do not live by the feudal code which honors people for the quality of the sheets they are born in. We look to the dignity of a man's spirit, and this man has shown a greater nobility than most of the secular knights who worship vanity and empty glory."

He turned to Bertran and smiled warmly at him.

"Are you ready to join us, worthy brother?"

"I am not, Mylord," Bertran replied with a new determination.

The Grand Master's smile faded.

"You've changed your mind?"

"I have, Sire."

William of Chartres looked at the three young people and understood.

"Is this the daughter of the man you seek?"

"It is."

"I wager that you choose to take her to him rather than remain with us."

"I do, Mylord, and I return this mighty sword to you," Bertran added as he unbuckled the scabbard.

"No, Bertran, you have earned it. Keep it in remembrance of our vows and the brotherhood which would have made you their own."

A shiver shot through Bertran's spine. For an instant, he longed to return to Castle Pilgrim and give himself to their sacrificial life. He had no idea what another future might hold, for Aimery still stood in the way and Adela would always be a headstrong noble who might never see him as anything but her father's serf.

He stepped back and looked at Adela. Her dust-covered, enchanting face cast its spell upon him once again. She was a part of him and he would never escape the desire to be with her.

"I must fulfill the mission which brought me here, Mylord."

"Then I will give you an escort to safeguard your journey. May the Almighty be with you and may you find the kingdom within which is promised to all who receive the Christ as their Master."

Saddened at the loss of a fine knight, the Grand Master

pulled in his steed's bridle and trotted away, rejoining the warrior-monks who awaited him.

Bertran watched them depart with a knot in his throat. It was a life he would have adapted to easily.

"Where is my father?"

Bertran turned back to Adela and walked up to her.

"You're as beautiful as ever, Adela. The desert has only made you blossom."

"Where is Lord Reynald?" Aimery shouted angrily.

"He is in Jerusalem, at the home of an Ismaili believer."

"We were headed there!" Adela stated with great excitement. "I wanted to pray at the Holy Sepulcher for a sign that would help me find him."

She hugged Bertran with a warm embrace. Aimery scowled at his ecstasy. He had never before experienced doubts over winning a coveted prize.

"You have found him for me, my dear Bertran! And we have found each other! How I missed you! I'd given up on everything we cherished."

"I would have found your father," Aimery stated somberly. "It would only have been a matter of time."

"You wanted us to return to France immediately!" Adela scolded. "But I knew that if I stepped onto the Holy Land, a miracle would happen!"

Bertran smiled to himself. Not even mighty Aimery could

conquer her indomitable spirit.

"The others are already on their way! There is no time to lose!" she exclaimed as the caravan gathered together to head through the Sinai.

With her usual exuberance, she hurried toward the caravan, followed by the young Arab who had made himself her slave. Aimery stepped up to Bertran.

"She's mine," the knight snarled. "We'll fight again in Jerusalem and this time, I'll gut you!"

19

The hill of Jerusalem the Eternal City lay between the valleys of Kedron and Hinnom which rise up from the Dead
Sea and the Wadi en-Nar, the Valley of Fire. Nestled in the
arms of Mount Moriah and Mount Ophel whose ridges descend to the Pool of Siloam, the mythic city had once been
a Jesubite village atop the Hill of Zion. For all its awesome
impact upon human history, Jerusalem was a town of no
more than three miles in perimeter, a little triangle of hills
and valleys separating the sea from the wilderness of Judea.
It was for these ancient stones and narrow streets that
countless followers of three religions across the centuries
had chosen martyrdom. Here the pilgrims would walk
along the Via Dolorosa whose steep inclines had soaked up
the blood of the holy man from Nazareth as he carried his
cross. Here the Son of God had shared a sacred supper
with the children of men in an upper room perched over
the busy streets. And rising above the place called Golgo-
tha was the monument for which the Crusaders had

suffered untold miseries, the Holy Sepulcher.

Upon reconquering the city, Saladin had wisely chosen to safeguard the holy sites of the Christian faith. And despite Muslim rule, pilgrims still managed to enter the gates and make their way through the marketplaces to the churches that enshrined the places they had sacrificed everything to find.

As they approached the Holy City, Aimery was flooded with a strange feeling which roared through him like a hurricane in full fury. His trained warrior's control was crumbling under the crushing weight of an inescapable realization. During their journey to Jerusalem, he had seen how deep and all-encompassing was the love between Adela and Bertran. Even they seemed unconscious of what the jealous knight was witnessing. They related to each other beyond words, as though their thoughts completed themselves in each other's hearts. They were kindred spirits, moving together with the harmony of birds in flight. Their love was timeless, uncontaminated by the transitory feelings of passing events.

Aimery knew that he could not compete with such a phenomenon. Neither his wealth, nor his prowess could win over a heart conquered by such a love. However many times he thrust his sword through Bertran, he would never manage to destroy his rival. Adela's heart was rooted in the

peasant's soul as though they were both of the same seed.
The knight's anger turned into immense sadness as he
came face to face with the one opponent he could not
champion. Yet his love for Adela only kept growing. No
matter how far he traveled, he would never find another
woman like the Baron's daughter. He was soul-sick and yet
he journeyed along with them, unable to give up, as though
driven by the momentum of winning to the bitter end. Giving up was simply not in his nature. He was possessed by a
tenacious spirit that could not let go once it had devoted its
energies to a particular aim. It was his glory and his flaw.
As they entered the Eternal City, Aimery repressed the
awareness of his unbearable loss by transmuting it into
rage. He had become a seething madman, unwilling to accept the inevitable.

Adela and her companions entered the city at mid-day and
found their way to the home of the Ismaili who was Lord
Reynald's host. She hardly noticed the ancient walls and the
aromas of jasmine and orange blossom that had filled the
city before Roman centurions wandered its streets. Bertran
was unimpressed by the town which for centuries had captured the imagination of humanity and sheltered some of
its greatest prophets. He knew by now that the truth of religion was not contained in externals, neither places nor

things, but in the heart of human beings.

They traveled quickly up the narrow streets jammed with people in every conceivable dress. Suleiman questioned merchants and beggars alike to find the home for which they had traveled so far. With every step, Adela felt her heart pump faster with unbearable anticipation. For eight long years, she had prayed that this moment might be given to her, and now that it was so near, she feared that it would be taken away at the last moment.

Aimery was also eager, but not to find the Baron. He feared that the power of Adela and Bertran's bonds of friendship would obliterate the more fragile romantic attraction she held for him once her father was found. He knew that only Bertran's death would separate them and open the way for his full possession of the woman he wanted.

They finally came to a small door lodged in a moss-covered wall in the old section of the city. Adela felt herself losing control as her whole body began to shake. Bertran turned to her but Aimery got there first and held her tightly. The rivals glared at each other, knowing that one of them would soon be dead.

Bertran knocked at the door and pulled out his medallion which would be the password for their entrance. After what seemed like an eternity, the door opened and a suspicious Arab face appeared in the crack.

Bertran dangled the chain before his eyes and the man immediately let them in. He quickly locked the door behind them and exchanged words with Suleiman.

"Tell him we've come for Baron Reynald," Bertran said.

The Arab looked at them with great surprise and then spoke in Arabic.

"He says that the Imam's friend is no longer here," Suleiman translated.

"He lies!"

Aimery grabbed the man by the throat and pushed him up against the wall.

"Tell me where he is this instant or I'll break your neck!"

"Aimery!" Adela screamed, "let go of him!"

The brash knight turned to her with a raging glare.

"Don't give me orders, Adela!"

"He'll be no good to us dead," she insisted, stunned by his violent tone.

"You can't trust any of these dark-skinned heathens, I tell you!"

Aimery shook him, banging his head against the wall. A sharp dagger suddenly appeared out of nowhere, and the Arab swung it at his assailant. The knight blocked it with his arm and smashed his elbow into the man's face. Before anyone else could react, he twisted the Arab's hand and tore the knife from his fingers.

"Stop!" Adela shrieked.

But it was too late. Aimery plunged it into his chest cavity and ripped the man open. The Arab crumpled to the ground with a groan.

"My God, why did you do that?" she yelled with rage and horror.

"No one pulls a knife on Aimery of Tours!" the proud knight responded, utterly unmoved by the taking of a life. Bertran rushed to the man's side and kneeled beside him. It was evident that he would be dead in moments.

"Ask him where we can find Lord Reynald," Bertran cried out to Suleiman. "Tell him we're here to take him home." Suleiman was so enraged at the senseless murder that he could hardly speak. He had joined with them precisely to get away from cruelty and death dealing. As though abruptly awakened from some powerful enchantment, the young man now found himself standing in the blood of an Arab brother, consorting with the enemies of his people and of his faith. He let out a cry from the depths of his soul.

"Talk to him, Suleiman!" Bertran shouted, "he's dying fast!" The young Arab knelt beside him and spoke in a quivering voice. The man shook his head negatively, choosing to leave this world as stubbornly as possible.

"Tell him the Mahdi wishes it!"

Suleiman looked at Bertran, wide-eyed. The revered messianic title was hardly every spoken by Muslims, and never by infidels.

"Tell him!"

Suleiman whispered to the man as he came in and out of consciousness. The words seem to revive him for a moment and he struggled to say a few words before exhaling for the last time. His limp body fell back in Bertran's arms.

"What did he say?" he asked Suleiman.

"He said...the Coptic monastery of Ein Karem...just outside the city."

He stood and walked to the door.

"What are you doing?" Aimery asked.

Suleiman turned to him with disgust.

"You will have to continue your journey without me. I will have nothing more to do with you!"

"Why? Because I killed one of your people? An Assassin no less!" Aimery shouted angrily.

"I left everything to join you in a noble endeavor. But you are no better than my father and his executioners! You are my enemy!" Suleiman yelled hysterically as he unlocked the door and rushed out into the street.

"I knew he was no good," Aimery muttered as he turned back to the others. "At least he got us here..."

He was interrupted by a violent smack which whipped his

head against the wall. Adela hit him again and again until he caught her hand in mid-air.

"You're a wild one, my sweet!" he said with a snicker. "But I'll tame you, you may be sure. I'll tame you."

He crushed her in his muscular arms and held her tight against his chest as she struggled to get away.

"Let her go!" Bertran roared.

Aimery raised his cold eyes, like a beast ready for the kill.

"She likes it here, boy."

"I said let her go!"

"What are you going to do about it?"

Just as Bertran leaped at him, the door flew open, revealing a patrol of Saracens.

"Seize them!" the leader ordered.

Aimery threw Adela aside and jumped back into the room, drawing his sword.

"Compliments of dear Suleiman, no doubt!" he shouted as he made his sword dance in the air.

Bertran pulled out his weapon and stood near him. The Saracens rushed in. Sabers and swords clashed with the terrible shriek of hissing iron. Adela ran to the back of the room, terrified. Her fear had come true. All could be lost now that she was within reach of her father.

The six Saracens formed a semi-circle around the young Franks and stabbed at them with spears and sabers. Their leader ordered one of his men to run for reinforcements. Bertran fought in a frenzy, realizing that all his hopes were on the verge of being destroyed. Next to him, Aimery reveled in the ecstasy of danger and the heat of fierce combat. He was intoxicated with the thrill of flashing blades and his supreme confidence kept him far from mortal fear.

Soon, another patrol entered the home. The Saracens were backing the young men toward the corner of the room where Adela watched on in terror.

"Find a way out!" Bertran yelled at her. "There must be a back door!"

Adela disappeared behind a hanging curtain. Several soldiers attempted to get passed them to pursue her but they were cut down in a fury of screaming swords. Four men of the first patrol already lay dead at their feet and the others were less enthusiastic about charging ahead. The room was too cramped for them to surround the Franks and they were forced to face them directly. But more soldiers kept arriving as the savage noise rose out into the street and word spread down into the market square that a battle was being waged under the shadow of the Dome of the Rock, one of Islam's holiest places.

"They'll be surrounding the house soon!" Aimery yelled out at his fighting companion. "Follow Adela and get her safely to her father!"

Bertran kept swinging and dodging the thrusting weapons of the enemy. He couldn't bring himself to abandon his rival to the sabers of the Saracens.

"Bertran! Do as I say!"

It was the first time that Aimery had called him by his name and the knight's voice was more of a plea than an order.

"She's yours! She always was and always will be! Now go and save her!"

Bertran backed up and Aimery leaped in front of him blocking the Saracens' passage. Bertran rushed behind the curtain and turned back one last time to see the brave knight fight his adversaries with incredible force and speed. His eyes welled with tears in spite of himself and he hurried to the back of the house where he found Adela trying to break the lock of a door.

"Stand back!" he shouted as he brought down his mighty sword over the lock. He kicked it open and rushed out into a little garden. They climbed over a wall of stone and leaped into the labyrinth of back alleys. They could still hear the clash of weapons echoing from the house.

* * *

The monastery was cut out of the steep wall of a great ravine along the path of a dry river bed. It was the last human habitat before the barren gorges of the Judean desert. This was the land where John the Baptist had found seclusion, the wilderness from which his solitary cry rang out, preparing the way of the Lord.

Great skeleton-like boulders rose up from the landscape as though warning all living things to stay away from these forsaken wastelands. The dark holes of cave entrances dotted the dusty faces of the rocks like giant Cyclops eyes looking out upon humanity in stern judgment.

It was in this remote refuge that Bertran and Adela reached the goal of their tempestuous journey.

As they hurried along the narrow mountain paths, Adela realized for the first time that he was no longer a peasant boy, but the noble knight with whom she would spend the rest of her life. Bertran saw in her eyes the presence of a compassionate spirit baptized by fire, the woman he had always known her to be. He took her by the hand. They both knew that nothing would ever separate them again.

An old man, with a giant white beard covering nearly half his body, opened the heavy gate of the monastery. He looked at them with great surprise for visitors were rarely seen in this forgotten place. His eyes widened with even

greater shock at the sight of a woman as he had not seen
one in some fifty years.

"You cannot enter here! " he said in a feeble but determined voice.

"We've traveled across the seas to come here, good sir, and
the gates of Hell will not stop us now!" Bertran responded.

"These are the gates of Heaven, my son."

"Then you will let us enter to take an old man home."The
little monk's wrinkled face softened.

"What do you mean?"

"This is the daughter of Lord Reynald, Baron of Vendome,
a wounded Crusader who has been away from home for
eight long years. We are told that he is here now."

"There are no lords here, my son, only servants of God."

"He is crippled and can no longer walk."

"There is such a man here, a man with no name. He lives in
the hermitage at the top of the rock."

"Would you take us to him?" Adela asked, begging for the
first time in her life.

"That I can do," the monk said with a gentle smile. "Follow
me."

He stepped outside the gates and they followed him around
the high walls of the monastery to the very edge of the
cliff. The old man pointed a crooked finger to a narrow,
winding pathway leading to the summit of the rock.

"What is he doing up there?" she asked as tears sparkled in her eyes.

"It was his request, my child. He wants to die alone with God. No one sees him anymore. Our brothers carry baskets of food to him once a day."

"Is he still alive?" she inquired no longer able to control the tears.

"The baskets return empty, so he must be. But I have never seen so unhappy a man."

Adela let out a moan as she broke down weeping. Bertran put his arm around her to support her.

"You're about to change all that," he said gently. "Your presence will heal his soul."

"What if it's too late?"

"It isn't!"

"How can you tell?"

"Because I'm sure that you are the source of his agony and of his joy. You are the one he longs for. Come, let's take him home."

They began the steep climb to the top of the great rock.

"Do you think he will recognize me?"

"He would know you in the blackest night. You are the light of his life."

"Why are you so sure?"

"I know..." Bertran said softly.

They reached the top of the hill and stopped a moment to catch their breath. A little stone hut stood at the far end of the plateau, shaded by yet another giant boulder which rose like a mighty hand calling forth the blessing of the Divine upon His children.

A harsh breeze came up through the crags of the ancient boulders and sounded a melancholic cry across the plateau. In the distance could be seen the rooftops of the Eternal City and the scraggly trees rising out of the Mount of Olives. In the center of this panoramic view of biblical events, there rose the cone-shaped hill of Mount Tabor whose summit had witnessed the Transfiguration.

This desolate plateau was a balcony seat overlooking the solemn stage on which the Creator had come among humans and made known His love for all time.

An empty food basket was the only sign of life on this lonely summit. Bertran and Adela slowly approached the little stone cottage that housed the man they had come so far to find. Adela took her companion's hand, needing courage to make the last few steps of the way. They approached the door. No sound came from within the one room hermitage.

Adela bit her lip as Bertran knocked at the door.

"Let a man die in peace!"

The voice was weak but could definitely be recognized as

that of Lord Reynald. Adela let out a cry which Bertran muffled with his hand.

"We mustn't overwhelm him. Let me go in first."

Adela would have protested but his determined expression silenced her for once. She leaned back against the dusty stones as Bertran opened the door and entered.

The small room was in darkness except for a ray of light coming from the heavens through a window slit like those of Frankish castles. A silhouette sat up on a bed of hay and blankets by the edge of the sunray. The beard was ungroomed and grown out, streaked with grey, but unable to hide the familiar features of the Baron of Vendome.

He wore the plain cloak of the monks and sat with his back straight as a spear. In the half light, his eyes seemed to glow with great serenity, though they were weighed down with heavy, dark circles. Bertran could tell that the noble man's spirit was fading away.

"Who are you?" Lord Reynald asked in a tired voice.

"Don't you recognize me?" Bertran asked, his heart pounding like never before.

In the silence of the mountaintop, the stone-faced lord studied him. Bertran tried to restrain his exuberance as best he could.

"Are you not one of the brothers from the monastery?"

He noticed the sword at his side and knew the answer to

his question.

"You look familiar...But I cannot tell...Why have you come to disturb me in my final hours?"

Bertran took a step forward.

"These are not your final hours, Mylord!"

A deep sorrow spread across Reynald's weary face.

"Oh, yes they are. I have lived too long. The Holy Land will soon have the parts of my body which it has not already taken."

"No, Sire. We have come for you."

"We?" he asked with surprise.

Bertran opened the door and Adela's outline appeared before him.

"Who is this?"

"One you have longed for and who has longed for you these many years, Mylord."

A tremor overtook the Baron's weakened body. He brought his hands to his face.

"This must be a final vision! You're angels come to take me to my last resting place!"

"We've come to take you home, father."

The young woman stepped into the room, tears streaming down her face.

"No! It cannot be! The Good Lord has granted me one last look at my beloved!"

She moved forward slowly and reached out to him. He raised his trembling hands toward hers. The long separated fingers of father and child met in the radiant sunbeam.

"Is it you?" he cried out from the depths of his soul.

"It is I, father!"

Their hands clasped with incredible intensity and it seemed that the whole mountain shook when the sorrowful man cried out with the joy of one reborn: "ADELA!"

She flung herself into his arms and they embraced like no two humans had ever embraced before. The heat of their love melted away years of pain and loneliness in an instant. Adela's tears fell on his hair and face like rain on parched soil. They laughed and wept and kissed and looked into each other's eyes, praising the mercy of God.

Bertran watched on, weeping great tears of joy. Eight years dissolved in a few moments of torrential love. When they were able to speak again, Lord Reynald held her away from him and admired the woman she had become.

"Is this my little girl? Is this the child I was so foolish to leave behind?"

She wept with happiness and kissed his cheeks. He turned to Bertran.

"And who is this young warrior who has brought you to me at the ends of the earth?"

"Why that is Bertran, father."

369

"Bertran? Bertran the peasant boy?"

"No, Bertran the valiant knight!" she said with great pride.

Bertran's soul leapt with ecstasy and he fell to his knees before his liege lord. The aged knight placed his hand on his head.

"You are my son now, Bertran. I bless you as a father, not as your suzerain."

Bertran kissed his hand and said nothing for emotion had blocked his throat.

"What madness brought you to me?"

"The same madness that will take you home to Tristan and the hearth that have missed you for so long!" Adela stated exuberantly.

"But I am...crippled...I can no longer walk."

Bertran rose and lifted him up in his powerful arms.

"I will carry you every step of the way!" he cried out. "Why wait any longer?"

"A moment, my children," Lord Reynald said softly.

He gestured for Bertran to take him to the window. Trembling like a newborn creature, he looked out one last time upon the land where the Christ had walked and prayed, been crucified and overcome death in the name of a loving God.

"This view has been my only companion for such a long time. It has inspired me and...transformed me. I want to say farewell."

A profound silence fell over them as they stared out at the breathtaking vista. The Holy Land stretched out before them, barren and harsh, but colored with a mysterious light that fell with special radiance upon the gardens of Bethany and Gethsemane.

The desert land became beautiful to the sparkling eyes of the three companions who pressed against each other in an unconquerable love. For it was upon these very stones that a young rabbi had revealed that such love was the way to the Kingdom of Heaven, a Kingdom whose gates had just opened within their hearts with the promise of new life. And they knew that nothing would ever separate them again.

THE END

www.ingramcontent.com/pod-product-compliance
Lightning Source LLC
Chambersburg PA
CBHW060153260626
47160CB00001B/244